Count Sergei threw the gla... it into small fragments, wit... any who wish to create disc... our feet and be trampled i...

When Kirsty heard his voice, she looked up, startled. Surely the voice was familiar? Could there be two men in Russia with just those deep yet softly threatening tones?

Afraid at first to seem too inquisitive—though, in the circumstances, she could hardly imagine why she should not be—she cast a quick glance up at her new husband. Her breath caught in a short gasp that was almost a sob. Her ears had not deceived her: this was indeed the man who had come to her aid in Archangel. This was the face that had haunted her unguarded moments!

CW01467248

Janet Edmonds was born in Portsmouth and educated at Portsmouth High School. She now lives in the Cotswolds where she taught English and History in a large comprehensive school before deciding that writing for Masquerade was more fun. A breeder, exhibitor and judge of dogs, her house is run for the benefit of the Alaskan Malamutes and German Spitz that are her speciality. She has one son and three cats and avoids any form of domestic activity if she possibly can.

Janet Edmonds has written two other Masquerade Historical Romances, *The Polish Wolf* and *The Happenstance Witch*.

COUNT SERGEI'S PRIDE

Janet Edmonds

MILLS & BOON LIMITED
15–16 BROOK'S MEWS
LONDON W1A 1DR

All the characters in this book have no existence outside the imagination of the Author, and have no relation whatsoever to anyone bearing the same name or names. They are not even distantly inspired by any individual known or unknown to the Author, and all the incidents are pure invention.

The text of this publication or any part thereof may not be reproduced or transmitted in any form or by any means, electronic or mechanical, including photocopying, recording, storage in an information retrieval system, or otherwise, without the written permission of the publisher.

This book is sold subject to the condition that it shall not, by way of trade or otherwise, be lent, resold hired out or otherwise circulated without the prior consent of the publisher in any form of binding or cover other than that in which it is published and without a similar condition including this condition being imposed on the subsequent purchaser.

First published in Great Britain 1986
by Mills & Boon Limited

© Janet Edmonds 1986

Australian copyright 1986
Philippine copyright 1986
This edition 1986

ISBN 0 263 75400 6

Set in 10 on 11 pt Linotron Times
04–0586–74,000

Photoset by Rowland Phototypesetting Limited
Bury St Edmunds, Suffolk
Made and printed in Great Britain by
Cox & Wyman Limited, Reading

HISTORICAL NOTE

PETER the Great, one of the most interesting rulers in history, Catherine, the Menshikovs and Gavril Golovkin, really existed and references to their lives are accurate. In portraying their characters I have endeavoured to adhere as closely as possible to what is known. The events in *Count Sergei's Pride* take place in 1707–8, and social customs in Russia at that time are taken largely on the authority of a gentleman called Olearius who travelled in Russia in the seventeenth century and was obliging enough to write about it.

Not only did Peter marry his mistress of several years in 1707 at a secret ceremony in the presence of a few close friends, but it remained officially a secret until 1712, when he married her again with all the pomp one might expect. After his death in 1725, Catherine ruled as Catherine I.

Alexander Menshikov outlived both his Tsar and his protegée though he remained in favour during their lifetimes and in fact ruled Russia through Catherine during her short reign. He had made many enemies, however, and when Peter II came to the throne in 1727, Menshikov's attempts to influence him resulted in his being exiled, first to the Ukraine and then to Siberia, where he died in 1729, aged fifty-six.

Many foreigners settled in Peter's Russia, particularly if they offered skills which Russians did not, at that time, possess. They lived in separate suburbs, and because Russians regarded all foreigners as Germans, the foreign quarter of Moscow was called the German Suburb. From at least the time of Ivan the Terrible, who died in

1584, to the present day, Russians and foreigners alike have needed passports and special permission to travel within the country. Similarly, Siberia has always been the place of exile for those who displeased their monarch.

St Petersburg—now called Leningrad—was Peter's creation, and in 1712 it was declared the capital in place of Moscow. The two-roomed wooden cottage in which Peter lived during the building can still be seen. Peter was determined to turn medieval Russia into a modern (i.e. eighteenth-century) European country. He made the boyars (noblemen) shave off their beards, cut the sleeves of their *kaftans* back to the wrist (the long trailing sleeves indicated that the wearer had no need to work), and abolished the *terem*—the custom of keeping women in seclusion which had come into force when Russia was ruled by Moslem Tartars (1240–1480). By Peter's reign, however, the *terem* could not be compared with a harem. He also, incidentally, decreed that a boyar could not marry unless he could produce a Certificate of Education!

During most of Peter's reign, Russia was at war with Sweden, but the exigencies of the plot have necessitated only fleeting references to this Great Northern War. Believe it or not, wheelbarrows were unknown in Russia until after Peter had seen them on his travels in England and Holland. Precisely how they arrived in Russia I have not been able to ascertain, so Alexander Benmore seemed as good a way as any. The only historical error I have knowingly—and deliberately—made concerns Prince Menshikov's palace, the building of which I have advanced by two years: it actually began in 1710.

Janet Edmonds

CHAPTER ONE

THE LIGHT of a thousand beeswax candles specially imported from Moscow flickered from the iron sconces on the wooden walls and in multi-tiered candelabra placed at intervals down the table.

Kirsty Benmore looked about her with all the interest to be expected from a sixteen-year-old at her first major social function. So this was the Governor of Archangel's idea of a western dinner party! Only good manners stopped her from giggling. For one thing, it was three o'clock in the afternoon, though the candle-light necessitated by the Arctic mid-winter outside made it seem later. The food, too, was hardly what one might have encountered on an English table: bear-meat and reindeer, and fish, fish, fish. But, most of all, it was the company that differed.

There were not many guests: Archangel was a small town with few resident Russians whose status warranted an invitation from the Governor, and even the necessary inclusion of the entire foreign community did not swell the number beyond that which could be comfortably accommodated at this admittedly long table.

Men heavily predominated. Although the foreigners had without exception brought the ladies of their household, it seemed that most of the Russian wives had preferred to remain in the seclusion of their *terems*, despite the Tsar's known objection to the custom, and looking at their menfolk, Kirsty was not in the least surprised that they had not compelled the attendance of their wives and daughters.

Apart from the Governor himself, who wore a

western justaucorps, and shivered, all the Russian men present wore the traditional *kaftan*. These long-sleeved, floor-length garments were, for an occasion such as this, of sumptuous brocades and damasks in the rich jewel colours so favoured by Russians, with the beloved crimson predominating. Sewn with gold and silver thread, embellished with fresh-water pearls, these *kaftans* gleamed and shimmered in the lambent candle-light with a barbaric splendour emphasised by glimpses of the fur linings which made such garments the only sensible wear in such a cold climate.

Of the boyars present, only one had deferred to the Tsar's decree to shave off his beard, the others without exception having preferred to pay the required tax and retain that adornment. It was that one exception to which Kirsty found her gaze returning. Of marriageable age by both English and Russian standards, it would have been unnatural if she had not taken a superficial interest in the men present, although it was, of course, unthinkable that she should marry outside the foreign community. Nevertheless, her lack of more than a very few basic phrases in Russian meant that she could neither comprehend nor participate in the conversation, and so she had plenty of time to study her fellow-guests of whatever nationality.

It was a pity that their neighbours and friends, the Harrow family, were too far down the table to talk to, and Kirsty could not help wondering how their youngest daughter, Mary, had reacted to being told that she was too young to attend. John and Margaret were there, though, both of them rather older than herself, and Margaret could at least converse with her brother, Kirsty thought wistfully, before resuming her scrutiny of those closer to her.

The clean-shaven boyar was not a young man—Kirsty supposed him to have been at least thirty—but he looked to be one of the youngest present, although it was hard to tell in view of the ageing effect of a profuse beard. Even sitting, he seemed to be tall, and there was something about his face with its high cheekbones and aquiline nose that drew her eyes like a magnet. Once, as she glanced across at him, she discovered that he was looking steadily at her. Their eyes met, and Kirsty, embarrassed, flushed and studied her plate instead. How dreadful it would be if he thought her forward!

The meal over, the Governor led the way into an adjoining room where a samovar stood ready to dispense hot water for the ladies' tea while the gentlemen continued to imbibe the limitless quantities of stronger beverages without which they would have declared the function a poor affair.

As the guests circulated, Kirsty's father instructed her not to let them become separated. 'I fancy this gathering will soon turn into the riotous affair that Russians expect: they are not accustomed to regulating their behaviour because of the presence of women. You will be safer at my side.'

Kirsty had no hesitation in heeding his advice: already the presence of women was attracting unwelcome attention in some quarters, and she found it necessary to keep her eyes down-cast in order to avoid drawing any of it upon herself. This enforced modesty did not, however, prevent her noticing that her conjecture concerning the clean-shaven boyar was correct: he was extremely tall, certainly the tallest man present, and his dark hair was clearly visible as he moved among the other guests. On more than one occasion, when Kirsty risked glancing up, he again seemed to be looking straight at her, though he made no attempt to approach.

It was not long before it became obvious that ribaldry was well to the fore. Kirsty did not need to understand the language to be aware of the nature of the raucous laughter that now rang out from time to time, and she moved instinctively closer to her father.

'I dislike the way things are moving,' Alexander Benmore said quietly. 'We shall take our leave as soon as we decently can.'

When that time might be was more difficult to decide, since the Russian custom was for the carousing to continue until the guests were snoring on the floor, and more than one foreign guest caught the eye of another with a questioning glance at the door.

Suddenly Kirsty was conscious of a hand on her waist, squeezing, while the sauce-streaked grey beard of an elderly boyar brushed the bare white skin of her neck as he peered over her shoulder in an apparent attempt to ascertain the depth of her décolletage under its lace fichu. She pulled back with a little cry, but his hold tightened and he uttered a remark, incomprehensible to her, which called forth hoots of laughter from his two companions.

Before Alexander could intervene on his daughter's behalf and put himself in the invidious and dangerous position of remonstrating with a man who outranked him, an iron grip descended on the boyar's arm and he was spun round in a manner that obliged him to loosen his hold on Kirsty's waist.

Relieved, she looked up to see that her rescuer was none other than the enigmatic man to whom she had felt so drawn. She had no idea what he was saying to her assailant, but the recipient was clearly anxious to avert the man's obvious wrath. It was strange, Kirsty thought, how much venom could be expressed so softly, for the younger man did not raise his voice, perhaps because the deep tones had a resonance that could be clearly heard.

As soon as the younger man relaxed his hold, the elder made his escape; Kirsty's rescuer at once turned on his heel and went back to his friends, neither waiting for

Benmore's gratitude nor making the brief leave-taking bow that would have been forthcoming from an Englishman in similar circumstances.

'Discourteous it may be to leave so soon,' Alexander said as he watched the young man cross the room, 'but we are returning home.'

His sentiments were apparently echoed by others of the foreign community, for they were not the only ones to take their leave of the Governor in the next few minutes.

For whatever reason, the Governor of Archangel did not choose to repeat his experiment of a western dinner, and in the three succeeding years Kirsty did not think that anything of any particular interest had happened in the little town. She often thought back to that afternoon, partly to reflect on the fact that it had driven her to learn Russian—never again would a remark made in her presence fail to be understood—but more frequently to allow herself the luxury of recalling the man who had so swiftly stepped in at the very moment when he was most needed. It was a trifle sad, though, that with the passing years her recollection of him became more dim, as though she recalled him through a veil which became less transparent on each successive occasion.

She sighed, not for the first time, and glanced up from her sewing. Was that her father, home already?

It was barely two o'clock; though, with the candles already lit, it seemed later. Kirsty often thought she would never become accustomed to the long, dark days of the Arctic winter which made candles or the dirty, malodorous oil-lamps a necessity for most of the waking hours. They were fortunate that her father's wealth —and his favoured standing with the Governor of Archangel—had at least enabled him to import bricks with which to build a chimney for their wooden house.

He found it comforting to think that if their home should burn down in one of the periodic fires that swept the community, at least it would not have been started by the over-heating of his own wooden hearth. Kirsty found this very small comfort, and preferred to appreciate the fact that a brick chimney enabled them to keep a fire burning twenty-four hours a day.

Widowed by the smallpox five years earlier, Alexander had appalled his family by taking his fourteen-year-old daughter to Russia, of all benighted places, to make his fortune. Kirsty's aunts and uncles threw up their hands in horror. Whoever heard of going to *Russia* to make one's fortune? The new colonies of America—ah, now that was quite another matter—but Russia? A land of barbarians and snow, with a Tsar as mad as a March hare, so they said. What fortune was there to be had among such heathens?

But Alexander was no fool. He had been in London when that same Tsar was lodged in Deptford, the winter the Thames froze over. People who had had dealings with Peter did not consider him mad, though his behaviour had certainly been barbaric on occasion, and Alexander knew of several who had been persuaded to throw in their lot with the young Tsar and take their skills to Russia for the building of a Russian navy and a new Russian city. True, Alexander's skills were not of that nature: he was a buyer and seller, and as such might not be quite so welcome as a craftsman would be, but he kept his ear to the ground and eventually sold everything he owned, bought two hundred wheelbarrows with the money, and shipped them, himself and his daughter to Russia, ignoring his family's protestations.

'Kirsty is all I have left,' he told them. 'She is quite willing to come with me.'

Tsar Peter had seen wheelbarrows for the first time in London and, although some had been made to his specification on his return, they had been badly constructed and were unpopular with his workmen. Alexander's, on the other hand, were sturdy, and when the Tsar heard of them he bought them all up, and their importer was permitted to remain in Russia, provided he was willing to move to the far north and trade in furs. This was just such an opportunity as Alexander had hoped for, and they had lived in the foreign quarter of Archangel ever since. As he was the Tsar's sole agent—for such he quickly became—their fortunes climbed, and he, at least, had no thoughts of returning to his homeland.

Kirsty had been by no means so set on staying in Russia: the country had been good to them, but all she knew was Archangel, and it was not the most congenial of places. Furthermore, her life was virtually restricted to the foreign quarter, and her circle of acquaintance was therefore extremely limited.

She was now nineteen—nearly twenty, in fact—and if circumstances had been otherwise, might reasonably have expected to have been married these two years past. Had they been in England or her mother's native Edinburgh, she would have been considered almost at her last prayers by now.

But in the foreign quarter of Archangel there was little opportunity to find a husband. Indeed, the only young unmarried man of her acquaintance was John Harrow, but he, with his parents and sisters, had recently moved to Moscow where he and his father were to supervise the continued paving of the city's streets. True, there were a number of widowers, and more than one had cast a speculative eye over Alexander's pretty daughter, but he knew too much about any of them to be willing to encourage their suit. Kirsty, reviewing them in her mind, had no reason to regret his stance.

It would be perfectly possible for her to marry a Russian, of course—after all, if it was true that Peter had secretly married his mistress, then the Tsaritsa was an illiterate Lithuanian peasant—but first it was necessary to meet one. This was an extremely unlikely occurrence for a respectable girl in a society where women were in practice, if no longer in theory, kept in the *terem*—the separate quarters where women met only husband, father, brothers and other women. So she continued to keep house for her father and to fill her days with a little visiting, some sewing, and, if the truth was told, quite a lot of sheer boredom. Each day had its predictable pattern, and for that pattern to be broken was an event in itself.

Never before could Kirsty recall her father's having returned so early, and looking across at the window, she half expected to see a blizzard whirl across the mica panes, not that any such change in the weather usually deflected him from the art of making money. The sky, though darkening fast, was as clear as it had been all day. There must be some other explanation for his premature return.

She rose from her chair. 'Are you ill, Papa?'

'Do I look ill?' he replied, the firelight catching his smiling face and painting it with a ruddy glow.

She looked at him thoughtfully. 'No, you do not. In fact, in that huge lynx cloak, you look like an Angora cat that has found a whole churn of fresh cream!'

He laughed. 'As I think I have, my dear . . . as I think I have. Though I have not yet ventured to drink it,' he added.

'If you wished to mystify me, Papa, you have succeeded admirably. What, pray, brings you home so early?'

'You do, my dear.' And her father's smile grew broader as her incredulity became apparent.

Kirsty looked at him speculatively before returning to her sewing. 'Very well, Papa, make a mystery of it if you will. I shall ask no more because I suspect that you will not long be able to keep it to yourself.'

Alexander looked with some exasperation at her dark hair bent over her sewing, apparently oblivious now to his very presence.

'You really can be the most annoying girl at times,' he said when she continued to fail to plague him with questions. 'In fact, you become increasingly like your dear mama, not only to look at but in your irritating habit of knowing me too well! I wish your husband joy of you.'

If that last sentence had been designed to bring her head up with a jerk, it succeeded with gratifying alacrity. This perhaps accounted for the satisfaction in Alexander's voice when he continued, 'Ah, that shook your composure, miss, did it not?'

'Let me be sure I understand you, Papa. Are you talking in general, or do you have a particular husband in mind?'

Unfastening his cloak, Alexander handed it to the servant, who stood by with a little tray on which stood a small silver measure of vodka and two glasses of steaming tea in silver holders. He took the warming vodka and tossed it back, Russian fashion, in one gulp, before instructing the woman to put the tray down on a side-table. Helping himself to one of the glasses of tea before handing the other to his daughter, he sat down opposite her and took a sip before replying.

'Do you not think it is time you were married?'

'Of course it is; but I am not precisely spoiled for choice here in Archangel, am I?'

'That is very true, and much of what choice there has been has also been totally unsuitable in one way or another. What would you say to a wealthy, handsome, young—well, youngish—husband?'

'I wouldn't believe it,' Kirsty said categorically, and

added, suspiciously, 'how -ish is "youngish"?'

'Thirty-two.'

So there *was* someone definite in mind. Kirsty wrinkled her nose. Thirty-two sounded rather a long way from nineteen. On the other hand, she was nearly twenty, and it somehow did not sound so far from that. It was, in any event, a great deal younger than it might have been, bearing in mind some of the suitors her father had rejected.

'Thirty-two, wealthy and handsome?' she said at last. 'And—clearly—he has your approval. Are there no drawbacks to this paragon? And am I to learn who he is?'

Her father looked doubtful. 'I do not know whether you would consider it a drawback, precisely. It all depends upon whether you had hoped to return to England. You see, he is a Russian.'

Kirsty's hands lay very still in her lap. 'I see,' she said. 'Pray continue, Papa.'

'He is an influential man, a boyar, though he styles himself "Count" in accordance with the Tsar's wish to westernise the Court. Count Sergei Ivanovich Borodinov.'

He paused expectantly, as though the name might mean something to his daughter, but it meant little.

'I have heard the name, I think,' she said. 'But I do not think he is one of the local nobility.'

'No, indeed. He has estates at Zubstovoy to the north of Moscow, and spends most of his time there and also in the capital—when he is not on manoeuvres, that is. He is a captain in the Preobrazhensky Guards.'

'A captain!' Kirsty exclaimed. 'Surely that is unusual?'

'He must be very able. Russians rarely hold rank above sergeant in that regiment, no matter how well born they may be, unless they have proved themselves.

Count Borodinov is well acquainted with the Tsar, though not among his most intimate friends. Nevertheless, such a marriage is an honour for you and can be of great value to me, as you may imagine.'

'From which I infer, Papa, that you have accepted on my behalf?'

'Oh, no, not at all,' her father hastened to assure her. 'Indeed, I told the Count I could not do so until I had asked you. He was surprised, since no Russian girl would expect to express an opinion, but the whole thing is somewhat irregular, you must realise: the Count came to me to ask for your hand, in the western style; normally these things are arranged between the parents, and the bride's father offers the girl to the intended groom. Doubtless, had Count Borodinov's father still lived, the matter would have been broached in the traditional way, for I do not fancy he is as enthusiastic as his Tsar about western ways.'

'Yet he seeks a western bride?'

'So it would seem. He indicated that the Tsar was happy for him to approach me on the subject, so Imperial approval is likely to be forthcoming.'

'What more has he told you?'

'You will, of course, move to Moscow. Indeed, it is there that the wedding is to take place.' He paused. 'He has also indicated that it will be necessary for you to adopt the Orthodox faith. I said I thought you would have few objections.'

Kirsty looked at him. Her father could rarely imagine any objection which might stand in the way of business for long, but she had to admit to herself that, baptised Protestant though she might be, it really made very little difference to her which branch of her faith she followed.

'I presume I am to have the pleasure of meeting this gentleman before giving you my answer?' Kirsty enquired. 'Do you know when he is to pay his respects?'

Alexander shuffled his feet and had the grace to look shamefaced as he answered. 'He will not be doing so. Count Borodinov remains in Archangel only until the morning, when he returns to Moscow. It is by no means usual for a Russian bride to see her groom at all before the wedding, so he did not consider it in any way necessary. I am to send him your answer this evening.'

'I am not a Russian,' Kirsty pointed out, 'and I rather feel that if Count Borodinov has his mind set on a western bride, he might at least make some concessions to western customs.'

'I did try to make that clear to him, but he seemed to think the sooner you became familiar with Russian ways, the better.' He saw Kirsty stiffen and bristle, and hastened to placate her. 'Do not have a false idea of him, my dear, he is very pressed for time. Quite apart from his many other advantages, he is most truly the gentleman —in the Russian mould, of course—and does not seem so apt to carry everything to excess, as do so many of his compatriots.'

'Neither of which is saying very much,' she remarked acidly. 'I think you had better leave me to think about this, Papa. I promise I will give you my answer in plenty of time.'

With that, Alexander knew he must be content. He was very well aware that, in his anxiety to promote the match, he had not phrased things in the most felicitous way. He had been very tempted to accept Count Borodinov's flattering offer as soon as it was uttered, but he knew his daughter well enough to guess that, had he done so, she would have refused point blank to go through with the wedding. From his knowledge of the man, he very much doubted whether Count Borodinov's pride would relish the thought of a bride who had to be dragged to the altar.

Alone in the room once more, Kirsty rose from her

seat and went over to the window. It was quite dark now, although it could scarcely be much later than three o'clock. The bitter Arctic wind howled round the wooden corners of the little township, and she felt grateful that it had not snowed for several days, for fresh snow would have been driven into impassable drifts that covered windows and doors.

There was nothing to be seen save her own reflection, dim in the thick panes, pale-faced and wide-eyed. She was small and slight with small bones and a pale, creamy skin enhanced by dark, almost black, hair, and large eyes, each grey iris with an outer rim that looked as though an artist had painted it with a perfect thin black line. The effect was to render startling an already beautiful face, but Kirsty herself was unaware of this.

She stared back, and her thoughts, though silent, were as clear and vivid as if she had been talking to that listening image.

The prospect of marrying a man selected by her father did not, in principle, worry her at all. It was, indeed, only to be expected, and a father was likely to be a far better judge of a man's character than a girl whose experience of the world was necessarily limited. She knew, too, that much as her father wanted this marriage, there would be no attempt to coerce her, should she decide to decline the offer. But what options were open to her? They were very few, she realised, and could see no prospect of their becoming more plentiful. If her father could be persuaded to return to England—or, for that matter, to let her return—the situation would be quite otherwise, but she dismissed that thought as soon as it occurred. Even if he were prepared to lay aside his lucrative business for a while, it was unlikely that Tsar Peter would permit him to do so, and if Peter were in favour of this suggested marriage, he would be equally unlikely to allow Kirsty to leave the country, since her doing so would indicate that a Russian boyar was not good enough for the daughter of a foreign merchant.

There were only three grounds on which she could reasonably decline this offer. If she had taken Count Borodinov in aversion—which, since she had never met him, could hardly be the case; if her father was aware of something to his detriment—and that certainly could not be so, for Kirsty knew that, no matter how much to Alexander's financial advantage a certain course of action might be, he would never knowingly put her own happiness at stake; or if she had formed an attachment elsewhere—and an attachment that was likely to result in a similar offer.

There was, of course, John Harrow. Not that she felt any attraction, but he was, she supposed, the most likely candidate for her hand. He was two years her senior and a pleasant enough young man, but given to acting very much on impulse in a way that made him seem much younger than she. Since John's father hoped to gain the Tsar's permission to send his three children home in order that the two daughters might themselves find husbands, it was unlikely that John himself would return a bachelor. Alexander had many times commented that young John needed a sensible wife to sober him down. The comment was true enough, and it was not a rôle Kirsty felt any inclination to fill.

So what reason had she for refusing Count Borodinov's offer? None, since the alternative might well be to remain unwed, a situation which might be perfectly bearable during her father's lifetime but would certainly not be so afterwards.

Briefly the reflection of a face seemed to flicker beside the reflection of her own. It was dark and handsome and very Russian, but the details were somehow blurred as in that of someone once seen and imperfectly recalled. The voice that accompanied it she recalled more vividly:

deep and quiet and implacable, yet with that almost musical quality that only Russian cadences can give. But the face and the voice had no name.

Kirsty shook herself. This was ridiculous! A girlish fantasy, no more. There was absolutely no reason why she should not marry Count Borodinov, and several why she should.

She turned from her reflection, and went in search of her father.

CHAPTER
TWO

As Count Borodinov had expressed a desire for the wedding to take place as soon as possible, all Alexander Benmore and his daughter needed were passports permitting them to travel to Moscow. In the meantime, Kirsty was to receive instruction, and baptism into the Orthodox church.

The Benmores were to stay with their friends the Harrows in the German Suburb, the foreign quarter of Moscow situated about a mile north-east of the capital's outer fortifications, and Alexander was anxious for them to be on their way before the spring rains turned the roads to Moscow into quagmires. They were lucky, and the journey by *troika*, though cold, was a great deal faster than could have been achieved by coach. Moscow itself was still in the firm hold of winter when they arrived.

It was Kirsty's first visit to the capital, and though she had naturally expected most of the buildings to be of wood, she was not entirely prepared for the size, splendour and ornate architecture of the numerous palaces built of that material, all interspersed with the humbler dwellings of the poor. Nor had she fully realised the visual impact of the hundreds of gilded onion domes that gleamed in the winter sun from churches large and small in every street.

She already knew that her own wedding was to be held, by gracious permission of the Tsar—who had already indicated that he would attend—in the little Church of the Deposition of the Robe. This small, elegant, single-domed building, tucked away between the great Cathedral of the Assumption and the Palace of the Facets inside the great Fortress of the Kremlin, had become the court chapel some fifty years before. That Count Borodinov's wedding was allowed to be held there was unusual, the more so since his bride was to be a foreigner. The rumours here of Peter's 'secret' marriage to Catherine were stronger than they had been in Archangel, and it crossed more than one mind that Peter might have been influenced by the knowledge that his wife—if she was his wife—was also a foreigner.

Kirsty had amused herself on the long journey south deciding on the nature of her bride-clothes, knowing that there would be no difficulty in finding a seamstress to make them. She was not pleased to find, on arrival at the Harrows', that her bride-clothes had preceded her.

'What can you mean?' she asked Margaret, the elder of the daughters, when the first effusions of greeting were done with. 'How can my bride-clothes be here? I have barely finished planning them!'

Mistress Harrow broke in gently. 'They were sent by Count Borodinov's order, my dear, and I have to confess that my daughters and I could not resist the temptation to look at them before laying them in the chest in your room.' She paused, and looked at Kirsty doubtfully. 'I do not think they will be quite what you had in mind.'

Mary giggled. 'I should not think Kirsty could have dreamed of such garments in a hundred years!' she exclaimed.

Bewildered, Kirsty looked from one to the other of them. 'What do you mean? They cannot, surely, be so outrageous?'

'Not outrageous,' Margaret assured her. 'Just outlandish. They are truly magnificent—barbaric, but splendid. Come, see for yourself.'

Kirsty needed no urging to follow her friend, and no sooner had the lid of the chest been thrown back than

she realised that Count Borodinov was making no concessions to his western bride. The garments laid out for
her inspection were, she realised, the traditional festive
costume of a boyarina.

The *sarafan*—a long, full, sleeveless dress that fitted
only on the shoulders and under which was worn a
delicately embroidered lawn blouse with long, full
sleeves—was of rich ruby damask, so heavily embroidered with tens of thousands of seed pearls that it
stood out stiffly and might almost, Kirsty suspected, be
self-supporting. Over it was to be worn a jacket of the
same material, which flared out from the shoulders to
just above the hip, its collar, hem, sleeves and fronts
edged with sable, the whole covered with embroidered
medallions of gold and silver thread and yet more pearls,
the meaning of whose symbolic design was lost on the
girls admiring the handiwork before them. Two *kokoch-
niki* were there as well: the tall, onion-shaped head-
dresses, so reminiscent of the gilded domes of the city's
churches, that were a flattering part of the national
costume at all levels of society, like the ubiquitous
sarafan. The smaller *kokochnik* was embroidered with
seed pearls and sat further back on the head, revealing
some hair at the front and all the hair at the back, but the
larger one, of cloth-of-gold embroidered with large
pearls and with one huge ruby at the base of the complex
central design, had a 'net' of pearls veiling the hair at the
front, and five long ropes of pearls at either side where
braids of hair might otherwise have been. A veil hid the
hair at the back and the whole head-dress was finished
off with a huge stiff bow behind. To complete the
ensemble were high-heeled, red velvet, pearl-
embroidered boots that reached to the knee.

'Barbaric' was one word to describe it. 'Magnificent'
was certainly another.

'But why two head-dresses?' Kirsty asked, trying on

each in turn. 'Could it be that Count Borodinov is actually giving me a choice?'

Margaret laughed. 'Alas, no! We asked our maid —who, I take leave to tell you, is overwhelmed by the magnificence of all this—and she says you go to the wedding wearing the smaller one and leave wearing the other. Apparently to cover your hair completely signifies the married state.'

Kirsty took little pressing to try on these opulent garments, and was very much surprised to find how well they fitted. The *sarafan*, of course, had only to sit on the shoulders and touch the floor, but it was precisely the right length, and the jacket fitted perfectly across the shoulders. The sleeves were perhaps a shade long, but nothing that could not easily be put right. Someone had furnished Count Borodinov with very accurate measurements, it seemed.

Looking at herself in the glass, she could not deny that these superb garments became her well, being entirely suited to her dark hair and creamy skin. What puzzled her was how she could be required to appear in such traditional dress, when the Tsar had decreed some years earlier that it should no longer be worn.

Now that she was actually in Moscow, Kirsty not unnaturally expected Count Borodinov to pay a morning visit, but he seemed determined to keep to the old Russian traditions. One would have thought that sheer curiosity might have prompted him to a prior view of his future Countess, but clearly, curiosity was not his besetting sin. He was certainly far from indifferent to the arrangements: not only had he supplied Kirsty's bride-clothes, but it soon became very clear that her father was to have no say in the proceedings. Count Borodinov intended to have every aspect of this wedding arranged precisely to his taste, and simply informed his future father-in-law—in the most tactful way possible, of course—of the steps he had taken.

This high-handed way of dealing with matters which did, after all, concern her fairly intimately, caused Kirsty more than a few qualms. There seemed to be an inflexibility and a determination about the Count's behaviour that boded none too well for the future. She had no real objections to marrying a Russian, and she was perfectly prepared to meet him more than half-way where customs conflicted, but she was not at all sure that she wished to be pressed quite so inexorably into a Russian mould. The same thought had occurred to Margaret Harrow and her mother.

It was Mistress Harrow who broached the matter one evening as they sat over their tambour-frames. 'Count Borodinov seems a very determined man,' she began hesitantly.

'That would certainly appear to be the case,' Kirsty agreed wryly.

'Are you sure—forgive me, for I know it is none of my business, but you have no mother, and I have always felt towards you as I do to my own daughters—are you sure this is a wise marriage?'

'Can anyone be sure a marriage will be wise?' Kirsty asked with a lightness she did not feel, for the question had been in her own mind for some while.

'You see, my dear, although you are very quiet and prettily behaved, I have often observed that you are quite as strong-willed as your father, and Count Borodinov's management of affairs so far does rather indicate that he expects a wife to be rather more submissive than I think you are inclined to be.'

'A doormat, in fact?' Kirsty said cheerfully.

Mistress Harrow demurred that that was not quite how she would have chosen to put it.

'But it is nevertheless what I think you meant!' Kirsty replied. 'I very much fear you may be right, but it is too late to draw back now, you know. We must just hope that he is open to argument when one meets him face to face. After all, he does not know me yet, and he surely cannot believe that I shall necessarily fit into his preconceived ideas of a wife—the very fact of my being a foreigner must lead him to expect something different, do you not think?'

Mistress Harrow had no such faith in the reasonableness of men, but wisely held her own counsel. As Kirsty had intimated, to draw back now would be to cause incalculable repercussions, not the least of which would be the probable banishment of the Benmores to England if they were lucky, to the east of the Urals if they were not.

Margaret was of a more romantic disposition than her mother. 'Papa and John say that Kirsty could charm the birds off the trees, if she set her mind to it. I am sure that Count Borodinov will pose few problems.'

'Let us hope that Master Harrow and his son are right,' Kirsty said, still determinedly cheerful. 'Just so long as my Russian Count doesn't expect me to live the rest of my life in a *terem*, I am sure I can contrive to be happy.'

The wedding was to prove a strange mixture of east and west. Because the bride's domicile in Moscow was in the house of a Protestant foreigner, it was quite impossible for the first part of the festivities, which normally took place in the bride's home, to be pursued in the normal way. It was equally unthinkable that they should take place in the house of the groom. The dilemma was solved by the Tsar, who decreed that he would take the part usually undertaken by the bride's father, and he also put the Terem Palace at the bride's disposal for the first part of the ceremonial.

So, on the afternoon of her wedding-day, Kirsty made

her way there in the closed palanquin provided by her groom and was shown into a private apartment where three *svakhi*, the serving-women deputed to perform their special function during the wedding, had been detailed to help her to dress.

In the evening, the priest led the groom's procession from his own house to the Terem Palace to be greeted by the bride's friends. At the forefront of these was the bride's proxy father, Tsar Peter, who graciously allowed Alexander Benmore to stand beside him to receive guests, although, as a foreigner who did not belong to the Orthodox faith, he could take no part in the ensuing ceremony.

When the groom was finally seated at the head of the table on which just three dishes were placed, Kirsty entered, so heavily veiled that she had to be led into the room and guided to the place beside him.

But it was the custom that the groom should not see his bride until the wedding night, and so, to preserve this secrecy, two boys stretched a sheet of red satin between the couple and held it there. This was the signal for the most senior *svakha* to play her part. Removing the heavy veil and the small head-dress, she combed Kirsty's hair and plaited it in two braids before putting the larger *kokochnik* on her head so that the bride appeared to be wearing a crown. Kirsty was able to remain for a while with her face uncovered, while the *svakha* moved over to comb the Count's hair.

Two of the Tsar's household then brought in silver salvers containing bread and cheese, which the priest duly blessed. At this point, the *svakha* covered Kirsty's face once more, and then the Tsar, representing her father, and an elderly Borodinov uncle, representing the groom's, stood up and ceremoniously exchanged the rings of the young couple.

Then Kirsty was led out of the room and the Palace

and across the few yards to the little church, closely followed by Count Borodinov and his friends. The bride and groom moved forward across the red satin on the floor of the church which indicated where the ceremony would take place, and came to a halt on that part specially marked for them. Kirsty peeped sideways up at her groom, but so thick was her veil that she could make out nothing except that he was very tall, and in dark clothes which seemed more western than Russian.

The two 'fathers' held ikons over the heads of the young couple, and while these holy pictures were being blessed, the rest of the congregation—standing, as was customary in Orthodox churches—lit candles which they held for the rest of the proceedings, the flames gleaming on the gold of the iconostasis so that the whole church seemed richly alive with colour and warm, glowing light.

Kirsty could not prevent the slight trembling of her hand as the priest joined it with that of her husband, and was in some sort comforted by the unwavering strength in the fingers that clasped her own while the priest repeated three times the question, vital to the ceremony, whether they wished to take one another and to live together in peace. Having received the expected answer, the priest, a candle in each hand, then led them in a circle, while crowns of flowers were held over their heads by their respective 'fathers'.

When they had completed their circuit, the priest exhorted them to 'be fruitful and multiply', and finally united them with the age-old proclamation familiar to Kirsty from Protestant weddings: 'Whom God has joined together, let no man put asunder.' With that, he drank from a glass of red wine, and the bride and groom followed suit. Count Borodinov threw the glass to the ground and trampled it into small fragments, with the declaration: 'In this way any who wish to create discord between us will fall under our feet and be trampled in their turn.'

When Kirsty heard his voice, she looked up, startled. Surely the voice was familiar? His previous responses had been monosyllabic, and now that she heard him utter a full sentence, she was indeed surprised. Surely she knew that voice? She glanced up at the tall figure beside her, but her veil, designed to be sufficiently thick to hide her face from her betrothed until they should be man and wife, was equally effective in preventing her from seeing more than his general shape.

The voice was the only indication of his identity. Could there be two men in Russia with just those deep yet softly threatening tones? An image flashed before her of a man in Archangel, so long ago, but there was nothing she could make out through her veil to tell her whether this was he. The voice, deep and caressing, was similar. She told herself to be sensible, common sense suggested that it must be pure coincidence.

Count Borodinov then took his bride's arm and guided her out of the church beneath a hail of hemp- and flax-seeds. He handed her into her palanquin before mounting his horse and accompanying his Countess to her new home.

The Borodinov Palace, in which Kirsty could expect to live for the greater part of her life, was a building about which she, not unnaturally, had a great deal of curiosity. As she felt her bearers draw to a halt, she could not resist the opportunity of twitching the curtains aside to catch a glimpse of it.

There was no denying its magnificence. Although built entirely of wood, it soared to three storeys, and with its onion-domed roofs and ornately carved windows, its horseshoe arches and latticed stairs, it looked like a palace from some oriental dream, an impression accentuated by the vivid colours in which it was painted.

Here was no restrained English taste: every piece of
exposed wood was painted—no doubt very necessary
for its preservation—in viridian and red, yellow-
ochre and russet; it called to mind some fairy-tale
gingerbread house and in its brilliant way it was as
appealing.

Her bearers stopped at the foot of a covered staircase,
its sides lattice-screened, that led into the huge entrance
hall, and Count Borodinov's proffered arm assisted her
from her palanquin and up the steps at the top of which
she was to stand beside—and slightly behind—him to
greet their guests.

This very western custom she found bewildering,
because in this setting it seemed incongruous. Was she to
regard her husband as a traditionalist, as had certainly
been her original impression, or as one of those determined to haul Russia into the modern age? It was
confusing, but she had little time to give the puzzle much
thought, for the first of their guests arrived almost before
the young couple had drawn breath.

However uncertain she might be as to her husband's
position in relation to the Tsar's ambitions for Russia
and his willingness to play his part in implementing
them, it was a simple fact that Kirsty could hardly
receive their guests in the western manner while her face
was still concealed. Neither did it seem appropriate, in
the public situation in which they now stood, to ask his
permission to remove her heavy veil. So, after a brief
hesitation as to the least conspicuous course of action,
Kirsty lifted the double layer of closely woven muslin
and threw it back over her head-dress. For the first time
she had the opportunity of snatching a glance at her
husband's face.

Afraid at first to seem too inquisitive—though, in the
circumstances, she could hardly imagine why she should
not be—she cast a quick glance up at him. Her breath

caught in a short gasp that was almost a sob. Her ears had not deceived her: this was indeed the man who had come to her aid in Archangel. This was the face that had haunted her unguarded moments!

Perhaps aware of her surreptitious scrutiny, he looked down, a smile in his eyes, though not on his lips. Embarrassed, Kirsty dropped her gaze, scarcely noticing that he wore the dark green uniform of the Preobrazhensky Guards rather than the traditional costume of a boyar, and felt her colour rise. As it did so, she was aware of a distressingly unquiet thought: no wonder he had not felt it necessary to pay a morning call—he had already known what his selected bride looked like. What arrogance it betokened that he had not extended the same privilege to her!

The first guest to present himself was that tall young giant who had played her father's part in the wedding ceremony, and Kirsty was naturally rather apprehensive at this, her first clear view of the young Tsar. So tall that he dwarfed the Count, himself some six feet in height, Peter also wore the uniform of his favourite regiment. Like most Russians, however westernised, he wore his own hair, and there was no sign of the facial tic that was said to come upon him in moments of stress. He was accompanied by a plump, dark-haired, pleasant-faced woman whom Kirsty correctly assumed to be the Catherine who might, or might not, have become the Tsar's second wife.

The bow Count Borodinov made to this couple was so deep as to be almost a genuflexion. Kirsty copied his example, and curtsied as low as her heavy *kokochnik* permitted. The Tsar raised her to her feet.

'We are pleased to make the closer acquaintance of our new "daughter". We trust you did not mind obeying our instruction to wear the traditional clothes of your new class,' he said jocularly.

'On the contrary, sir, I was delighted,' she assured him.

'Generally, as you may be aware, we prefer western clothes to be worn, but it seemed more appropriate on this occasion that you should be seen to emphasise your acceptance of life as a Russian.'

Kirsty curtsied again. 'I am greatly honoured that you have not only attended our wedding but graciously played so important a part. It will be something to tell my children—that the Tsar himself took my father's part and held my crown of flowers.'

'A crown can be a heavy burden,' he replied, but any solemn portent that might have been read into his words was belied by the cheerful smile that accompanied them: this ruler might find the crown a burdensome item, but it was not one he would willingly relinquish.

The Tsar and his consort took their place beside the bridal pair, and joined with them in welcoming the assembly to what was to prove a very western style of wedding-breakfast. These guests, unlike those of the Governor of Archangel, comported themselves much more in the western mode, and though the eating and drinking were hearty and the dancing owed little to the west, nothing was carried to quite the excess that Kirsty's other experience might have led her to expect. Indeed, she began to feel considerably more optimistic about her future. If Count Borodinov was intent upon obeying his emperor's explicit intructions to emulate the west, perhaps he had chosen her because she would be so suited to help him to carry it through. Kirsty smiled with a contented pride: if that had been his reason for offering for her hand, she would make sure he was not disappointed. It would be her particular pleasure to help her husband and his household to make the difficult transition that the Tsar required.

When the time came for the newly-married couple to

be raised to shoulder height by their guests and marched through the house to the bedchamber with the ribaldry that such events always provoke. Kirsty felt quite cheerful.

But when the door had closed behind them, the sounds of revelry receded, and she was alone for the first time with the husband she barely knew, her cheerfulness and optimism evaporated, to be replaced by an inevitable shyness. There was nothing missish about this: she knew well enough what was expected of her, but she had never before been alone with any man except her father, and was suddenly quite desperately anxious to get to know this handsome man first.

Count Borodinov's first action once they were alone was to remove his full-skirted coat and his boots and exchange them for a heavily embroidered *kaftan* of the kind so disliked by his Tsar. Then he moved over to a little table and poured two glasses of honey-coloured liquid, one of which he handed to his bride.

'Mead,' he said curtly.

'Thank you, sir,' she murmured, and sipped the wine gratefully. The relaxed warmth that would follow in its wake would ease the uncertainties of this night.

He watched her as she did so, and Kirsty, conscious of his scrutiny, glanced up, to be disconcerted by his impassive gaze. Then he stepped forward and removed the heavy *kokochnik* from her head, placing it on the table beside the mead. He gently unfastened and removed her sable-edged jacket and threw it on a chair beside the hearth. His long fingers, strong and sensitive, ran through her curls so that her hair hung over her shoulders, accentuating the pale, fine-boned beauty of her face.

'That is better.' There was satisfaction in his voice. 'Only a husband should see his wife's hair so loose and free.'

Once again the deep voice remembered from Archangel stirred Kirsty's heart. It was strange, she thought, that so simple a thing as a voice could have so devastating an effect. Strange, too, that she should so clearly have remembered the voice, whereas the face had begun to dim. She smiled shyly up at him and was for the first time able to scrutinise thoroughly the man she had married.

Count Borodinov was tall and long-limbed, the lean-ness that accompanies such a build being echoed in his face with its high Slavic cheek-bones and aquiline nose. The angle of the cheek-bones set his grey eyes at an angle that recalled the features of the Tartars who once ruled this mighty land, a similarity enhanced by his dark hair. Dressed as he now was in a *kaftan*, itself an inheritance from the days of Tartar rule, he looked more barbarian than European, and Kirsty dropped her gaze, confused: in his western uniform he had looked simply as unusually handsome officer; now she felt that the essential Russianness of the man had suddenly been underlined, and she realised in her heart for the first time what her head had told her before: that the gulf between Russian and European was huge, and to throw a bridge across it might prove a difficult undertaking indeed.

Watching her in his turn and puzzled by the sudden dropping of her frank gaze, Sergei led her quietly to the ornately carved and painted bed.

'Will you not be seated?' he asked gently. 'We have the night before us, and I, for one, do not propose to remain standing for its duration.'

'I am sorry. I did not think.' Kirsty's confusion brought colour to her cheeks. It had not occurred to her that he might simply be waiting to follow her lead, and in the absence of chairs—a western item of which perhaps Count Borodinov disapproved—she had not thought to use the bed as a substitute.

Briefly, gently, Sergei lifted her fingers to his lips. 'It does not matter. We scarcely know one another. How, then, could you anticipate?'

His words brought a little smile to his bride's lips. 'I think it was the absence of chairs,' she told him. 'I know it sounds foolish, but I just didn't think.'

'Tomorrow the carpenter will present himself and you will instruct him in what you wish him to provide,' he said quietly.

Kirsty's confusion returned. 'Oh, no . . . I didn't mean . . . I wasn't hinting . . .'

'This is your home now. It will be ordered as you wish. If you would prefer chairs in the western style, then they shall be provided.'

'You are very kind,' Kirsty murmured.

'Not at all. I wish my wife to be happy—and before you thank me for my consideration, remind yourself that it is an essentially selfish wish. For if a wife is happy, then the husband is likely to be so, too.'

Kirsty began to feel slightly less tense. It seemed that her husband had sufficient humour to laugh at himself, for though his voice was perfectly serious, there was a warmth and a gleam in his eyes which belied it. The mead, too, was having its effect, and she felt comfortably warm within and without, and with that general warmth came a further relaxation of the tension inevitably attendant upon an occasion such as this.

Observing this, Sergei reached for the mead and replenished his own glass. 'Will you have more?'

Kirsty hesitated, and then nodded. The mead's effect was far from unpleasant, and, besides, one little corner of her mind was glad that the glass gave her something to do.

Sergei looked at her questioningly. 'Are you accustomed to mead?'

Kirsty shook her head. 'I cannot recall drinking it

before: Papa used to bring in wines from France—and Hollands for himself. Ararat milk, he used to call it,' she added inconsequentially.

'Then I must have a care not to give you too much,' Sergei commented. 'It would never do to have you fall asleep on your wedding night.'

He meant the words harmlessly enough but regretted them as soon as they were uttered, for he sensed the restraint that returned to Kirsty's manner. He touched her cheek with his forefinger. 'A thoughtless remark,' he said. 'Forgive me.' She smiled, albeit doubtfully, and he was prompted to add, 'It is my first wedding night, too, you know.'

This time Kirsty chuckled. 'To tell the truth, that had not even occurred to me,' she confessed.

'Then in that respect we stand on equal footing, do we not?' he asked, pleased to have been able to retrieve the situation so easily. He was a little taken aback to be rewarded with a distinctly speculative eye.

'Do we?' Kirsty countered. 'Not entirely, I would imagine.'

Touché, Sergei thought, surprised. Could it be that his English bride might be rather sharper than he was accustomed to in a woman? But he kept his thought to himself. He laughed briefly. 'I take your point.'

There was a silence between them then, a somewhat self-conscious silence during which Kirsty was happy to have her mead to sip. Sergei watched her for a few moments. 'You take your mead very seriously,' he said at last. 'I hope it meets with your approval.'

'Yes, I like it,' she said, and then giggled. 'We are making small talk like two strangers who have only just been introduced.'

'Is that not what we are?' Sergei replied. 'I know we had met before—"encountered" is perhaps a better word—but we are hardly acquainted with one another. I imagine conversation becomes easier with time.' He took her hand once more and kissed it, and then, to Kirsty's confusion, turned it over and kissed the pulse in her wrist. He looked into her eyes, and reading there a warmth which perhaps accounted for the trembling of her fingers, he touched her cheek gently and then turned her unresisting face towards his own. His kiss was brief and gentle, and when Kirsty's hand fluttered uncertainly to his shoulder, its successor was long and lingering and tender. There was nothing more natural in the world than that he should gently take her wine glass from her or that his embrace should become closer, stronger.

Kirsty's heart sang. Somewhere, at the back of her dreams, this was how it should be; this was what she had imagined, and her body moved instinctively to his. As if he had only been waiting for the encouragement of such implied compliance, Sergei took her head between his hands and his mouth descended upon hers with an unexpected hardness. Unexpected, but not unwelcome. Kirsty's heart beat faster as hitherto unsuspected feelings seemed to take over her body, and when Sergei's hard kisses forced open her mouth that his tongue might explore it, her head swam.

This was not the gentle courtship she had envisaged, yet, unimagined as it was, it was not distasteful. Her hands reached out for him, and as he felt their fluttering touch, he swept her into his arms and she felt his body, strong and urgent, pulsing against her own. Then, suddenly, he broke away and was discarding his robe, his shirt, his breeches.

'Come,' he said. 'We have work this night, and clearly we are neither of us averse to it.'

Kirsty stared at him, uncertain at first, not of what he expected of her, but of the manner of it, and then she dropped her eyes at the unfamiliar sight of a man beside her, naked.

Sensing her hesitation, he laughed softly and pulled her gently to her feet. She was reassured by the tender, lingering kiss he bestowed upon her before, in one deft, practised movement, he pulled her *sarafan* over her head. Now he held her close and tight, their bodies touching through the thin cotton of her blouse and shift in a way that both disturbed and excited her newly-aroused senses. Then his hand was at her neck, and suddenly one swift gesture ripped her blouse and chemise so far that they slid down round her feet.

'Like Venus rising from the waves,' he said softly, pressing her once more towards him, and Kirsty, conscious as she was of her nakedness, nevertheless could not repress a thrill of excitement and a sudden welcoming of the submission that moulded her to him.

With no warning, he lifted her in his arms and laid her on the coverlet of miniver and stood briefly, looking down at her before half-sitting, half-reclining beside her, his hand caressing tenderly her fast-awakening body.

'My God, how you are beautiful!' he whispered, and then he lay beside her, his mouth on hers, his hands gently, arousingly, exploring her body.

Her response to the cajolery of those strong fingers was instinctive: her hands caressed the strong muscles of his shoulders and her thighs parted languorously in response to his questing touch.

The next she knew was the searing tip of his manhood, piercing, thrusting, tearing her apart, and, all langour gone, she screamed and screamed again and then moaned as his rhythmic desire slaked itself. A sudden thrusting surge and it was done, and he lay within her, spent, for some moments before affording her the release she sought.

He smiled down at her and turned her face gently towards him, intending to kiss her, to fondle her until his vigour returned, thinking the next time to enjoy his bride more slowly and perhaps to coax her to heights of ecstasy.

He was startled at the blank face he looked down upon, and that there was no response to his kiss, only a stiffening at his touch. He raised his hand to lift a tendril of dark hair from her moist brow and was shocked to see the tears slowly coursing down her cheeks. When she turned away from him without a glance, the shock turned into a hurt which flickered briefly but unseen in his eyes and transformed itself into an urge to retaliate.

He raised himself on one elbow and stared down at her, weeping silently at his side and trembling like a silver birch in an Arctic wind. At last he spoke.

'At least we know you came to your wedding-bed a virgin.' His voice was harsh and unfeeling. But there was nothing unfeeling about the way he covered her trembling body with the miniver counterpane, though Kirsty in her misery was aware only of the harsh displeasure of his voice.

There was no coaxing to heights of ecstasy that night.

CHAPTER
THREE

WHEN KIRSTY awoke, her husband had gone and the events of the previous night might have been but a nightmare, had she not felt so stiff and sore. She lay on the borders of wakefulness for several minutes before the mists of sleep cleared and she knew that those events had been no nightmare. Alone and unobserved as she was, she felt herself flush with the degradation of her memory, a degradation of which her aching body was ample testimony. Perhaps such pain was inevitable— she had heard as much in hints and whispers, here and there. But why had he left her thus arbitrarily? Did he not realise the pain and anguish he had caused? Kirsty felt the tears pricking her eyes again and with them came an even less welcome thought. Had he left her in disgust at her reaction? How had her husband expected her to react to an action, the sheer physical violence of which had been so totally unexpected? Was this not how other women reacted? For Kirsty had no illusion that she might be the first woman in Count Borodinov's life.

Turning these thoughts over in her mind brought her no consolation, and it was with relief she heard the respectful tap at the door which announced a serving-girl with hot chocolate.

'Sergei Ivanovich requests that you join him when you have bathed and breakfasted, that the wedding gifts may be examined,' she said.

Count Borodinov's palace had its own bathroom, and as Kirsty felt her aching body ease, she acknowledged that such a luxury was worth every *kopek* of the fee payable to the Tsar for the privilege of private bathing.

There was much giggling among the serving-women as they laboured to comprehend the intricacies of their new mistress' western clothes, but at last it was done and they led her to the huge dining-room where the wedding gifts—or those that were small enough to be brought in—were laid out.

The room was low-ceilinged with low, horseshoe doorways, and every inch of wall and arch was richly ornamented with painted and gilded foliage and flowers and the stiff, formal ikons that, until so recently, had been the only permitted form of decorative painting. The gifts rivalled the room in magnificence, and Kirsty knew that it was not customary to retain them all but to return those that were not wanted to their donors.

Count Borodinov was waiting for her, pacing the inlaid wooden floor in a boyar's flowing *kaftan*, its heavy fur collar humped over the wearer's shoulders so that they echoed the curve of the doorway.

He stopped as she entered, and frowned.

'Were there no Russian garments in your coffers?' he asked harshly.

'You know there were, sir,' she replied stiffly, as she recalled the unhappy events of their last meeting. 'I understood, however, that the Tsar has decreed that only western clothes shall be worn.'

'Within these walls, I prefer it otherwise, but no matter.' His voice grew harsh. 'Doubtless you feel more comfortable in those. However, it will please me if sometimes you wear the *sarafan*.'

Kirsty inclined her head. 'Then I shall do so, sir,' she said.

He looked irritated. 'Do not address me thus. It is not seemly.'

She flushed. 'You must forgive my ignorance, Count. How should I address my husband?'

'My name is Sergei when we are alone. In front of

others, whether serfs or Tsar, I am Sergei Ivanovich. You will be called Christina Alexandrovna. The servants may call you that or they may prefer "*barinya*" —"my lady". You will be referred to as the Countess Borodinova.'

'That much I knew.'

He looked at Kirsty curiously. 'When we first met —an event I suspect you scarcely remember—you spoke no Russian at all, and in the circumstances, that was probably just as well. Yet now you are fluent, if not perhaps perfect. Can you have learned so much since your father arranged this marriage?'

Kirsty smiled tentatively. 'Perhaps I should lie and say I have, but the truth is otherwise: I do indeed recall our first encounter and have been grateful for your intervention ever since. But I must confess to a strong curiosity as to just what that unpleasant old man said, and I was determined never to be at such a disadvantage again, so I set about learning Russian. Our impending marriage added impetus, I need hardly add. I had not, of course, expected that I would ever be in a position where I might ask you what was said.'

He laughed. 'Your curiosity must remain unsatisfied, Christina Alexandrovna. I would not repeat it even, to my wife. That such a remark was made at all brings credit to neither my country nor my class, and you will go to your grave in ignorance of it.'

There was an implacability underlying the laugh in his voice which persuaded her to let the matter drop: it was not, after all, of any major importance, but his next words served only to discompose her.

'I am glad my intervention on that occasion was appreciated. Was it gratitude that inspired you to agree to our marriage?'

It might have been—and something more besides —had I known it was you, she thought, but, incurably truthful, she blushed. 'Alas, I must confess that I did not know that the man desirous of our alliance was the one who had earned my gratitude.

His face clouded imperceptibly. 'Then it would perhaps be unwise to ask what prompted your acceptance.'

Kirsty stared at him. 'Why should it be unwise? It is customary in both our countries for marriages to be arranged for the convenience of both parties. The only difference I am aware of is that in Russia girls do not seem to have the opportunity to decline.'

'Yet you did have such an opportunity and chose not to exercise it. I can only infer that the alliance suited your convenience.'

'Which is precisely why I assumed the offer was made,' she retorted. 'After all, my father is a wealthy man, and I came well dowered. Was that not the reason?'

Any hope she might have cherished as to his answer was immediately dashed. He shrugged. 'What other reason might there be?' The question seemed rhetorical, and the tone indicated that he had in some strange way withdrawn from her. Kirsty changed the subject.

'Are these, then, our gifts?' she asked, turning to the array before her.

'They are splendid, are they not?' he commented ironically. 'Influenced, no doubt, by the fact that we need few of them. Samovars, for example. I think we have so many that we certainly do not require three more. I have, however, decided that one shall be kept for use by you in your own quarters.' He gestured towards the three huge silver urns. 'You shall choose which it shall be.' His tone was magnanimous.

Kirsty shot him a glance, wondering if the magnanimity, too, were ironic in its intent, but decided not. She did not realise that, in allowing her any choice at all,

Count Borodinov was making a great concession to his wife's foreignness. She looked at the three ornate silver samovars. There was really very little difference between them. They were all equally heavily ornamented and were probably equally efficient at heating water. She turned to her husband. 'In truth, I have no preference. Is there one that, by reason of the donor, you would prefer me to keep?'

She realised as she spoke that she could not have said anything that would have pleased him better. He pointed to one that was, if anything, very slightly smaller than the others.

'This one. It is a gift from an elderly aunt who can ill afford to have bought it, and so when I must pay within the year for those gifts we keep, I shall be able to value it at a greater price than it can have cost, and thereby enable her to accept money to ease her lot that her pride would otherwise prevent her from accepting.'

'Then that shall be the one,' Kirsty declared. 'You may tell her, if you will, that I shall think of her with great affection whenever it is used.'

There was no mistaking the warmth in his eyes. 'Come,' he said. 'There can be no doubt that we can deal well together,' and he took her hand. But at his touch, the memory of last night's pain came flooding back, and he felt her fingers stiffen and saw that her face was rigid with apprehension. He let her hand drop, and his face hardened. The gulf between them that seemed, however briefly, to have narrowed, now yawned as wide as ever. How little he knew of this Englishwoman whose fragile beauty had entranced him since the first time he had seen her! She had left him in no doubt that it was a marriage of convenience, but now that she had his wealth and status, could she not at least meet him half way? The wedding gifts were safer ground. He gestured towards them.

'I have decided upon which we shall not keep, but

if there is anything here that you particularly like, you have only to say. There are two other gifts.' He strode over to a window and flung open the casement, beckoning her to join him.

In the courtyard below stood a ponderous western travelling carriage, and beside it a groom holding two long-headed, curly-coated greyhounds of the type used for hunting wolves.

'The carriage is a gift from your father—a gift in the English tradition, as he stressed when it arrived, and therefore it shall be kept. The hounds will be returned. I do not like them.'

'Oh, no!' Kirsty cried. 'You cannot say so! Of all the gifts I have seen, they would give me the greatest pleasure. When I was a child, we had a dog that I loved dearly, but we could not bring it with us and the opportunity for another never arose in Archangel: dogs are not much kept as pets there, I fancy.'

'Nor anywhere in Russia, save by those who will appear western in their ways,' he said shortly. 'But if a pet is what you want, the wife of a fellow-officer has a little pocket spaniel that whelped some two weeks since. I will get one of those, provided you keep it out of my way. These two are not pets. They are hunting-dogs, and would be spoiled for their work.'

'You do not understand,' Kirsty protested. 'I have never seen their like outside this country and they are so beautiful! Of all the dogs I have seen here, these wolf-hounds are the ones I have most admired, but when I begged Papa to get me one, he told me that only the nobility might own them. Now I have the opportunity.'

'Nevertheless, they are not suitable. We have some on our country estate, and you will see them when we move there. These will be returned.'

'But these are a gift; that makes them different,' Kirsty insisted. 'Besides, you have just told me I might have whichever of the presents I wished. Well, I have decided: I shall have the hounds.'

'What sort of wife is it who picks the one thing guaranteed to displease her husband?' His voice was cold.

'An English one,' she retorted before she had given herself time to think. 'And what sort of a husband is it who goes back on his word?'

'Not a Russian one,' he said stiffly. 'I request you, however, to keep them out of the house when I am in it.'

'You will not see them outside the stable block, I promise,' she assured him.

'Very well. We shall speak no more on the subject of wedding gifts. Come with me to see your quarters.'

Without waiting to see whether she followed and without pausing to usher her through doors before him, he strode through the palace. Kirsty had assumed that the room where she had spent the wedding night would be her bedroom, a prospect which did not altogether delight her, but he led her to another wing of the house where a single door led to a comfortable suite of rooms overlooking the courtyard but with no windows facing the outside. The rooms were as ornately decorated as everything else she had seen, there was a private bath, and it was all as opulently comfortable as the most ardent sybarite could wish.

'This is your *terem*,' he said. 'Naturally, when I am from home, you will be at liberty to make free of the palace—how else can you keep house, after all? But when I am home, you will confine yourself to your *terem* except by invitation; when I have guests, you will naturally not be seen.'

Kirsty stared at him, aghast. 'A *terem*? Do you seriously expect me to remain in seclusion like some Turkish concubine?'

He shrugged. 'It is the Russian custom.'

'And I am not a Russian!' she flared. 'You must have known when you offered for me that such seclusion would be quite unacceptable to a westerner!'

'I did not expect that seeking to please her husband would also be unacceptable to such a one.'

Kirsty's eyes were pleading as she laid her hand upon the brocade sleeve of his *kaftan*. 'Indeed, sir . . . Sergei . . . I do not mean to displease you, but seclusion . . . the *terem*! I beg you, do not condemn me to a life of such boredom! I shall behave with absolute circumspection, I promise you, but leave me at least the freedom I had in the German Suburb.'

'Where women have a freedom most Russians find quite unnatural. As for boredom—why, it does not seem to bother Russian women, and you will have your hounds to keep you company, will you not?' he added bitterly.

Kirsty hesitated, unsure how to broach what was in her mind. 'And tonight?' she said at last.

'Tonight? Rest assured, Christina Alexandrovna, you will not be disturbed. An heir we must ensure, but that can wait until you have schooled yourself to overcome your revulsion.'

'But I don't . . . it isn't . . .' Kirsty floundered.

He looked at her coldly. 'Your body told me all I needed to know. At least I can credit you with no dissimulation. Be grateful that I do not demonstrate my affection in what is said to be the time-honoured way of my people.'

'I do not understand.'

'It is said by some foreign observers that Russian husbands hold it to be a great sign of affection that they beat their wives.'

'If it is true, then you have amply demonstrated your true feelings,' Kirsty whispered.

'It is not a custom that I have ever felt had anything to

commend it, even were it carried on, but you will doubtless interpret matters as you please. I am on duty, and shall leave you now. Ask for anything you want: the servants are here for your convenience.'

He turned, and swept out too quickly to see the pleading hand outstretched towards him as if to pluck him back. The door closed behind him, and Kirsty was left alone in the *terem*.

CHAPTER
FOUR

IN FACT, Kirsty found plenty with which to occupy herself in the next few days through the simple necessity of familiarising herself with the running of the palace. Sergei's military duties kept him often away, and since, when he was at home, he treated her with an icy, distant politeness, she was not altogether sorry to see so little of him. He did not come near her bedroom, and she found her feelings about this to be distinctly mixed: on the one hand she gradually ceased to steel herself for sounds of his impending arrival and its consequences—consequences which she had managed to convince herself could only be painful; on the other, it was scarcely a boost to her self-confidence to have a husband who could so easily dispense with her company.

Her first visitor was Alexander Benmore, who allowed himself to be shown over her new home and made the appropriately appreciative noises, but seemed somehow preoccupied. The tour of inspection finished, they sat down on divans while the samovar was brought in and Kirsty dispensed tea. Now that she was no longer drawing his attention to this feature or that, she became more strongly aware that her father's thoughts were elsewhere.

'What is the matter, Papa?' she asked. 'You seem to have something on your mind.'

He sipped his tea carefully before replying. 'It is nothing that need worry you. It is simply that I am disappointed to have had my stay in Moscow curtailed so suddenly.'

'So suddenly? Are you not to remain here, then? When must you leave?'

'You had not heard? Permission to remain has been withdrawn. I am to return to Archangel within the week. A pity: I had made some useful connections here and hoped to be allowed to transfer my business to the capital.'

'Why has it been withdrawn so suddenly? What reason were you given?'

'None, as is usually the case. However, I have, as I said, made some useful connections and was able to suggest in some quarters that, while I shall obviously comply with the order, I would like to have an idea as to the reason. It appears that Count Borodinov has something to do with it.'

'Sergei? How should that be?'

Alexander shrugged. 'So far as I have been able to ascertain, he feels that you will find it easier to adapt to Russian ways if foreign influences are removed from you.'

Kirsty looked at him, perplexed. 'But I thought Tsar Peter wished to encourage western influences, Papa? Can Sergei be influential enough to be able to persuade his Tsar to overcome his ideals so easily?'

He smiled, a shade grimly. 'I doubt that your husband does have so much influence with the Tsar. But there are plenty in positions of power who do not like the westernisation of Russia, and some are able to revoke passports in the name of the Tsar, if not to issue them.'

'Will you appeal against this decision?' Kirsty asked.

'Not I. The matter is not so crucial that I would risk losing the patronage I have enjoyed so far—and it would be very much at stake were I to offend in certain quarters.'

This there was no gainsaying, and Kirsty had, in any

case, realised that it was extremely unlikely that her father would be allowed to stay in Moscow indefinitely. She would have liked him to have remained a little longer, but since it was not to be, she must make the best of it.

Alexander looked at her with some sympathy. 'Do not forget that our good friends the Harrows are in the German Suburb, and are likely to remain there,' he reminded her. 'I know Mistress Harrow and her daughters are always willing to receive you.'

Kirsty was also aware of this, and smiled a little absently as she assured her father that he need not worry about leaving her to her new life so soon. She had no illusion that she might be able to reverse the order that would send him back to Archangel, but she could certainly let her cold husband know her feelings on the subject.

She knew she had until the following afternoon to consider how best to approach the matter, and when the Count returned home, he was extremely gratified to see his wife in a traditional *sarafan*, a fact which earned her a marginally warmer greeting than she was becoming accustomed to. When he found that the meal laid before him consisted largely of the food he liked best, he became positively expansive. There was a smile in his grey eyes that brought Kirsty's heart into her mouth, but she kept her own eyes modestly downcast until, his meal finished, he laid his linen napkin aside and his hand over hers, feeling it flutter, but not stiffen. The smile became warmer.

'Tell me, Kirsty, was it by chance you served my favourite dishes?' he asked, his voice almost teasing.

Kirsty looked up at him innocently. 'No, sir, it was not. I determined to please you and consulted the cook. She was delighted to advise me as to those recipes most calculated to please you, and between us we planned the meal. Did it indeed meet with your approval?'

'Most assuredly it did, as does your modest—and very Russian—appearance.' He lifted the hand that lay captive under his own and raised it gently to his lips. 'Come, Kirsty, let us withdraw to the Divan Room.'

Kirsty was happy to follow him into the low-ceilinged, heavily ornamented room whose function corresponded to an English withdrawing-room, though it was, because of the couches that lined the walls, a great deal more comfortable.

Sergei led her over to a divan, but before she could sit down, he drew her gently to him and, tilting her chin gently, kissed her lightly upon her upturned lips. There was no stiffening this time, he noticed with satisfaction and relief, no feeling that she might withdraw from him. Thus emboldened, he put his arm round her tiny waist, invisible under the voluminous folds of the *sarafan*, and pulled her more firmly against him. This time there was nothing light about his kisses, nor was there any reserve in her response. Her arms crept up around his neck and her eyelids closed, the long black lashes like crescent moons upon her ivory cheeks.

Then he lifted her in his arms and laid her unresisting body on the broad expanse of the couch, and half-lay, half-sat beside her, gazing down upon the delicate beauty that now was his in name if not perhaps in heart. He longed to touch, to feel, to caress those enticing curves, the more voluptuous because she was so unaware of their great power of enticement. But he hesitated. He was her husband; he could do as he would; and yet . . . he dreaded that one ill-advised move might destroy this burgeoning sensuality and replace it with the rigid shock which pain and fear had already once induced. And so he stayed his caresses, contenting himself with gentle kisses and welcoming the response they brought. His fingers played with the single button that secured the collar of the lawn blouse beneath the *sarafan*.

'This Russianness becomes you,' he said, and there was more warmth in his voice than Kirsty could remember hearing before.

'I am glad you are pleased,' she said. 'I fancy it would not so please your Tsar.'

His face clouded. 'In the privacy of my own home, I feel I may do what I like.'

Kirsty looked at him, curious. 'Tell me, Sergei. If you feel so strongly about all things Russian—as you clearly do—what led you to offer for a foreigner?'

He looked down at her in silence for a moment. If only he could know what was in her heart! This evening it was almost as if . . . and yet he could not escape the knowledge that, by marrying him, she had acquired a station in life and wealth beyond her imagining, and her father had acquired a son-in-law of influence: how improbable it had to be that any other consideration could have induced her to agree to the wedding.

'Perhaps it was to please my Tsar,' he said at last.

'Perhaps,' Kirsty agreed. 'Yet I do not think you are a man to take so drastic a step for no greater reason than that.'

'Have a care—some would say it were treason to suggest that there could be a greater reason than a desire to please the Tsar!'

'But you are not, I think, one of them.' Kirsty was silent for a short time. 'Tell me—is your influence with the Tsar so very great?'

No sooner had she spoken than she sensed a caution in his manner. He shrugged. 'Minimal, I should think.'

'Indeed? Yet he came to our wedding.'

'A whim, no more. We were honoured that he should do so and others will doubtless read much into it, but the

fact remains that he took a fancy to come, and came
—that is all there is to it.'

'Do you say, then, that you have no influence over
him?'

'None at all. It is true that his ear is there and I might
have access to it should I wish, but few people can exert
influence upon him. His is hardly an indeterminate
character, you know.' He paused. 'Does my influence
—or otherwise—in that quarter concern you?'

'Only in one respect. Papa was here yesterday. His
passport to remain in Moscow has been rescinded, and
he understood that it was at your instigation.'

'Indeed? And why should I wish to see him gone?' The
ice had entered his voice, and already Kirsty was regretting that she had broached this topic and thereby
destroyed the accord that had so briefly and so happily
lain between them. She could hardly avoid pushing it to
its conclusion now, however.

'He had heard it was to remove foreign influences
from me, that I might the quicker conform to the
Russian pattern of a wife.'

'I see. Hence the *sarafan*, the dinner and your singular
—and unprecedented—compliance this evening.' His
words cut her like a whiplash. 'I presume the intention
was to prove that you were fully Russian, and that
I should therefore immediately use my influence to
ensure your father's continued stay in Moscow. Is that
it?'

Kirsty tossed her head defiantly. 'And if it were,
would that be such a bad thing?'

'On the contrary. It is an excellent scheme: in future I
shall know I have only to observe your dress and the bill
of fare to be put upon my guard against favours requested. I am only sorry I had not realised what was in
store for me tonight: I was for a brief time taken quite off
my guard.'

'This is ridiculous,' Kirsty protested. 'It was not like that at all!'

'Was it not? I bow to your better understanding of your own motives.' The voice was ironic, making it perfectly clear that her protestations had been discounted.

'You make me sound like a devious, scheming hussy!' Kirsty exclaimed.

'You do me an injustice, my dear. I have never regarded you as a hussy.' Sergei's voice was infuriatingly smooth.

'Neither am I scheming or devious,' she insisted. 'If I were, I should have acted much more subtly and you would not have been aware that the ground was, so to speak, being prepared.'

'That argument almost convinces me! What a pity you did not realise that I was sufficiently alive to the time of day to see through your more simple plan.'

'But I did not have a plan!' Kirsty protested, exasperated.

'Do you really expect me to believe that this unwonted compliance with my wishes and your pleas on your father's behalf are quite unconnected?' Sergei's polite incredulity was intolerable.

'Yes . . . No. Oh, I don't care *what* you believe. It is true I hoped you might be able to intercede on Papa's behalf—that is obvious, since I raised the matter—but as for the rest, it just seemed that . . . I don't know how to explain it . . . I thought you would be pleased,' she finished lamely.

'How very kind.' The voice was acid. 'Forgive me if I remain unconvinced.'

Kirsty stared at him with something approaching dislike. 'You are impossible!' she said at last.

'I am sorry you should think so,' he replied, his voice holding no hint of regret. 'It is not, I believe, a generally held view. As to your father's predicament, I do not know who his informant was; I can only say that he was mistaken. Yet I cannot regret what has been done. You have chosen to marry a Russian. Very well. Had your father given you no choice in the matter, I would be disinclined, out of sheer humanity, to force you to adopt a culture not of your choosing. But you had the choice. I do not care how "western" a face you present outside these walls in accordance with Imperial decree, but within them, you will be as Russian as I demand.'

'And my own wishes on the subject are of no account?' Kirsty demanded.

'None whatever.'

'Then I suggest, Sergei Ivanovich, that you should have considered more carefully before you offered for me. Such total submission to a husband's will as you require is alien to an Englishwoman.'

His face, like his voice, was cold and hard. 'As to that, I fancy you delude yourself. It is, in any case, beside the point. Whatever you were born, you have chosen to be a Russian wife, and a Russian wife I shall make of you, though I die in the attempt.'

'Take care, then,' Kirsty flashed at him, angry now as she had not been before. 'For you may very well do so—and there would be precious little mourning from your widow.'

'So long as she has ensured that I have an heir, why should I be concerned?' he retorted.

'An heir?' Kirsty said flatly.

'An heir,' he repeated. 'Surely you are sufficiently aware of your responsibilities as a wife to realise that that is foremost among them?'

'Yes, of course, but I thought . . . I hoped . . .'

'I hope you did not delude yourself that, after one disastrous night when your revulsion was made abundantly clear, I would refrain completely from expecting you to fulfil your chief purpose.'

'You make me sound like a brood mare,' Kirsty said with revulsion.

'Crudely put, but in essence accurate enough,' Sergei replied. 'After all, you have hardly shown yourself to be the loving help-meet, have you?'

His hands suddenly closed in a vice-like grip and he pulled her towards him, kissing her savagely and without preamble in a way that made her twist and writhe in his grip in an effort to free herself. Her efforts were unavailing: if she had sensed the strength in his hands before, now she knew it. She knew, too, that it was anger that drove him, but she found no consolation in the knowledge, for she could not think of any means whereby to assuage that anger. Her lips were bleeding from his assault upon them and her wrist would be severely bruised, but she knew as he forced her back upon the divan that such minor injuries were the least she had to fear.

She guessed his intent, and fear of a repetition of the pain of her wedding night lent strength to her renewed struggles, but these seemed only to refresh his anger and strengthen his resolve. She was still struggling when he took her with a force and determination that seemed to pierce her being, and she screamed and tried to writhe away, but his hard, muscular body was more than a match for her. Her screams rang out as she felt as if she was being torn apart. But screams had no meaning: they served only to stoke the fires of Sergei's anger, and both of them knew no servant would dare investigate their cause. All Kirsty could do was to long for the blessed release which would eventually come. The wait was interminable and unutterably painful, and when he withdrew, she was close to unconsciousness.

This time there was no attempt to cover her so that she

might sleep. Sergei did not even glance at her dishevelled body. He left her there without a word, later to drag herself unaided back to her *terem*. On this occasion, as never before, she welcomed the seclusion of her own quarters. When she awoke next day, stiff and sore, it was to be greeted with the news that Sergei Ivanovich had left the house hours before. She could not regret it.

For the next few days Kirsty remained in the *terem* on the excuse of a chill. The Count made no attempt to visit her, nor, so far as she was aware, did he make any enquiries as to her well-being. He certainly sent no messages of concern. When finally she emerged from her self-imposed seclusion, he greeted her with a frigid politeness which was devoid of compassion or the slightest degree of concern.

The days of isolation had served to suggest to Kirsty that she could be considered to have goaded him into his possession of her that evening, and, had there been any indication on his part that he, too, had acted with a violence that he perhaps regretted, she would have been happy to make some attempt to bridge the gulf between them. But he gave no indication of anything save a preparedness to treat his wife, at least in front of the servants, with the courtesy due to her by virtue of being his wife. Apart from that, he did not speak to her unless he had to, and sought her company not at all.

Kirsty felt empty and hopeless. She longed to be able to do something that would magically put everything right. It seemed as if this marriage, brief as its life had so far been, was beset with misunderstanding. Kirsty treasured the memory of Sergei's early tenderness, and nothing that had happened since, no amount of aggression or pain, could entirely expunge that memory. She sought desperately in her heart for some way of turning time back, of recapturing those moments, so brief in retrospect, but so dear. If that could but be done, she thought, the painful memories would soon be wiped out.

How it was to be done was the problem. After their recent conversation, any attempt to appease him, by demonstrating her willingness to abandon her western ways in the privacy of their own home, was doomed. He had concluded that her first essay into that approach had been a cynical attempt to win him over so that he might use whatever influence he had on her father's behalf. She now realised that the things she had said in a sudden flash of temper arising out of his own cynicism would only have served to confirm him in his opinion. She was quite sure he would distrust any further attempt of a similar sort and was honest enough to acknowledge that she had only herself to blame if he did. Her tongue was a deal too sharp. It always had been, of course, but Sergei had not grown up with it as Alexander had, and therefore he was presumably unable to make the allowances that her father, with affection and understanding on his side, had done. But it seemed as if Sergei himself had no desire to make the effort needed to lower the barriers between them, and in the absence of any conciliatory gesture from her husband, Kirsty could not think how to proceed.

So she retreated further from him, spending most of her time in the *terem* with the two wolfhounds, Misha and Belka, taking good care that, if she knew Sergei was likely to be home, they were returned to the stables. She even considered trying to rejoin her father, now on his way back to Archangel, but knew it to be impossible —she could not imagine permission to leave her husband being forthcoming even if she dared approach the Tsar to ask him. As for her leaving without it—she did not know what the punishment might be, but that it would be terrible she did not doubt, any more than she doubted that she would be brought back to suffer it.

It was not to be expected that a girl of Kirsty's spirit could long tolerate the tedium induced by this circumscribed existence, and her thoughts soon began to turn with nostalgia to her life in the foreign quarter of Archangel and her brief stay in the German Suburb of Moscow. The recollection of the freedom and bustle of that earlier life reminded her also of her father's comment that Mistress Harrow and her daughters would be happy to receive her.

Once the idea was in her mind, the temptation to pay them a visit was almost overwhelming, and she resolved to ask Sergei's permission to go. Second thoughts brought her to a different decision: if she sought his permission and it was refused—as well it might be, since he seemed to want her to lay aside her western connections—she could not go without openly defying him, and that was hardly likely to lead to better relations between them. On the other hand, if she chose to assume that there could be no objection and simply went, telling him about it afterwards if the opportunity arose, he might be angry, but since he had not forbidden such a visit, he could hardly accuse her of disobedience. Therefore the least she could do would be to travel to the German Suburb in a way compatible with his views.

Thus Kirsty ordered her palanquin to be brought round that afternoon. After much thought about what she should wear, she decided against traditional Russian dress and wore instead a modest dress of amber satin with a jacket of rich brown velvet. The palanquin was too low to accommodate the tall head-dress or *fontange*, so she contented herself with a small lace scarf pinned to her dark hair by way of a cap. A pair of gloves of soft kid completed her toilette; she debated whether to wear a mask, but decided that, since between palace and palanquin, and palanquin and house, her complexion was unlikely to be ravaged by the elements, it was a protection she could safely manage without. She made sure that the curtains of the palanquin were drawn so that she travelled in the seclusion appropriate to the Countess Borodinova, and considered it no small blessing that the German Suburb was only two miles from the palace. Had it been further, the tedium of a long journey with nothing to look at would have been intolerable.

The Harrows were surprised and delighted to see her. Her bearers were sent round to the servants' quarters for refreshment, and she was led into the comfortable sitting-room that Mistress Harrow and her daughters had made very much their own. Master Harrow was from home, but his son John naturally joined their visitor. Kirsty had known the Harrows ever since she first came to Russia, and having thought of John more or less as an older brother, had never felt the least constraint in his company. Quite suddenly now, she saw him in a different light, and realised that this man might well, had Count Borodinov's offer not come when it did, have been her husband. She blushed as he bowed over her hand, and he himself was startled at the change he observed in her. It was true that the blush overlay a pallor he did not think he had noticed before, but Kirsty's whole bearing was suddenly more confident. The girl he had known in Archangel and, more briefly, in the German Suburb before her wedding was gone, replaced by this quietly elegant woman. It now occurred to him that this woman, had he realised it in time, would have been a highly desirable as well as a highly eligible wife. Why had it never struck him before? Perhaps, having been brought up so much as brother and sister, he had never really noticed her burgeoning maturity.

If he held her hand a little longer than convention

permitted, only his mother noticed, but she was more concerned with Kirsty's appearance. She, too, had noticed that the new Countess was rather paler than she used to be. Unlike her son, she also noticed the dark shadows beneath her visitor's eyes.

John led Kirsty to the stiff-backed sofa and invited her to be seated. 'I am glad I happened to be at home today. My sisters have frequently wondered whether you would find time to pay us a visit, but I had not imagined I should be fortunate enough to be here when you did.'

'It is I that am fortunate in finding so many of my dear friends at home,' Kirsty replied before turning to Mistress Harrow. 'I hope my coming thus, on an impulse, has not inconvenienced you in any way?'

'How could it do so?' John exclaimed before his mother's disclaimer had a chance of being uttered. 'You are always welcome here.'

'You are kind to say so, but, all the same, it might not have been convenient. I should have sent to enquire,' Kirsty said doubtfully.

'John is quite right,' Mistress Harrow assured her. 'You know us well enough not to be offended if, on your arrival, you find us on the verge of going out, or not here at all, and I confess my daughters and I have frequently speculated upon your new life. I hope you are finding that marriage suits you?'

'It must suit any woman to have charge of her own household.' This remark, the truth of which was un-arguable, left whole areas of marriage uncovered. Mistress Harrow made no comment but drew her own conclusions, and even John looked rather more sharply at Kirsty. For some reason he found he was not at all sorry that she had not burst into a eulogy on the delights of marriage.

His sisters noticed nothing untoward in Kirsty's answer, and Mary could contain her curiosity no longer.

'Is your palace *very* grand?' she asked excitedly.

'Mary! Such vulgarity! Kirsty, I beg you will forgive my daughter such an ill-bred question!' Mistress Harrow implored.

Kirsty laughed. 'Yes, Mary, very grand—and, like my bride-clothes, very Russian and very barbaric.'

'Is it huge?' Mary persisted, to her mother's resigned dismay.

'I think you could fairly call it that, though I no longer get lost in it!'

Mary's questions might be the despair of her mother, but they served to ease Kirsty's seeming tension, and when the kettle had been brought in and the macaroons sampled, Kirsty felt so very much at home that all constraint virtually disappeared and she was able to relax and converse in a way she had almost forgotten.

Her hosts—the ladies in particular—were agog to hear about the luxuries of her new home and sighed longingly at the thought of a private bathroom.

'It has always seemed to me,' Mistress Harrow said wistfully, 'a great pity that foreigners coming to the German Suburb over the years have not, before building their houses, taken more note of the traditional Russian customs relating to buildings. I doubt if there are many foreigners who could not afford the Tsar's fee for the privilege of a private *banya*, and it is such a to-do to bring in a bath, have it filled and then emptied again, that it quite destroys any gratification there might be in knowing oneself to be clean! Of course,' she added hastily, 'I cannot approve of the Russian custom of bathing every week: there must be a limit to the extent to which it is wise to wash away the skin's protective oils, but I must confess that if we had such a private *banya* here, I should be tempted to bathe as often as once a month.'

John Harrow smiled. 'There are plenty of public baths in Moscow, Mama. You could always visit one of them.'

His mother looked shocked. 'John!' she exclaimed. 'Have a mind to your tongue! As if your sisters and I could even contemplate the notion of bathing, naked, in the public eye. You should be ashamed of yourself for even thinking such a thing! What will Kirsty think of you?'

'Only that he was joking,' she assured her. 'I cannot imagine John thought you would take his suggestion seriously.'

John smiled warmly. 'How well you understand me! Mama is never quite sure when I am joking. What a pity you are not more often here to set her right!'

'Indeed, I should like to visit more frequently, and now that I am more conversant with my domestic responsibilities, I hope I may do so, though not for the purpose of explaining your jokes to your mother.'

Somewhat mollified by this exchange and by her daughters' sympathetic laughter, Mistress Harrow smoothed her ruffled feathers. 'You will always be welcome, Kirsty. I assume that Count Borodinov has no objection to your pursuing an acquaintance in the German Suburb?'

'What objection could he have?' Kirsty countered.

'He is known to be something of a traditionalist,' Mistress Harrow replied cautiously. 'I have even heard it suggested that he was behind your father's sudden return north, so that you might more quickly adopt Russian ways.'

'I have heard that, too, and it is untrue,' Kirsty told her, but there was a certain stiffness in her manner that Mistress Harrow suspected was not due to a dislike of inaccurate rumour.

'He is *very* handsome,' Mary sighed.

'And you are far too young to be considering such matters,' her mother replied sharply.

Margaret came to her sister's rescue. 'I don't think

anyone can escape noticing it. Mary should learn to be a little more circumspect in her remarks, I agree, but there is no denying that Count Borodinov is a very handsome man—and very rich, too.'

'Master Benmore was indeed fortunate to secure his interest,' Mistress Harrow agreed, noticing that Kirsty made no comment but seemed rather ill at ease at having her husband thus discussed. 'Kirsty, more tea perhaps?'

Kirsty accepted the change of topic with relief and smiled gratefully at John as he took her cup to be refilled. Mistress Harrow watched them carefully. Remembering the casual sisterly light in which her son had always previously regarded Kirsty, his current solicitude was unexpected. She must remind him that the friend of his youth was now a married woman, even if she suspected that all was not well with the marriage. She was quite sure that Kirsty was not happy. Had they been alone, she would have risked the charge of presumption and asked Kirsty bluntly how things were: having stood for so many years in place of a mother to her visitor, she felt she would have been failing in her duty not to do so. But they were not alone, and having once turned the conversation, she could approach the subject only from the most oblique angle. Mistress Harrow reckoned without her younger daughter's lack of circumspection.

'You really are very lucky, Kirsty,' Mary said. 'They say Count Borodinov has strenuously avoided matrimony until now, and there are many disappointed hopes in Russia—if not broken hearts—as a result of your good fortune.'

'That will do, Mary,' her mother said repressively.

'You know, we have been most remiss,' Margaret interjected. 'We have been talking about the Count without asking Kirsty the only really important question —how he does?'

'Count Borodinov is very well. He sees to it that I lack

for nothing,' Kirsty added, feeling that perhaps a rather fuller answer was called for.

'Oh dear!' Mistress Harrow was clearly dismayed. 'I know I have no right to pry, my dear, but that answer does not precisely suggest that all is well, you know.'

'If you, who have been so much of a mother to me, have not the right to pry, then no one has! I know you have only my interests at heart. The truth is that I see very little of my husband—his military duties keep him from home much of the time—and I imagine it will take some time and no small effort on both our parts to find a balance between the expectations of our different cultures.'

'Is there, then, so great a gulf?' Margaret asked.

'Greater than I had imagined,' Kirsty told her. 'Bridging it is not made easier by the conflict between Count Borodinov's traditionalist views and his need to conform to the Tsar's intention to bring western ways to his empire.'

'That would certainly make matters more difficult,' Mistress Harrow agreed. 'I recall we suspected that he might wish to adhere strongly to his own traditions when we saw the bride-clothes he had provided, and were more than a little uneasy when your father was ordered back to Archangel. On the other hand, he has allowed you to visit your foreign friends, and that must be taken as an optimistic sign.'

Kirsty coloured and looked somewhat abashed. 'To tell the truth,' she said, 'he does not know I am here.'

Mistress Harrow was shocked. 'You have not visited us against his wishes? Oh, Kirsty, that would be very, very wrong.'

'Oh, no, nothing like that. I simply omitted to ask him. The confines of the *terem* are so dull that I determined to see some familiar faces.'

'Terem!' It was John Harrow's turn to be startled. 'Do you mean to say that he keeps you in seclusion?'

'I have the rest of the palace, of course, when he is not there, although that is no more interesting than the *terem*—and the *terem* is extremely comfortable, you know. But I do find it very tedious to have nothing to do but drink tea, eat sweetmeats and sew. I supervise the running of the palace, of course, but there is very little need even for that.'

'If you find it dull now, when it might reasonably be expected to have the interest of novelty, what will it be like a year hence?' Margaret asked.

'Hush, Meg,' her mother interjected. 'You should not say such things.'

'Why not?' answered her unrepentant daughter. 'I should have thought it was quite important to think ahead.'

'Margaret is right,' Kirsty said. 'It has suited me, for one reason and another, to make use of the *terem* until now, and I fancy it will always serve some purpose. But I do not think I can tolerate it as a way of life, and I am determined that I shall not be kept in seclusion—and the sooner Sergei Ivanovich realises that, the better,' she added defiantly.

Mistress Harrow shook her head. 'That is no way to approach the matter,' she said. 'You must seek to win him round, and not to behave in a manner that can only antagonise him.'

'I am sure you are right. However, I have not so far proved myself particularly adept at "winning him round", and no matter how I try, antagonism tends to be the result. On one thing I remain determined: either Count Borodinov abandons the idea of a formal *terem*, or I suspect I shall be obliged to abandon Count Borodinov.'

Even as she spoke these words, Kirsty realised that

the sentiment expressed was one which was—or should have been—unthinkable, let alone inexpressible. She could not be surprised at the shock and barely concealed dismay on Mistress Harrow's face or the incredulity on those of her children. Mistress Harrow was determined to mitigate the impression Kirsty had created.

'Come, come, my dear,' she said in as conciliatory a tone as her surprise permitted her to assume. 'You cannot mean that precisely as it sounded. To be sure, the *terem* must be a frustrating institution, but as you have admitted, it has its compensations. I am sure you and Count Borodinov will come to an acceptable compromise. Now, can I press you to another cup of tea?'

The hint was taken, the subject dropped and the conversation reverted to the firm ground provided by social trivia. The subject of Kirsty's relations with her husband was not referred to again until she came to take her leave, and then only obliquely.

'You are always welcome here,' Mistress Harrow said. 'But it would be better, another time, to let Count Borodinov know of your intentions. There should, after all, be nothing between a man and his wife that hints of . . .'

'I think you mean deception,' Kirsty remarked ruefully.

'I am sure you would never seek to deceive him,' her hostess said gently. 'But you must agree that there was a lack of openness about your visit today.'

'You are right, as ever. Would you be happier if I assured you that I shall tell him of my visit when I return?'

'A great deal happier,' Mistress Harrow replied.

'Then I shall do so.'

In the absence of his father, it was naturally John Harrow who handed their guest into her palanquin, raising her hand to his lips in farewell, as was the English custom. His parting words were not, however, customary. He lowered his voice. 'I deeply regret that all is not well. Be assured that, should you need assistance, I am here. You have only to speak.'

Surprised and not a little embarrassed by the intensity of his tone, Kirsty could only murmur her thanks and wave goodbye to his mother and sisters before drawing the curtains round her and instructing her bearers to set off home.

There was plenty to occupy her mind, not least her own unpremeditated declaration. It was true that the *terem* had proved a sanctuary for which she had cause to be grateful; it was also true that she had protested to Sergei on that first tour of inspection that she did not wish to be confined to her own quarters. However, nothing in her subsequent behaviour would have led him to suppose that she had not come to terms with his desire that she should live in seclusion. It had suited her purpose to do so for a time, but she suddenly realised, even as she spoke to the Harrows, that she could not bear to be so circumscribed for much longer.

Her ability to persuade Sergei to see her point of view, she doubted. She doubted still more her ability to persuade him to agree to any plans she might have to lead a more open life. As to her abandoning Count Borodinov, it was unthinkable—yet she had thought it. She was not at all sure what the punishment might be for a wife who left her husband, but she had a tolerably good idea that it might be very drastic indeed. Certainly her father would be exiled and lose all he had come to Russia to acquire, while Sergei would undoubtedly become a laughing-stock. The thought of so proud a man thus brought down was not one she could contemplate with equanimity, yet she was unable to accept permanent life in a *terem*.

She thought of John Harrow's parting words, and found comfort in them. She could not immediately imagine any way in which he could help her present predicament, but she was grateful for the sentiment expressed. She thought back over her visit and John's part in it with something approaching wonderment. He had been attentive and warm, quite different from the impulsive young man she had always thought him—and quite different from the coldly polite man she seemed to have married. She could not help feeling a tinge of regret that Sergei no longer showed such warmth and attentiveness, and that feeling led on, unbidden, to a further regret that John's warmth and sympathy had not been apparent until it was too late: had there been any sign of them in Archangel, her present situation might be very different.

It was her present situation she had to deal with, of course, and she had to admit that she had not so far proved very adept at persuading her husband—rather the reverse, in fact—to do anything he did not want to do. But there must be some way, and she had to find it.

Sergei was home that evening, and she joined him for dinner with some trepidation. There had been an understandable constraint between them since her last disastrous attempt to improve relations, and to that constraint was added the necessity of keeping her promise to Mistress Harrow that she would tell him of her visit.

He watched her toy with the food on her plate. 'Is the meal not to your liking, Kirsty?' he asked, not unkindly. 'We can send for something else if you would rather.'

'Not at all. It is simply that I do not seem to be very hungry.'

'You are not ill, I hope.' It was a statement devoid of feeling.

'I fear it is more likely due to too many macaroons,' she ventured.

'Macaroons?'

'Yes. I hope you do not object, Sergei, but I visited Mistress Harrow and her daughters in the German Suburb this afternoon, and they plied me with tea and macaroons, which seem to have quite ruined my appetite for dinner.'

There was no immediate answer, and when he next spoke, Kirsty had the feeling that he chose his words with care.

'I should have preferred to know of your intent, so that an armed escort could have accompanied you,' he said. 'But I would not want you to think that I wish you to cut yourself off from your former friends. I hope your visit was enjoyable.'

Kirsty felt sufficiently encouraged by these words to expand upon her visit.

'It was not premeditated or arranged at all, but I knew Mistress Harrow would not mind that. I travelled in the palanquin: it is more comfortable than the coach but interminably slow, and I must confess that, with the curtains drawn, it is not the most interesting mode of travel.'

His laugh was so genuinely warm that Kirsty's spirits lifted. 'I imagine it must be deadly dull,' he said. 'I confess that I had never given the matter thought before. If you choose to visit again, I suggest you take the coach your father gave us: it will be faster, so at least the boredom will be shorter.'

'Then I may go again? I should certainly like to do so, and Mistress Harrow expressed a wish that I should.'

'Of course you may. Have I not just said that I do not wish you to cut yourself off from your friends?'

There could be no doubt that this had been a most

encouraging exchange, and when Sergei suggested—somewhat tentatively, Kirsty thought, or was that her imagination?—that she should bring her tambour-frame and sit with him awhile, she was happy to do so. Although they did not talk much, it was in some indefinable way a most companionable evening, the most pleasant of her married life, and Kirsty was almost sorry when it was over and fatigue bade her say good night to her husband and beg him to excuse her.

He took her hand and raised it to his lips, retaining it for a little longer than she expected.

'If you are tired, then you must indeed retire,' he said. 'I have no wish to see you become haggard simply by keeping me company.'

'I did not mean that!' Kirsty was alarmed that he might have misunderstood her. 'It is just that today has been much busier than other days, and so I am rather tired.'

'Then to bed with you, and may you sleep undisturbed until the sun is up.'

There was no hint of criticism in his voice, or any attempt to detain her. 'Then good night, sir.'

'Good night, Christina Alexandrovna,' he replied, and the formality of the name sounded strangely affectionate on his lips.

Next morning the storm burst, the more devastating because so totally unexpected. A trembling Anna woke Kirsty from a deep and dreamless sleep, her voice urgent and anxious.

'Christina Alexandrovna, you must wake up!' she said, shaking her mistress.

'Good heavens, what on earth is the matter?' Kirsty asked her.

'Sergei Ivanovich insists that you attend him now,' the girl said.

'Why? What has happened?' As Kirsty spoke, she

swung her feet out of bed and reached for the *kaftan* she wore in place of a robe. 'Is there water for me to wash?'

'There is not time, Christina Alexandrovna. He will see you now.' The girl was holding the door open.

Puzzled as to what might merit such urgency, Kirsty ran down the stairs to where Count Borodinov paced the length of the great entrance hall.

'Sergei,' she said, her voice alarmed as much at the fury in his face as at the urgency of the summons. 'What has happened that I may not even make myself presentable before obeying your call?'

'Such innocence!' he stormed. 'One would almost believe you had no idea what has happened!'

'But in truth I have not!'

'Indeed? Did you imagine I would not discover your perfidy?'

'My *what*?' She had no idea what he was talking about, and anyone less angry than Sergei would have realised how genuine was her incredulity.

'I give you credit for being a first-rate actress,' he said bitterly. 'You tricked me completely last night, and if I didn't know better, I'd swear you had no idea what I am talking about this morning!'

'But I do *not* have any idea what you are talking about,' Kirsty protested. 'I beg you, Sergei, what is this all about?'

'So I must spell it out, must I? Very well. Yesterday you visited the Harrows, did you not?'

Kirsty nodded.

'To be precise, if I recall your words—and do, please, correct me if I err—Mistress Harrow and her daughters?'

'That is so—I told you about it.'

'You did, indeed, but that was only part of it, was it not?'

Kirsty was still puzzled. 'I do not know what you mean!'

'You failed to mention that there was a gentleman present, did you not?' His voice was grim.

Kirsty's puzzled frown cleared and she gave a little laugh. 'Is that all? It was but John Harrow, their son. You know that Mistress Harrow and her daughters have been like mother and sisters to me, John has, in the same way, been the brother I never had.'

'But he is not your brother, and you chose to conceal the fact of his presence.'

'I did not "choose to conceal" it: I took it so much for granted that it did not occur to me that it was significant. I went to visit Mistress Harrow and her daughters. I was surprised, it is true, to find that John was also there, but it had no special importance—after all, our families have been friends for many years.'

'Then they will be friends no longer.'

Kirsty stared at him. 'What do you mean?'

'Precisely what I said. I was perfectly happy for you to visit your friends when no proprieties were ignored, but to find my own servants sniggering over my betrayal is something I cannot and will not tolerate.'

'What betrayal? What can lead you to such a ludicrous suggestion? What was there for servants to snigger over?'

'I went to the stables to give instructions that you will in future use the coach, rather than the palanquin, whenever you wish to pay a visit to your friends, and the head groom—who has known me since boyhood and therefore takes liberties that others would not dare—asked me if I intend to encourage your visits! It turns out to be the gossip of the servants' quarters that you were handed into your palanquin by a man—who added insult to injury by kissing your hand! This is now, I remind you, the prerogative of your husband.'

Kirsty stared at him, dismay in her face and despair in her heart.

'I am sorry, Sergei,' she said. 'But it is our custom that the senior man present should hand a guest into her conveyance. I assure you that nothing was done that did not accord with absolute propriety. The presence of Mistress Harrow must surely indicate that?'

'Not to a Russian.' He paused. 'I would like to believe you. I am loath to think you set out to deceive me, yet the evidence cannot be denied: you concealed the fact of Master Harrow's presence.'

'I cannot accept that,' Kirsty protested. 'Concealment implies a deliberate hiding of the fact, and that is not the case—any "concealment" was entirely inadvertent. I have already explained that I took his presence so much for granted that it simply had no significance—no more than my failure to mention it.'

'It sounds plausible enough,' Sergei said grudgingly, though there was nothing in his tone to suggest that he was convinced. 'Nevertheless, you will remember in future that no man other than your husband—and your father, should he return to Moscow—may have any part, however insignificant, in your life.'

Kirsty was about to protest at the unfairness of such a decree, but bit her tongue, deciding it was not worth the risk of being forbidden to visit the Harrows, a ban that would almost certainly follow any such protest on her part.

'Very well, Sergei Ivanovich,' she said with a meekness she was far from feeling. 'I shall give Mistress Harrow advance notice of any intent to visit her, and ask her to ensure the absence of both her husband and her son. It will seem very strange to her,' she added, 'I can only hope she will not be offended.'

'You need not worry yourself that Mistress Harrow may take offence,' Sergei said stiffly. 'The occasion will not arise. You will pay no more visits to the German Suburb.'

He strode out of the palace, leaving Kirsty dumbfounded.

CHAPTER
FIVE

KIRSTY WAS initially speechless at Sergei's parting stipulation which effectively cut her off from any communication with westerners, but her immediate second reaction was blazing fury. So much for her attempts at conciliation! So much for Count Borodinov's willingness —or perhaps it was his ability that was lacking, she thought savagely—to come to terms with the inevitable complications caused by his decision to take a bride from the foreign community!

So angry was she that it was on the tip of her tongue to order the horses put to so that she might repeat her visit of the previous day. She refrained largely because such an action could only make things worse, and, besides, the coachman might refuse to take her to the German Suburb, and that was an indignity to which she had no intention of submitting herself.

She paced angrily up and down the ornately inlaid floor of the great entrance hall, her fury feeding upon itself and growing, as a fire feeds upon itself and grows. She dared order neither carriage nor palanquin to take her to the German Suburb. Very well. She would show Count Borodinov what his unreasonable restrictions could lead to. She ran upstairs to her room and threw open her coffers, tossing over *sarafans* and gowns alike until she came to what she was looking for. She dressed quickly in one of the morning toilettes she had been used to wear in Archangel, and over it put the heavy cloak of russet wool, its hood and edges trimmed with beaver, that she had customarily worn to go out in the days when she was not expected to live like a Russian. She hesitated a moment before taking her mask, and was about to put it on when she thought again, and slipped it instead inside her beaver muff. Thus attired, Kirsty swept out of the palace and into the stable yard.

'Fetch my hounds,' she ordered.

The groom was disconcerted. Never before had the Countess herself appeared for her hounds: it had always been the accepted practice to send a message requesting they be brought to the house. Consequently, he looked quite blank. 'The hounds, *barinya*?' he repeated.

'Yes, the hounds. Leash them. I am taking them out.'

'No, *barinya*.' The groom was shocked 'That's my job, *barinya*. I walk them eight versts a day. It is enough.'

'And have you done so today?'

'No, *barinya*, but . . .'

'Then do as you are told.'

Long inured to the vagaries of his masters, the groom did as Kirsty bade him, and she took Misha and Belka, coupled in the traditional way to one leash, out of the stable yard and into the crowded, muddy streets of Moscow.

Kirsty set off at as brisk a walk as the streets and her long skirts allowed, fuelled by the anger that put determination in her step. It was therefore several minutes before she realised that she was attracting considerable undisguised interest from passers-by. Western clothes always attracted some interest, as she knew from the days when, in Archangel, she had visited the markets outside the foreign quarter. The interest exhibited on this occasion, however, far exceeded anything she had experienced before.

Then she realised that Misha and Belka were the cause. Only the nobility owned borzois, and her clothes proclaimed the fact that she was no serving-girl exercising them in the course of her duties. Despite the Tsar's decrees on the matter of seclusion, the ladies of the nobility were not customarily seen unveiled in public, and certainly did not stride through the streets accompanied only by a brace of hounds.

Suddenly conscious of the speculation her action would cause and the gossip that would ensue, she fumbled in her muff for her mask. To put it on in the middle of a crowded street would occasion even more remark, it was true, but at least her identity would be concealed for the rest of her walk. But, with the need to retain the muff in one hand and the leash in the other, it was no easy matter to extract her mask and put it on. Just as she thought she was about to succeed, she was jostled from behind and dropped it in the mud. She picked it up and stared at it in dismay: she could hardly wear it now.

As she stood there, uncertain whether simply to discard the soiled mask or to tuck it, muddy as it was, back in her muff, she became aware that a man in knee-high western boots was standing before her. She glanced up and breathed a sigh of relief on perceiving John Harrow.

'Master Harrow! You can have no idea how pleased I am to see you!' she exclaimed.

'If your pleasure matches my surprise, I am flattered indeed. What brings you here with only your dogs? Or is there a maid close by?' His eyes strayed across the crowds, but could see no one who appeared to be in attendance upon the Countess.

Kirsty flushed. 'I am alone, and I must admit that I am fast regretting it.'

'So I should imagine. Whatever came over you, Countess? Does your husband know what you are doing?'

Kirsty's flush deepened. 'I hope not—and I hope he does not find out. We had a . . . a somewhat frank discussion this morning, and I was so angry that I determined to walk it off. I could not bear the thought of just sitting idly all day.'

John caught her hand, and his voice was warm with sympathy. 'I do feel for you in your unenviable situation, but you will acknowledge it was an ill-advised way of relieving your anger.'

'I realise it with increasing force as every minute passes,' she said ruefully. 'But what do I do now? I must return to the palace, I suppose, before any more harm is done, but I think it is going to take rather more courage to do so than it did to storm out.'

'Then you will permit me to accompany you, I am sure.'

Kirsty hesitated. She certainly did not relish the thought of returning on her own, but neither was she in favour of returning home on the arm of the man whose innocent presence at her recent visit to his home had so infuriated Sergei. It would be bad enough to return on the arm of any man other than her husband, but to do so on John's would be regarded by Sergei as a deliberate insult, should he come to hear of it. She had little hope that he would not: too much attention had already been drawn to her public escapade, and, besides, it was highly probable that one of the servants might recognise her escort.

As she hesitated, a horseman, resplendent in a pale dove-grey justaucorps, its huge cuffs turned back and secured with silver braid and silver buttons, drew rein beside them. Under a beaver tricorne, a thin and calculating face beamed at them.

'It is the Countess Borodinova, is it not?' a smooth voice inquired.

Kirsty could hardly deny it. 'You have the advantage of me,' she said. There was something decidedly familiar about the man, but she could not put her finger on it, and must only trust that he would not be offended at her forgetfulness.

'Alexander Danilovich Menshikov,' he enlightened

her. 'I attended your wedding, but I think you were too preoccupied on that occasion to remember all your guests. And who is your attentive escort?' the silken voice went on. 'I fancy I have not had the pleasure of your acquaintance, sir.'

There was nothing for it but for Kirsty to make the introductions.

'Harrow,' the Prince mused, 'I think I have heard the name. In what way do you serve the Tsar, Master Harrow?'

'My father and I are supervising the paving of Moscow's streets,' John told him.

'Indeed?' Prince Menshikov flicked a speck of mud from his sleeve. 'One cannot but hope that the project is soon completed.'

John flushed at the implied criticism. 'We work as fast as we can, but our labourers are unskilled and therefore slow. It is our hope that their speed will increase with their experience.'

'A hope that others must echo. A pleasure to have met you, Master Harrow. Countess Borodinova, you will excuse me, I am sure: the Tsar's business calls.'

Observing the concern and dismay on his companion's face, John took her arm. 'Whatever is the matter?' he asked. 'You look quite worried. For my part, I consider it an honour to be addressed by the Prince.'

'Quite possibly you do,' Kirsty said sharply. 'I, however, can think of no person I would not have preferred to encounter in my present position: as a guest at my wedding, he must be well acquainted with my husband. Who knows what he may not tell him? Let us be gone before we meet anyone else.'

There was a mulish set to her mouth that John did not recall ever having noticed before, and he thought it wisest to accede to her suggestion. He was anxious to convey to his parents and sisters the gratifying news that he had been introduced to the powerful Prince Menshikov. Who knew what such an introduction might lead to?

But first he had to escort Kirsty home from this extraordinary walk she had embarked upon. He was very much afraid that Count Borodinov would not be entirely happy to see his wife arrive home accompanied by another man. Kirsty seemed to have no high opinion of her husband's reasonableness, but John had little doubt that he could satisfactorily explain the situation to him, and was already forming in his head the words with which to do it.

It was probably just as well that he was to have no opportunity to pronounce them. Kirsty, knowing that Sergei had left the house, and wishing to minimise any chance of a servant's recognising her escort, dismissed him before they actually reached the palace.

'It is only a few yards, and if you are concerned for my safety, you may stand here and watch until I am safely through the coach-house gates,' she told him.

'But this is not at all the thing!' John exclaimed. 'I cannot take my leave before handing you over to your husband's safe keeping!'

'You speak as if I were a piece of delicate glass! It really will be better if I go on alone. Besides, I was not the only person to storm out. As like as not, Sergei isn't there. Thank you very much for being so obliging as to escort me thus far, but, truly, John, you will now serve me best by doing as I bid.'

There was an appeal in Kirsty's eyes which he could not ignore, and so, reluctantly, he stayed where he was until he saw her pass through the gates.

Kirsty silently handed her dogs over to one of the grooms, and ignoring their curious stares, ran indoors and up to her rooms where she tore off her muddy clothes and her completely ruined shoes, for she had quite forgotten to wear pattens. Then she flung herself on her bed and wept.

Why, oh why, had her evil genius driven her to an action which must be attended by so much public observation? Sergei was bound to hear of it, and his anger was likely to be greater than she had yet seen. Nor could she blame him. In retrospect, she almost thought a defiant trip to the German Suburb would have been preferable. Her only consolation was that she had the rest of the day to compose herself and decide how best to convince Sergei that she genuinely regretted her action.

Kirsty's consolation was short-lived. She had been in the palace barely an hour when the door of her chamber was unceremoniously thrown open and Sergei stood there in his green regimentals and his mud-bespattered boots. His face blazed with fury, and he still held his riding-whip in one leather-gauntleted hand, slapping it against the palm of the other in pent-up anger.

'So, madam, you choose the seclusion of the *terem* as if it were some holy sanctuary. Or did you fondly imagine I should not come to hear of today's little escapade?'

Sergei expected the face she turned to him to be startled; he would not have been at all surprised to read defiance there; he had not expected it to be tear-stained and puffed with crying. Disconcerted, much of his anger dissolved in the need to understand this unexpected turn of events.

As Kirsty saw him, the tears which she had thought to have under control at last welled forth. 'Oh, Sergei, I am so sorry!'

He could not disbelieve her. There was no dissimulation in her voice, and her face told its own story. But his anger was still there, fuelled by the memory of Prince Menshikov's gloating eyes when he happened to mention, in the presence of so many, the extraordinary chance of his happening upon Christina Alexandrovna and her attentive escort.

'For precisely what are you sorry, Countess? For the fact that I found out? For having had the misfortune to meet Menshikov? I cannot believe you regret doing anything that you knew would meet with my displeasure.'

'You may believe what you will! Nevertheless, I do regret it. I regret all those things, and more. Most of all, perhaps, I regret my own temper which reacted in such a way to your prohibition. The prohibition was unfair, but I should not have done what I did.'

'And when did you come to this conclusion, may I ask?'

'About a hundred yards from the palace. It was the stares of the passers-by that made me realise the enormity of what I was doing.'

'I would rather it had been your own sense of propriety,' Sergei said stiffly.

'Would you rather I had pretended it was?'

Sergei was silent a moment, considering. 'No, I think not,' he said at last. 'I prefer the truth, however unpalatable.'

Kirsty looked at him apprehensively. 'I must tell you that it was John Harrow who escorted me home. I know you will dislike that, but I was by that time very grateful for his attendance, and if it is any consolation to you, I think he was as shocked as you at my action.'

'I will attempt to be consoled by that fact. I had heard of his presence.'

'From Menshikov?'

'From Menshikov.'

They looked at each other in silence. What more could be said? Almost tentatively, Sergei reached out a gloved hand and lightly touched his wife's tear-stained cheek.

'I told our noble Prince that you had almost certainly been taken ill on your walk and that, if it were so, I should stand in Master Harrow's debt. That will remain my explanation. I think perhaps you would be happier resting now. I shall send Anna to you.'

Her husband was certainly less angry when he left the room than when he entered it, but Kirsty could form no very real idea of his feelings when the door closed behind him. If she had hoped that the lessening of his anger would result in Sergei's lifting his prohibition on visits to the German Suburb, she was disappointed, and resigned herself to busying herself with household affairs and playing with Misha and Belka, who seemed most willing to leave the Spartan comforts of the stable block for the luxury of the *terem*.

The groom who had charge of the dogs grumbled that they would become spoilt, but Kirsty refused to be deflected from her intention to have some sort of companionship, and simply said 'Nonsense,' and brought them in.

The groom appealed to his master, whose views, Kirsty knew, were the same as the servant's, but Count Borodinov merely shrugged and said that the hounds belonged to the Countess, and if she wished to make fools of them, so be it.

Kirsty's situation was aggravated since she had no acquaintance among Russian women whom she could visit, and it did not seem to occur to the wives of Sergei's fellow-officers that she might welcome overtures of friendship. Nor did it occur to Sergei to suggest to his brother-officers that their wives could ease Kirsty's transition from foreign resident to Russian wife. The officers were frequently entertained at the palace, and Kirsty saw to it that everything was done that should be done and everything that was provided was of the best, but these entertainments were in the Russian style, which meant that the gatherings were exclusively male, and consequently the sounds of roistering inebriety clearly penetrated the *terem* walls. Kirsty, therefore, felt no desire to be present. It was the very fact that they took place and were invariably reciprocated that increased her sense of isolation and her loneliness. The cold formality of her relations with her husband might have suggested to an observer that they had established a mutually acceptable footing for their marriage, but this was not what Kirsty looked for. She was perhaps to outward appearances the wife her husband wanted, but her heart was desolate. Surely there could be more?

As time passed, she found it increasingly difficult to decide just why Sergei had wanted to marry her in the first place. More than once she determined to ask him, but then, face to expressionless face, her courage failed, and her desolation and despair increased.

When, after breakfast one morning, Count Borodinov sent a servant to request his wife's attendance, she assumed he was planning another party for his friends. To her surprise, he handed her a gold-embellished invitation card in the western style. She read it and handed it back to her husband.

'Well?' he said. 'Do you wish to go?'

'It is from the Tsar!' Kirsty exclaimed. 'Surely, whatever the wording, it is a command!'

'It would certainly be difficult to decline. If you should dislike the idea, you could plead illness.'

'Certainly not!' Kirsty's tone left her husband in no doubt on the subject. 'I shall enjoy it above all things—a dinner party in the English style! Oh, Sergei, you cannot mean you *wish* me to plead illness?'

He laughed. 'I do not think I could be so unkind as to deprive you of the obvious pleasure it will afford you, and at least I shall not have to blush at your ignorance of western ways! You must be fittingly dressed, of course.

Do you know a good seamstress in the German Suburb who can turn you out in the height of English fashion?'

'In the German Suburb?' Kirsty flushed at the unhappy memory of the last time that place had been mentioned between them.

'Where else? I would have you put every other woman in the shade, and a Russian dressmaker would not be sufficiently *au fait* with the English mode.'

'There is indeed a good English seamstress there, but an even better French one, and it is said that the court of the Sun King sets the fashions for Europe now. May I go to her instead?'

'My dear, I would not presume to dictate to you upon the subject of western fashion. Go to whichever you will—but be sure she knows that neither expense nor effort is to be grudged.'

Madame de Fontainebleau—Kirsty could not entirely believe that the dressmaker had ever legally acquired quite so grand a name—was delighted to dress the beautiful wife of so rich a man as Count Borodinov. She produced the latest *poupées fameuses* for her client's inspection, the life-sized dolls that came each month from France dressed in the latest fashions. Together they discussed what should best suit the young Countess. Red, of course, was fashionable and had the added advantage of being very much in favour in Russia, but on the other hand they had to bear in mind that, for those very reasons, it would be worn by most women present. Madame was not inclined to recommend the pretty paler colours that were just becoming acceptable: rose pink, pale blue or a delicate lemon were, indeed, most attractive, but the Countess's colouring was somewhat striking, and she rather fancied something a little stronger. What did the Countess Borodinova think of this?

With the air of a conjurer she whisked the dust-cover

off a bolt of velvet of a rich, dark, sapphire blue. She unrolled several ells of it and held it against Kirsty and turned her towards the looking-glass. Kirsty was convinced. Nor did the two women have any difficulty settling on the most suitable style, though this in itself posed a problem which Kirsty felt it advisable to refer to her husband.

She went to find him before he left next morning, and if he was surprised that his wife should thus seek him out, he betrayed no sign of it.

'I consulted Madame de Fontainebleau,' Kirsty said. 'That is the French dressmaker from the German Suburb, you understand, and we have decided on the fabric and the style.'

Sergei looked slightly surprised at these words. 'I am pleased to hear it, but you do not have to keep me informed on the matter, you know.'

Kirsty chuckled. 'I know, but there is one aspect of the style of which I should prefer to have your approval before Madame de Fontainebleau makes it up. I fancy you may not be happy about it.'

'Indeed? I confess my curiosity is aroused.'

'It is currently very fashionable to have an extremely low and wide *décolleté*. Madame says this can be filled in with lace, but it would spoil the effect.'

'Then let us take no such risk,' Sergei said. '*Décolleté* it shall be. Doubtless I shall withstand the shock. May I enquire as to its colour?'

Delighted—and no little surprised—at the ease with which she had secured his approval, Kirsty told him. 'We did give serious consideration to red,' she added, 'but it will be worn by so many that we both felt the sapphire would be more striking.'

'I would not have it otherwise,' Sergei told her, taking his regimental tricorne from his body-servant. He paused and looked down at her, and Kirsty wondered whether it was sympathy she saw in his eyes. 'You are really looking forward to the reception, I think,' he remarked at last.

'I am indeed,' Kirsty assured him. 'You cannot know how different a complexion it puts on everything to have something to look forward to.'

'You think I cannot?' he said enigmatically, but not unkindly, and lightly kissed her finger-tips before leaving the house.

When Kirsty presented herself before him on the evening of the Tsar's dinner, she had good cause to be pleased with her appearance. The lace chemise beneath the sapphire velvet broke the colour at neck and wrist and set off the ivory of her skin to perfection, while the warm richness of the velvet was complemented by the gleam of the matching satin underskirt. A wired *fontange* gave her the height she lacked, and a deceptively casual dark curl over her shoulder seemed to be the finishing touch. Sergei was dressed in the western style, too, but soberly in a deep crimson.

'I dare not risk outshining Peter Alexeyevich,' he said. 'My wife shines for both of us. There is but one thing lacking.'

Kirsty was taken aback and not a little disappointed. She had put so much into looking her best, and now he thought there was something lacking! She opened her mouth to speak, and saw that Sergei was smiling and holding something out to her. It was a small wooden box with a design of delicate beauty enamelled on the lid.

'Open it,' he said.

Kirsty did so and gasped, speechless. It was beautiful: a necklace of sapphires set in gold and surrounded by pearls. Sergei lifted the heavy collar from its velvet-lined box and clasped it round her neck, then stood back and surveyed her.

'That was the finishing touch which was lacking,' he

said. 'The result is perfection. Shall we go?'

Overcome by such compliments from so unexpected a source, Kirsty could only nod.

The occasion turned out to be as much a reception as a dinner, with rooms set aside for various entertainments. The Tsar, just recently returned from Warsaw, stood at the head of the staircase with Catherine at his side, raising once more all those questions as to whether she was still his mistress or had he, as some rumoured, married her, despite the fact that the Tsaritsa Eudoxia lived, albeit in a nunnery? The Tsar was courtesy itself, and had not forgotten the last occasion on which they had met.

'Countess Borodinova,' he exclaimed. 'And as charming in the English style as in our traditional costume at your wedding! You are a lucky man, Sergei Ivanovich,' he added, turning to the Count. 'A woman who can move with equal ease in two so different worlds is a rare object.'

'Rare indeed, sir,' Sergei answered, and Kirsty shot him a quick look. Had she detected a note of irony in his voice?

The Palace of the Facets was crowded. It seemed as if everyone who mattered in Russia was present—and quite a few who didn't. Some of the faces seemed vaguely familiar to Kirsty and she assumed they had been at her wedding. There was also a number of guests from the German Suburb, though it seemed the Harrows had not been invited, and it was quite clear that the majority of guests looked to these foreigners for guidance as to the correct etiquette.

This was particularly noticeable where the Russian ladies were concerned: it was very apparent that they were unaccustomed to mixed gatherings such as this, but their husbands and fathers seemed oblivious to the fact and did nothing to make them feel more at ease.

Among these guests who were very much at ease was a tall, thin man who, unlike Sergei, obviously experienced no qualms about outshining his Tsar. His gold-embroidered red coat gleamed with orders and decorations, not least of them the broad blue sash of the Order of St Andrew across his chest. He wore a white wig in the French style, and a large diamond pin adorned his cravat. His pencil-thin moustache was not in the usual Russian style: such Russians as wore one preferred a longer, fuller one that drooped at either side of the mouth—and this man's gave an unpleasantly calculating look to an already thin mouth. Kirsty recognised him at once: it was Prince Menshikov.

It seemed to her that 'calculating' was a word that fitted him well. His smile was blandly pleasant, but it failed to reach his eyes, and her initial reaction on seeing him was that he missed nothing, and was shrewdly assessing his fellow-guests as though to decide where their usefulness to him lay. That having been her impression, she was not particularly surprised that he should make his way through the other guests towards them, and address her husband.

'Greetings, Sergei Ivanovich,' he began, his eyes not on the man to whom he spoke, but on Kirsty. 'How pleasant to see your English Countess, of whom we have heard?'

Sergei bowed, a polite, if somewhat tight-lipped smile on his face. He turned to Kirsty. 'Permit me formally to introduce Prince Menshikov, whom, I believe, you have met. Alexander Danilovich, my wife, Christina Alexandrovna.'

The Prince bowed over her hand. 'I compliment you, Sergei Ivanovich,' he said and his calculating eyes never left Kirsty's face. 'You were fortunate indeed to discover so fine a diamond—or perhaps a sapphire?—in the sterile wastes of Archangel.'

Sergei bowed his acceptance of the compliment, but Kirsty felt he was not altogether pleased. She had no idea why this should be, since any favourable remark from such a quarter was not to be lightly set aside. Alexander Menshikov, only recently created a Prince of Russia, was a very powerful man indeed whose influence was known even in the foreign quarters of the Empire's most outlying cities. He had been, despite his reputedly humble origins, a close friend of the Tsar since boyhood and remained, it was said, one of the few people who could deal with Peter's sudden rages. The gossip was that Catherine, the Tsar's mistress (or possibly wife) had earlier been Menshikov's mistress. Whether or not that was so, she had certainly been part of the favourite's household, and it was there that Peter had met her.

Menshikov was known to be totally corrupt and dedicated to amassing great wealth, something he was reputed to do at every opportunity and by any means, despite the Tsar's well-known disapproval of corruption. He had the ability to charm the Tsar out of his disapproval, and since he also served the Tsar's interests before his own, knowing that his own depended upon continued Imperial favour, his many enemies felt that his position was well-nigh impregnable. This did not make them like him the more, but they took very good care not to offend the man who had the ear of Peter Alexeyevich.

Dinner was served in the English style; that is to say, the guests sat round the sides of one long table with the Tsar at its head. There was much speculation as to whether Catherine would sit at the foot: were she to do so, it would be taken as a tacit acknowledgment that the Tsar had married her. But Peter had no intention of ending speculation in that way, and Catherine sat on his right.

Apart from the Tsar's own position, there was no

resemblance to an English seating arrangement and no consideration of precedence given. Unless invited by the Tsar to take a particular place, guests sat where they would, which, Kirsty supposed, at least made the meal less of an ordeal for those Russian women unused to mixed gatherings: they could sit beside their husbands and not be obliged to make conversation with men who were total strangers.

Count Borodinov and his wife were among the favoured few invited to sit sufficiently near the Tsar to make possible conversation with him and his consort. Peter saw no reason to restrict his remarks to those on either side of him and was perfectly happy to conduct a shouted conversation with someone several places away. The resulting uproar—since his example was emulated further down the table—caused Kirsty some amusement: it meant that the meal bore very little resemblance to the soberly conducted dinner parties it was designed to copy.

Initially, Kirsty took little part in the conversation: the opinion of a woman as to the likelihood of the Tsar's finally overcoming King Charles XII of Sweden was hardly likely to have much weight when compared with that of seasoned campaigners.

Then the subject of the conversation changed. The Tsar looked down the long table.

'What a pleasant change it is to see the ladies gracing the evening, like so many iridescent butterflies. I fancy we impoverish ourselves by keeping them in seclusion.'

Prince Menshikov smiled. 'Their presence has certainly added a lustre to the occasion,' he said with a smile that was directed not only at Catherine who sat opposite him but moved to Kirsty, who was placed on his right.

'I rather think our presence has made the occasion less roisterous,' Catherine remarked. 'Most of the gentlemen seem to be behaving with a little more circumspection than I fancy is usual at such festivities.'

'Let us hope they do not find the restriction on their behaviour irksome,' Menshikov commented after surveying his fellow-guests briefly.

'They must adjust their ideas,' the Tsar said in a voice that brooked no contradiction. 'I wish to see the ladies more frequently at Court. I can see no virtue in the *terem*.'

Menshikov laughed. 'I beg leave to disagree, Peter Alexeyevich. Where else but in a *terem* would one expect to see virtue?'

Peter turned to Kirsty. 'Tell me, Christina Alexandrovna, is there less virtue in the freedom of the foreign quarters of our cities than in our *terems*?'

'I think not, sir,' Kirsty told him. 'Those who wish to be unvirtuous will find the opportunity wherever they are.'

Sergei intervened. 'Nevertheless, my dear, I think you will agree that the opportunities are fewer in the *terem*.'

'Indeed they are!' Kirsty was oblivious to the decided interest Prince Menshikov was showing in this exchange between husband and wife. 'There are opportunities for very little in a *terem*. One may sew, of course, and eat sweetmeats and gossip, but I am sure that a wife who mixes more generally must have a greater range of conversation and thus be a more interesting companion to her husband.'

'Well said,' Catherine remarked. 'I have travelled widely with Peter Alexeyevich, and he talks to me much as he would to any of his friends. It is a good basis for companionship.'

The Tsar beamed at her and patted her hand. 'But you are an exceptionally sensible woman, my dear.'

'How fortunate you are, madame,' Kirsty exclaimed,

'to have the affection of a man who allows your talents to flourish!'

'I am sure Count Borodinov would not wish yours to be hidden.' Menshikov's silken voice set her on her guard, and she did not miss the sly glance he shot across the table at Sergei. Did this man really think she might be led into saying something disloyal to her husband?

She smiled up at the Prince. 'Indeed not, or I should not be here.'

The Tsar broke in. 'Do you live in the *terem* in the Borodinov Palace, Christina Alexandrovna?'

'For much of the time I do, sir. It does have its advantages, but it is not a way of life I would wish imposed upon me,' she added, not entirely able to keep a hint of defiance from her voice, and she saw a flush rise on Sergei's cheeks.

The Tsar did not appear to notice. 'Neither my mother nor my sister allowed themselves to be trammelled by the confines of the *terem* and were the better for it in many ways, although in Sophia's case it perhaps led her to take too much upon herself.'

'It is a situation that most Russian women would take time to adjust to,' Catherine reminded him gently. 'We shall need to model ourselves upon those of our foreign sisters, to whom such freedom is customary,' and she smiled across at Kirsty.

Kirsty blushed. 'I would not presume to set you an example, madame. You do as well as any, and have no need of guidance.'

'You see, Sergei Ivanovich,' the Tsar said triumphantly. 'What *terem*-reared Russian girl of such tender years would have the ability to make so diplomatic an answer in such a situation? Such a one would blush and giggle and sit dumb-struck.'

Sergei inclined his head towards his sovereign. 'We

are both fortunate in our ladies—as, too, is Alexander Danilovich.'

Menshikov smiled his acknowledgment of the compliment to his own recently-acquired wife, who, like Catherine, had never allowed a *terem* to keep her confined.

'However,' Sergei went on, 'it is no secret that the *terem* is a Russian tradition I would be loath to lose.'

The Tsar did not seem too pleased at this direct opposition from a very junior officer. 'I very much fear you will have to learn to live without it, Sergei Ivanovich. Just as you boyars have had to learn to live without your beards and your long sleeves.'

Darya Menshikova had taken no part in the conversation but now she leant across the table towards Kirsty. 'Can you imagine Count Borodinov with a long boyar's beard?' she said, seeking to divert the Tsar's mind from anything bordering on the contentious.

Kirsty stared at her husband appraisingly for a few moments. 'To tell the truth,' she said at last, 'I do not think I should have been inclined to marry him if he had had one.'

Even Sergei, whose face had grown steadily grimmer, was obliged to laugh at this, and it seemed that Darya and Kirsty had, between them, hit just the right note, for the Tsar clinched the conversation good-humouredly by commenting, 'You see, Sergei Ivanovich? Had you not abandoned that particularly Russian tradition, you would not have been so lucky.'

The conversation moved to safer ground after that, and it was not long before the meal was over and the guests moved to participate in the other entertainments. Kirsty circulated with the ease of one accustomed to do so, and knew that Sergei, never far from her side, had no cause for complaint. It almost seemed, on occasion, as if he were proud that his wife was so much at ease when so many, older, Russian women clearly were not.

Nothing was said during the brief coach-ride home, and once they were indoors Kirsty sank on a divan and kicked first one and then the other little sapphire satin slipper into the air and wriggled her toes in their silk stockings before the heat of the stove.

'I *have* enjoyed myself,' she sighed. 'Yet I am not at all sorry to be able to relax once more.'

'Does it give you enjoyment, then, to make a fool of your husband?' Sergei asked stiffly.

Kirsty sat up straight, all relaxation banished. 'I did not do so,' she protested. 'How can you say so?'

'You disagreed with me in public.'

'On a subject on which we also disagree in private. Would you prefer me to lie? Or to disagree with the Tsar? Which would you prefer?'

'Neither, of course, as you very well know. You do not have to volunteer information which makes it perfectly clear that we disagree.'

'It was but one small remark, Sergei,' Kirsty pleaded. 'You read too much into it—much more, I am sure, than anyone else present.'

'Not more than Menshikov,' he told her. 'He has found what he will regard as a weakness and will use it for his own ends.'

'Does he have some grudge against you?' she asked, surprised.

'I have given him no cause to bear a grudge, except that I was born to money and rank and he was not. That is sufficient. There is nothing personal in it, simply a desire to demonstrate his power—a power that nobody doubts, in any case.'

'Oh, Sergei, I am sorry, but what was I to know of the position? I did not think so small a remark would distress you, and would not have said it—at least, not in such a place—had I known how displeased you would be. I will keep a close watch on my tongue in future.'

'If you kept a close watch on your thoughts, your tongue would take care of itself!'

Kirsty stared at him in amazement. 'My thoughts are my own!'

'On the contrary, they are, like your body, mine. I have had precious little satisfaction from the one. As to the other, you will adopt the views of your husband —and those include the retention of the *terem*, whatever the Tsar may decree.'

'That sounds to me suspiciously like treason,' Kirsty remarked.

'Nevertheless, that is the situation, and you would do well to remember it unless you wish to emulate the Tsaritsa Eudoxia and enjoy your remaining years in a nunnery.'

Kirsty stared at him aghast, and realised, as she saw his lips white with rage, that he was a great deal more angry than she had appreciated. Her initial impulse to discomfort him in a way he would not forget waned as she realised that to do so with Sergei in his present mood would hardly be conducive to any improvement in their mutual understanding. When she answered, it was in a voice from which she had managed to expunge any hint of retaliation.

'I am sure you speak in anger,' she said gently. 'I have said that I am sorry my remark should have distressed you and that I will take care in future. But, Sergei, do you truly want a wife who does not think for herself and who is as much at your disposal as . . . as a samovar?'

He looked down at her and she fancied some of the grimness left his mouth, though his laugh was short and humourless.

'If that is what I wanted, I am most certainly disappointed,' he said.

It was a remark that hurt her more than threats of a nunnery could ever do.

Sergei looked at his wife and was startled to see that she looked as stricken as if he had slapped her. Would he ever understand this exquisite creature? His acquaintances had warned him of the dangers of marrying a foreigner, and he had certainly not expected these outbursts of independence amounting to defiance. He had known how advantageous such a marriage would be from Alexander Benmore's point of view, but sometimes—just sometimes—he had the feeling that his daughter might not have married him simply for her father's sake. There had been times when there was a warmth about her that could not, surely, be due entirely to his wealth and position? And now, for instance: what had he said to cause so stricken a look? Her next words told him.

'It has never been my intention to disappoint you, Sergei Ivanovich,' she said in a small voice. 'Can we not somehow establish a compromise when our views and expectations differ so extremely?'

'You have misunderstood me,' he said gently. 'I did not say I was disappointed. I said I should have been, had I expected a wife who was prepared to be regarded in the same light as . . . a samovar, I think you said. Such a wife would be very convenient, no doubt, but her attraction would wane within a week, as the Tsar found when he married just such a one. My only disappointment is that we have not managed to deal better together.'

'It is a disappointment we share. I think perhaps neither of us realised how great an adjustment to each other's ways we needed to make.'

'A Russian does not expect to make an adjustment to his wife's way,' Sergei replied, but it was a simple statement of fact, and not a rebuke.

'Which probably causes no problems—when his wife is also Russian. Remember, I would not expect to have to make such adjustments were my husband English. Sergei, we must compromise before we tear ourselves apart.'

He turned from her and paced over to the window looking out on the dark courtyard. What she said was true and eminently reasonable, and yet—where the seclusion of his wife was concerned—how could he compromise?

Sergei turned his back on the window and faced his wife across the room. 'If I may have your word that you will leave if a man is present,' he said, 'I am prepared to allow you to resume your visits to your friends in the German Suburb. But the *terem* remains.'

Knowing how great a concession this represented, Kirsty forbore to ask him to reconsider that final stipulation. Better by far to prove her willingness to obey him in the small matter and return to the larger one later. She said simply, 'Thank you, Sergei, you have my word. And now, if you have no objection, I will to my *terem*: it has been a tiring evening.'

As she rose from the divan and passed him on her way to the great carved door, she half thought that he would stay her, and looked up at him doubtfully, wondering if he had more to say. It appeared not, for he simply bade her good night and opened the door for her. She murmured her thanks as she passed through.

Would she ever understand this man? It became increasingly difficult to know what he wanted from her, and always, at the back of her mind, was the tantalising memory of the man she had glimpsed during the first part of her wedding night. Then she had thought she knew why he had married her, but glimpses of the tender side of her husband were becoming increasingly rare, and she no longer felt equipped to guess why he should have married a foreigner at all, let alone why it should have been she. There must be some way of pleasing him, some middle way, yet she seemed unable to stumble upon it. At all events, the pleasure she had had in the evening was now quite driven away, and she made her way to her quarters in such low spirits that Anna, the maid who had waited up to undress her, concluded that western-style dinners were not such fun as people made out.

Kirsty was not to know how long Sergei remained behind, wrapped in thoughts that were the mirrors of her own, before retiring to his own rooms.

CHAPTER
SIX

KIRSTY WAS longing to see the Harrows again and in particular to tell them about the Tsar's reception, but on the other hand, she felt it wiser not to take too sudden advantage of Sergei's partial change of heart. Consequently she spent the next day—or what was left of it once she had woken up, bathed and breakfasted—in her quarters playing with Misha and Belka.

The following day, however, she ordered the carriage put to and, taking care to pull down the blinds with which Sergei had had it fitted, was driven out to the Harrows' house.

Mistress Harrow was surprised and delighted to see her.

'The girls have gone out, but will be back shortly,' she told Kirsty. 'I know they will be eager to ask you all about the Tsar's dinner, which, you must know, has been the talk of the German Suburb. But come in and take a dish of tea: I shall be glad of the company.'

'Are you alone, then?' Kirsty asked, suddenly feeling too embarrassed to ask directly whether John Harrow or his father were at home.

'Completely,' Mistress Harrow replied cheerfully. 'My husband and son have been busy these last few days, leaving at dawn and not returning till after dusk. The girls begged me to go with them, but sometimes, you know, it is blissful to have the house to oneself, so I told them to take a servant instead and I have had an hour or two of peace.'

'Upon which I have intruded,' Kirsty said ruefully, but Mistress Harrow was having none of that.

'And very welcome, too,' she assured her. 'Do not be imagining me to be some sort of recluse *manquée*. I had just decided that peace and quiet had lasted long enough and was hoping the girls would soon be back, so your arrival was most opportune. Just in time to prevent my feeling myself deserted and ready to fall into a fit of the dismals.'

Kirsty could not but laugh at the vision thus conjured up of the ever-cheerful Mistress Harrow in a fit of the dismals. 'I do not think you are often cast down,' she said, 'and some tea would be most welcome.'

Mistress Harrow led the way to the sitting-room, which, furnished as it was in the English style, always made Kirsty feel at home. The caddy had scarcely been unlocked when Mary and Margaret came in, as delighted as their mother to see their guest.

'We were talking about you only yesterday,' Mary began. 'We heard that you and Count Borodinov had attended the Tsar's dinner and cannot wait to hear all about it at first hand. Is it true he has married the Lithuanian peasant?'

'Shush, Mary, watch your tongue. If he has, that is no way to speak of the new Tsaritsa.'

'But, Mama, it is true! They say she has even changed her name from Martha to the more Russian Catherine to please him!'

'It is not more Russian,' Margaret corrected her younger sister. '"Marfa" is a well-established Russian name. Though not, perhaps, one found in the first circles,' she added.

'Precisely.' Mary was triumphant. 'But is it true? Kirsty, you should know if anyone does!'

'It is perfectly true she is called Catherine,' Kirsty told her. 'As to whether they are married, I cannot say.'

'But you will have seen the seating arrangements,' Mary persisted. 'Was she at the end opposite the Tsar?'

Kirsty laughed. 'You can tell nothing from the seating arrangements! People sat where they would unless the Tsar directed them to a particular place. I assure you that, but for the fact that the company was mixed and sat round one long table, it little resembled an English dinner party. For one thing, the guests all talked at once unless directly addressed by the Tsar, in which case, of course, everyone in the immediate vicinity held their peace while he spoke.'

'Did you have agreeable neighbours at table?' Mistress Harrow enquired.

'Indeed, we were most fortunate. The Tsar requested our presence near the head, where our immediate neighbours were the Tsar himself and Catherine, and Prince and Princess Menshikov.'

Margaret looked serious. 'Exalted company, indeed,' she said. 'What is your opinion of the Prince? He is both feared and mistrusted, they say.'

'He was most affable,' Kirsty said cautiously. 'One would hardly expect otherwise on such an occasion, though, would one?'

'You did not much care for him!' Mary exclaimed.

'Shush, girl!' Her mother sounded cross. 'You really must learn not to say the first thing that comes into your head! You cannot expect Kirsty to say anything that, if it got back to the wrong ears, might prejudice her husband.'

'How should anything get back from here?' Mary looked surprised.

'Walls have ears,' her mother said, 'and people working in a foreign household invariably pick up more of the strange language than they are usually given credit for. And now, let us hear about you, Kirsty,' she went on, changing the subject. 'We are all sorry it has been so long since your last visit.'

Kirsty coloured slightly. 'It is not always easy to get

away,' she said. 'My thoughts have been with you, however.'

'I should have thought a great lady such as you have now become would be able to get away whenever she liked,' Mary interjected.

'You are mistaken,' her sister reproved her. 'Kirsty has a large palace to oversee, and although it will be well staffed, a good housewife will always keep a finger on the pulse.'

Kirsty smiled at her gratefully. 'You can have no idea, Mary, of the hundred and one things that always seem to need doing. I had thought the palace would run itself, and it did to begin with, but it soon loses momentum if one seems to be paying it no attention.'

'That is always the way,' Mistress Harrow said with feeling. 'And if houses did run themselves, how then would we fill our time?'

Before anyone had time to answer, the door flew open and John Harrow burst unceremoniously into the room.

'I *thought* it was the Borodinov carriage I saw turn into the avenue!' he exclaimed. 'I guessed it must be Kirsty paying us a visit.' He turned to her. 'It is so long since you have been, and to think I might have missed you, had it not been for that chance glimpse!' He stopped, suddenly hesitant.

When she saw who it was who had burst, un-announced, into the room, Kirsty's colour heightened and she immediately rose to her feet, mindful of her promise to Sergei.

'I am glad to see you well, John,' she said, and turned to her hostess. 'Mistress Harrow, you will excuse me if I make my farewells. I declare, time runs on, and I had no idea it was so late.'

Mistress Harrow and her daughters looked at her in some amazement. Mary was betrayed into saying, 'So soon?' but no one took this up, and she noticed her mother and sister exchange glances she did not understand. Mindful of earlier reprimands, she held her tongue, determining to seek an explanation when their visitor had gone.

John was oblivious both to the silent communication between others of his family and to Kirsty's obvious unease.

'It is not late at all,' he assured her. 'You may easily stay another half-hour. It is simply that I am back earlier than is usual.'

'Nevertheless, I must be on my way,' Kirsty said. 'Pray have my carriage sent round.'

As Mistress Harrow reached for the bell, a blood-curdling scream rang through the house. The occupants of the room stared at one another.

'What in heaven's name . . . ?' began John, and then the door burst open and a flushed and tearful maid bobbed a curtsy.

'A thousand pardons, lady,' she said to Mistress Harrow. 'But cook has upset a bowl of boiling fat on her arm. Come quickly, *barinya*, she could die from it.'

Without a second thought, the three ladies of the household rushed to the nether regions, leaving the door open and Kirsty alone in the room with John.

'In this crisis, it obviously behoves me to be gone,' she said. 'If you can find a maid or a footman to escort me to my carriage, I shall take my leave.'

John took a step towards her, 'There is a constraint between us that never used to be there,' he remarked.

'I was not then a married woman,' she pointed out.

'To be sure, but does that change in your situation necessitate your leaving the instant I appear?'

'It does when my husband is a Russian,' Kirsty replied.

'I see. He would keep you in seclusion?'

'Something like that,' Kirsty admitted. 'Certainly he

would not approve of my being alone in a room with you like this.'

'Neither would my mother, had Tanya not had an accident.' His voice became more urgent. 'Kirsty, does it suit you, a girl of spirit, to be as restricted as your words suggest?'

Torn between a natural inclination to truthfulness and loyalty to Sergei, she temporised. 'I knew when I married Count Borodinov that a degree of seclusion would be expected,' she said.

'A degree! You are hardly ever away from home!' John exclaimed.

'You cannot know that,' Kirsty protested.

'Can I not? There is little you do that I do not know, at least outside the walls of your sumptuous prison, and it is rarely enough that you are allowed forth.'

'You speak too freely,' Kirsty told him stiffly. 'Years of childhood friendship do not permit such liberty—or such impropriety.'

'Very well! It is not my wish to distress you, but let me just say this: I have known you since you came to Russia and have an affection for you at least as strong as any brother's. I do not believe the secluded life of a Russian wife will long suit you. Should you wish to flee the *terem*—and, by definition, Russia, since you could hardly remain here—you have only to get word to me, and somehow I shall try to help you.'

He gave her no time to reply, which was just as well, since he left her bereft of words, but instructed the footman to order the Countess's carriage brought round. Hardly had the man set off on his errand than Mistress Harrow returned from the kitchens.

'My dear, my deepest apologies for thus running off and leaving you with John. I trust you came to no harm? Not that it is likely,' she added hastily, 'but it was remiss of me to leave you unchaperoned.'

'I fully understand,' Kirsty replied. 'My carriage is at this moment being called. You will wish me to perdition at this time of crisis, I know. How is Tanya?'

'She will live. It was but a few drops of fat—painful enough, to be sure, but hardly warranting such histrionics as we were treated to. You will come again, will you not?' She sounded anxious.

'When it is possible, I shall do so,' Kirsty assured her, and took her leave, bidding Mistress Harrow to convey her good wishes to Margaret and Mary who were still attending to the cook.

There was plenty to occupy her mind during the drive back to the Borodinov palace, and she was grateful for the drawn blinds that enabled her to think without distraction. She hated the *terem*. Not the quarters themselves, or even the idea of having a part of the house that she could regard as her own: on the contrary, it was an idea with much to recommend it. No, it was the concept that a woman must be kept apart from the society of all but other women that she found intolerable. For a woman of her rank it meant, for example, that she could not go out, as the Harrow sisters had done. Forbidden the company of men, she heard no business talk, no politics, no philosophy. It was true that her own position was more isolated than that of a Russian woman would have been because she did not have a wide acquaintance of female friends and relations on whose society she could call. Nevertheless, Kirsty had always enjoyed listening to discussions between her father and his business associates and seeking clarification from him afterwards of matters which had puzzled her.

All this was gone, and since Sergei seemed to have little desire for her company, she had no opportunity to converse with him. She fully intended to shake off her shackles, but until John Harrow's words, it had never crossed her mind to do so other than by ultimately persuading her husband that they were unnecessary.

John had presented an alternative solution. It was so drastic that Kirsty was at first inclined to dismiss it as ludicrous, but then a disquieting thought struck her: what if she failed to persuade Sergei? He had not, after all, proved very flexible in his views up to now.

If she fled for good and all, she would be placing herself entirely under John's protection. This was hardly a wise thing to do, since he, too, would also be obliged to leave Russia and she would be dependent upon a man who had lost the means to support her. John was an honourable man, but she did not love him; nor, having known Sergei, could she ever do so.

Since the time Sergei had come to her rescue in Archangel she had regarded him in much the same light as a knight from the days of chivalry. When she had realised whom it was she had married, her heart had been unable to believe such a happy coincidence. She had loved him at that moment and longed to be free to love him since, despite his treatment of her which had ranged from the violent to the frigid. If only she knew why he had married her! She did not even know if he was aware, when he offered for her hand, that she was the girl to whose rescue he had come that evening. If only she could make him love her, she thought, the spectre of the *terem* would surely fade. But how did one set about such a task? And if one failed, did one remain in misery or take flight back to one's own country?

Whatever one did, she was quite sure one did not let one's husband find out from servants about the unexpected appearance on the scene of John Harrow. She was tempted to conceal it—sorely tempted—yet if her previous unintentional concealment had provoked his wrath, how much worse it would be if it were deliberate.

She broached the subject at dinner. 'I visited the Harrows today,' she began.

'Indeed? I hope it was an enjoyable visit.'

'Not particularly. That is, it was at first, for they were agog to hear about the Tsar's reception, but—well, it became rather embarrassing.'

Sergei's smoked sturgeon paused momentarily on its way to his mouth.

'I am sorry. In what way were you embarrassed?'

'Mistress Harrow, her daughters and I were enjoying a dish of tea when John came in, unannounced and unexpected. There was nothing I could do about it,' Kirsty went on, feeling how feeble an excuse it sounded, 'except send for my carriage and go.'

'And did you do so?'

'Of course—and Mistress Harrow saw me into it. I think she realised that John's presence made things a trifle difficult for me.'

He looked at her curiously. 'And why are you telling me this? You must know it is hardly news likely to delight me.'

Kirsty tossed her head defiantly. 'If you must know, I would rather you heard it from me than from the servants.'

Sergei laughed. 'Very wise. Tell me, had you not feared I should learn about it from another source, would you still have told me?'

Kirsty thought for a few moments. 'In truth, I don't know,' she said at last, and was surprised that he laughed again.

'That is undoubtedly an honest answer,' he told her. 'It goes no small way to reassuring me.' He reached across the table and took her hand. 'Come,' he said. 'Let us go to the Divan Room. I have something to tell you.'

Glancing up at him curiously, Kirsty allowed herself to be led to the small room furnished with backless sofas that gave it its name. Such a room was, Sergei had told her, one of the few civilised customs that Russia had adopted under the Tartar yoke, and Kirsty had to admit that the divans themselves were a great deal more comfortable than the stiff-backed, rigidly upholstered sofas and armchairs currently fashionable in the German Suburb. Of course, she reflected, the comfort was to an extent dependent upon one's clothes: the stiffly upright Western seats were easier to cope with when one was wearing the rigid corset demanded by western clothes. This evening, however, she had changed into the shapeless, comfortable *sarafan* and so, free from the restraints of a corset, was in no way incommoded by the low, deep seats.

The samovar was brought in and the flames beneath it lit. When the servants had withdrawn, Kirsty turned to her husband.

'You had something to tell me,' she said. 'From your tone, it is important.'

'We are ordered to St Petersburg. We leave within the week.'

'St Petersburg!' Kirsty exclaimed. 'Do we have a house there? You have never spoken of it.'

'We do not.' His voice held a hint of grimness. 'I very much fear you will have to be housed in a log cabin. I believe, however, you may be permitted to return to Moscow very shortly. It is at the special request of Catherine that you are to come. I have already set in train the building of a stone palace there since it is only a matter of time before all nobles are ordered to do so, and I am optimistic that I, too, will be able to return to Moscow before winter sets in: even the Tsar does not remain in his new city during the winter months.'

'Why should Catherine have requested my presence?'

He shrugged. 'It seems that she has taken a liking to you,' he said. 'That there is some purpose behind this visit, I am sure, though I have no idea what it might be. I hope you will not find the journey too tedious.'

CHAPTER
SEVEN

SERGEI'S HOPE was unfounded. The autumn rains were turning such tracks as existed into quagmires that trapped the wheels of the lumbering carriage sometimes axle-deep. In vain did Kirsty point out that she was a perfectly competent horsewoman and that, if Sergei would but provide her with a mount, they could make good time, but he would have none of it. It took them three weeks to reach the future capital.

Kirsty's heart sank at what she saw before her. Although some houses of brick and stone were gradually going up and there was some evidence of a design to the whole, almost all the existing completed houses were of wood: some of them, like the Tsar's tiny cottage, painted to look like European houses of brick. Sergei had secured a two-roomed cabin for his countess, and laughed ruefully when he saw her face fall.

'Pray God, you will not be here long.'

'Pray God, indeed,' she replied absently, looking around her. There was already a hint of winter in the air, freezing the marshy swamp that was to become one of the beauties of Europe. Sergei showed her the site of their future palace on the bank of the Neva, but all there was to see were the massive foundations being sunk into the swamp, and Kirsty could form no idea from them of what the city would look like.

Next day Kirsty found out why they had been ordered to this unhealthy swamp. With no prior—and no subsequent—announcement, in the presence only of a few close friends and, at the request of Catherine, of the Count and Countess Borodinov, the Tsar married his mistress. It went without saying that Prince Menshikov, close friend and confidant of Peter Alexeyevich, was present. He drew Sergei and his wife aside, his face stern and his eyes hard—no sign of the bland courtier of their previous meeting.

'You are honoured indeed to have been present on this occasion,' he began.

'We are very conscious of the fact,' Sergei told him. 'It is an honour we shall treasure.'

'Then treasure it in private,' the Prince told him shortly. 'This marriage is not to be made public: Peter Alexeyevich does not feel the time is right for any but a privileged few to know it has taken place. A privileged few who, because of the fancy of Catherine, include you. I advised against your presence: nothing personal, you understand, merely an uncertainty as to your, and, forgive me, but more particularly the Countess Borodinova's, ability not to gossip.'

'Surely you are aware that there has been speculation in Moscow that the wedding has already taken place?' Kirsty asked.

'Speculation, yes, and it will continue, but it must be neither confirmed nor denied. Do you understand that?'

'I am sure we both realise the importance of acceding to the Tsar's wishes,' Sergei said. 'You may rest easy on that score.'

Menshikov bowed. 'I am sure I may. The Tsar returns to Moscow tomorrow. You may follow when you will.'

When he was out of earshot, Kirsty turned to her husband. 'I shall not be sorry to return, but all this way for a wedding! Why did it not take place in Moscow?'

Sergei shrugged. 'There is little doubt that this new city will become the new capital of Russia. If that is so, it has a symbolic significance.' He paused. 'Your father would be well advised to see if he cannot obtain permission to transfer his business activities from Archangel to this swamp. It is said that merchants from the west will be encouraged to transport their goods through St Petersburg instead of Archangel.'

The journey back to Moscow was every bit as tedious as the outward one, and Kirsty was only too happy to retire to her *terem* and sleep the clock round.

When she felt sufficiently refreshed from her journey to join her husband at breakfast, it was to receive the news that the Tsar was to give a ball to which they were invited.

Kirsty sighed. 'So soon! Is his energy limitless?'

'So it is generally believed,' Sergei told her. 'Furthermore, it does not occur to him that others are less energetic. Another visit to your Madame de Fontainebleau is called for, I fancy—but, Kirsty, keep a watch on your tongue.'

The ball was spectacular, and Kirsty, in cloth-of-silver and diamonds, was the cynosure of too many eyes to please her husband, and when the Tsar himself sought her hand for the gavotte, Sergei was torn between this honour to him and the dislike of seeing another man, even the Tsar, leading his wife down the room.

The composition of the ball's programme had caused much heart-searching among those responsible for drawing it up. Because of the traditional seclusion of women, there were no Russian dances suitable for such a function, and Russian guests, both male and female, had little idea how to perform any of the strange mixture of western dances that was finally included. Dancing-masters from the German Suburb had been much in demand from the moment invitations had been received, and sufficient foreign guests had been invited to ensure that the floor was never empty. Among them, Kirsty was pleased to see, were the Harrows, and she asked Sergei, somewhat tentatively, if she might present them to him.

It was not an entirely felicitous idea. Sergei's unsmiling formality did not fit in with the social small-talk such
an occasion warranted, and it seemed to Kirsty that he
was particularly displeased that the party should have
included John, though how it could be otherwise was
impossible to conceive. The Harrows were certainly
conscious of the constraint, and found it necessary to
circulate among their other acquaintance sooner than
friendship might otherwise have expected.

Scarcely had the Harrows moved on than Prince
Menshikov, still the blandly smiling courtier,
approached. 'May I hope, Sergei Ivanovich, to venture
where the Tsar has trod?' he asked.

Still irritable from his introduction to the Harrows,
Sergei was unwisely curt.

'Express yourself plainly, Alexander Danilovich,' he
said. 'What do you want?'

Menshikov's eyes narrowed, but his voice was as
bland as ever. 'Why, to lead Christina Alexandrovna
into the pavane, what else? Do I have your consent?'

For a brief moment, both Menshikov and Kirsty
thought it would be withheld—and so it would have
been had Sergei not been at least as fully aware as the
Prince of the probable outcome. Like any Russian, both
men were entirely dependent upon the Tsar's continued
favour for the retention of their lands, their serfs and
their wealth, and though, through his marriage to
Kirsty, Sergei was now an object of the Tsar's attention, the fact remained that Menshikov was Peter's
childhood friend, his closest adviser and his undoubted
favourite. Only if one wished to finish one's life in the
Siberian wilderness did one anger the Prince. Sergei
had no such wish.

He bowed. 'I should deem it an honour,' he said.
'Kirsty?'

She curtsied. 'And I also. I fancy there are not many

foreigners who can claim to have danced both with a Tsar and a Prince of Russia in the same evening.'

Menshikov's smile grew broader. 'I compliment you, Sergei Ivanovich, on the acquisition of a wife who knows so well how to please, and allied to such beauty, too—a rare combination. You must hold yourself very fortunate.'

'I do, I assure you, Prince. I am fully aware of the good fortune that has always so far attended me.'

'Then we must hope it sees no need to desert you, Count.' Menshikov bowed, and turning from Sergei, raised Kirsty's hand briefly to his lips. 'Until the pavane, Countess.'

She inclined her head. 'I look forward to it.'

It really needed nothing else to set the seal of Sergei's disapproval on the evening. The ball was a glittering occasion; by almost any criterion one might apply, it was a success. As a means of westernising Russia, such a ball as this was certainly one of the more pleasant.

Had Sergei not been married, he would have enjoyed it, he acknowledged to himself. He acknowledged, too, that had his wife been some plump Russian dumpling, he would have felt less strongly than he now did. But his wife was not. She was the most beautiful, the most desirable woman he had ever seen. He thought he knew why she had married him, but he had hoped she might look beyond his wealth and his rank, and there had been times when he had thought perhaps she did so, when he suspected there might be a passion there equal to his own, could it but be aroused. Yet she recoiled from any but the most superficial touch, and such efforts as she had made to ease relations between them had seemed to stem more from a desire of a strife-free life than from anything else. He looked forward to the coming summer when he could take her to his country estate, away from outside influences. Perhaps there, among the orchards of Zubstovoy, they could establish the understanding he longed for.

He watched her execute the stately steps of the pavane with the ease of one accustomed to them, and observed that Prince Menshikov was hardly less familiar with them, thanks to his extensive travels in Holland and England. Kirsty moved with grace, from time to time smiling across at her partner, occasionally blushing at some unsought compliment, and Sergei inwardly cursed his own stubbornness in refusing to learn the steps of any of these courtly dances. It was a stubbornness that now placed him at a disadvantage. It would not happen again: he would learn. At the next ball, his wife would dance with him.

It was well after midnight when they returned home, having left the ball as early as Sergei dared.

Kirsty looked tentatively up at him as they entered the house and the servants relieved them of their cloaks.

'I do not think you enjoyed the ball, Sergei Ivanovich,' she said.

'It was a brilliant occasion,' he said shortly.

'To be sure, it was,' she agreed, 'but that is not to the point. I think you disliked it.'

'I should have liked it well enough had you not been there,' he said bluntly.

'Thank you.'

'I am sorry, Kirsty: I did not mean that you gave me cause to blush; on the contrary, you did me great credit. I simply cannot stomach seeing another man—other men—enjoying the company of my wife.'

'In your presence, Sergei,' she reminded him quietly. 'There was no impropriety, you know that.'

'By your standards, perhaps. Not by mine. Kirsty, can you not see? I do not *wish* to share you. You are mine. I wish it to remain like that.'

Kirsty stared at him, wonderingly, and took a step

towards him, laying her hand upon his brocaded sleeve. 'I am no less yours because I dance with someone else in your presence.'

He caught her to him then and his heart soared as he felt no resistance to his embrace, only a softening of her body against his, as if the door of paradise might swing open.

As Kirsty's arms reached up and she felt his soldier's body hard against her own, her heart, too, leapt. This was closer to her dreams. She longed for the moment to linger, lest its passing should destroy the mutual happiness she sensed could be theirs if nothing were to disturb the delicate balance of these moments.

But it did. A grinning servant, who lacked the sense to withdraw at such a time, coughed and enquired whether Sergei Ivanovich needed anything further that night.

'Your absence,' his master snapped, and the man withdrew, but the mood was broken, the moment gone.

Perhaps that was no bad thing. Kirsty thought. The gulf that stretched between them was in part due to their entirely different expectations, but it was also because they did not know each other, that despite a brief encounter in Archangel, they were strangers, and they had done little since their wedding that could be calculated to change that state of affairs. So she smiled shyly at her husband and bade him good night.

'Good night, Kirsty,' he said, and then hesitated, unable to banish his evil genius entirely. 'John Harrow is a handsome man,' he added.

'Pleasant enough,' Kirsty said, surprised. 'I would not describe him as handsome, precisely.'

'You knew the family in Archangel. I am surprised you did not marry him.'

Kirsty laughed. 'Since he did not offer, I could hardly do so.'

Sergei's face clouded. 'Does that mean you would have done, had he done so?'

Since, in Archangel, it had never crossed Kirsty's mind, she did not take the question seriously, nor did she realise how seriously it was meant. Instead, she laughed again. 'As to that, Sergei Ivanovich, we shall never know!'

Sergei's face hardened, and there was an ominous whiteness about his mouth which she had never seen before and would not be sorry never to see again.

'So you laugh at me, do you, Countess?' He spat her title out as if it were an insult.

'No!' Kirsty exclaimed. 'Such was not my intent. It was merely a light reply to a question I did not take seriously.'

'You do not regard your involvement with another man as serious?'

'There is no involvement! For goodness' sake, Sergei, you asked me a purely hypothetical question to which there can be no certain answer. I have never been "involved" with John Harrow, and in Archangel I certainly never considered him as a future husband.'

'"In Archangel",' her husband echoed. 'From which I infer you have so considered him since leaving there.'

'How could I? I am married to you!' But Kirsty flushed, partly in anger and partly because she knew she had been regarding John Harrow in a different light in recent weeks.

As the colour rose in her cheeks, Sergei chose to construe it as a tacit admission of a preference for the man he was fast coming to regard as his rival.

'I am sorry, Countess,' he said icily. 'Had I been less precipitate with my advantageous offer for your hand, you might have received and accepted that of Master Harrow, and we should not have entered upon our present disastrous course.'

Giving her no opportunity to reply, Sergei strode out of the room, slamming the door behind him. Kirsty stared after him in disbelief. Was all that because he had thought she was laughing at him? Yet the only other interpretation was jealously, and how could jealousy exist without the prerequisite of love? Saddened and defeated by her inability to understand her husband, Kirsty betook herself to her own lonely bed.

Next morning, her cup of chocolate was accompanied by a note. In it Sergei informed her that he would be away on manouevres for two days—and she was forbidden to leave the palace on any pretext until he returned.

Kirsty read it in deepening despair. No sooner did she and Sergei seem to be approaching some sort of understanding than something happened to put them back almost as far as they had been to start with.

But despair was not an emotion Kirsty willingly entertained, and her mood very soon changed to anger. She ripped the little note to pieces and flung them across the room—an unsatisfying gesture, since they simply floated delicately to the floor, a fact which did nothing to assuage her wrath. How *dare* he leave so curt a message! And how *dare* he go back on their previous agreement —and without a word of either consultation or explanation! To do so in such a cowardly way, too: to send a note which she would receive only when he was safely out of the house!

Furious, her cup followed the note and smashed with gratifying impact against the door. Kirsty watched its contents trickle down the wooden panels for a few moments before sending the saucer to join its companion. She found added satisfaction that a service of fine china much treasured by Sergei was now no longer complete. That will teach him! she thought.

Really, the man was becoming intolerable! It would serve him right if she immediately ordered the carriage to take her—with the blinds up, of course—to visit the Harrows. It would really be very satisfying to do that, especially if she sent him a curt note of her own, as soon as she returned, telling him what she had done.

Even as her mind dwelt with some gratification on the picture of his impotent fury when he read her note, Kirsty knew she would not do it. She was at a loss to understand why his pride could not bear the thought of her dancing with other men. If matters were otherwise between them, she might have thought him jealous, but that could not be the case. No, it could only be pride, and she had a strong suspicion that, however tempting her contemplated action, it would be more likely to render their differences irreconcilable than to bring him to his senses.

As it happened, matters were to be taken out of her hands. A note arrived later that day requesting the pleasure of her company on the afternoon of the morrow, at the Tsaritsa's apartments to take tea with Catherine and some of her friends.

Kirsty knew she had no choice but to go: politely worded as the note might be, it was none the less a command. She knew that Sergei, could he be consulted, would have no option but to lift his ban for the occasion.

The problem was that he could not be consulted, and Kirsty felt she could no longer hazard a guess as to what his reaction might be when he learned she had disobeyed him. True, disobedience on this occasion was not quite the same as that which she had so briefly contemplated, but it was still disobedience.

She turned the matter over in her mind for some time before a solution occurred to her: she would send Catherine's note to him by messenger, enclosed with one of her own explaining that she felt she really had to accept, and regretting that his military duties precluded her discussing it with him first. If he objects to that, she thought, he is unreasonable indeed.

Kirsty dressed for the occasion in the western clothes that would be expected at Court, but travelled in the closed palanquin which she knew would be her husband's preference, and thus, once more, she found herself entering the Terem Palace, the private palace of the royal family.

There were some half-dozen women with the Tsaritsa in a large drawing-room furnished in the western style, which sat strangely against an architecture essentially Russian. All of these women Kirsty had seen at the Tsar's dinner, but only one, apart from Catherine herself, was known to her, and that was Darya Menshikova. The Menshikov influence was very noticeable at the little tea party, for another of the women was the recently widowed Anna Golovina, sister to the recently elevated Prince.

Not knowing quite what to expect of the tea party, Kirsty was agreeably surprised to find that the conversation, far from being limited to matters domestic, ranged across politics and the seemingly endless campaigns against Sweden. Both Darya and Catherine made a point of accompanying their husbands on their campaigns whenever possible and had, it seemed, been doing so for some years before their respective marriages. Consequently they were remarkably well informed on military matters, and she found their comments both interesting and informative.

She was, however, extremely bewildered by some of the things she learned, especially when she tried to relate them to her own experience: she had accepted that Russian women, particularly those of a certain class, expected to live in seclusion, and that the Tsar was desirous of changing that. But it was perfectly clear that both Catherine and her close friend Darya had not only not been living in seclusion but had enjoyed a freedom far, far greater than would ever have been accorded any western woman, and Kirsty was honest enough to admit to herself that she was more than a little shocked by what she learned. Perhaps her views were not so very far from Sergei's, after all. And perhaps—a sobering thought —his implacable views stemmed partly from a fear that she might wish to emulate the ladies of the Imperial entourage. If that were the case, she should have little difficulty in persuading him that he had nothing to fear.

Kirsty enjoyed both the company and the converse, and only regretted that she had little to offer because she felt her lack of contribution to the discussions made her a dull companion. She had been relieved to find that only women were present: at least that would mitigate any displeasure Sergei might exhibit on his return, and it was reassuring to discover that these extremely emancipated women had not entirely abandoned the traditional ways of their people.

This reassuring thought was discarded when the door opened and Prince Menshikov walked in, entirely un-announced and apparently entirely at home, accompanied by friends, not all of whom were married to the ladies present.

His appearance was greeted with cries of pleasure from most of those in the room, and Kirsty smiled politely as he bowed over her hand.

'A charming addition to such a parure of diamonds,' he said, his voice as silkily smooth as she remembered it.

It was perhaps an overly florid metaphor, but it was, she supposed, kindly meant, so she smiled shyly and thanked him. She expected him to move away then, similarly to compliment others of those present, but instead he drew her hand unwillingly into his arm and led her very slightly apart.

'I confess to surprise that your husband permitted you

to come,' he said. 'Indeed, I warned the Tsaritsa that he would not.'

'My husband is on manoeuvres. Were you not aware of that?'

'Ah! I see! Sergei Ivanovich knows nothing of this visit!'

'On the contrary, I have advised him of the invitation and of my intent to accept.' There was an element of haughtiness in Kirsty's voice which was intended to depress. It failed.

'I am sure the estimable Count will appreciate that,' Menshikov said. 'I would I had been there to see his face when your note arrived.'

A wiser woman would have smiled and said no more, but Kirsty was not yet familiar with Prince Menshikov's tactics. She had been warned about him, it was true, but she was anxious for him not to have any confirmation of his implied suggestion that all was not well with the Borodinovs' marriage. So, instead of letting the matter drop, she bridled.

'I cannot imagine what pleasure that might have afforded you. Indeed, I very much doubt whether you would have learned anything at all.'

'How very true! It has often been remarked that Count Borodinov has a positive genius for maintaining an inscrutably blank expression when it suits him.' His voice became soft and sincere. 'Come, Christina Alexandrovna, let us not fence: we both know Sergei Ivanovich is less than enthusiastic about Peter Alexeyevich's plans to make Russia a country that can compare with anything in Europe. No one was more surprised than I that he should take a foreign bride. The Tsar, of course, was delighted. "Mark my words," he said to me, "this will be the making of Sergei Ivanovich." I confess I have seen little indication of a change in his views, and had not expected to see you here. I can only felicitate you on your extremely shrewd tactics!'

'There were no "tactics", as you call them,' Kirsty replied. 'There was no reason why I should not come, and I am quite sure Sergei would not have wished me to offend the Tsaritsa by declining. I did the only thing possible in the circumstances.'

'Precisely. The circumstances being, as I understand it, that after the ball he forbade you to visit.'

Kirsty stared at him open-mouthed. 'You cannot know that!' she said.

'Can I not? I am sure you are right. Had I known it, I should naturally not have dreamed of suggesting to our Tsaritsa that she should invite you, since—had I known it—to do so would have put you in an invidious position.'

Kirsty's mind was racing. If Menshikov knew of Sergei's directive, and she could not deceive herself into thinking it was a chance guess, then it could only mean that some member of their household was in the Prince's pay. Perhaps the best thing to do now was to play the naïve innocent; it would not, after all, be so very different from her performance in the conversation up to now, she thought ironically.

She lowered her lashes and glanced up at the Prince from under them. 'I see you understand my problem only too well,' she confided. 'Do you think he will be very angry?'

'Not if you look at him like that. But you must educate him, you know. You must wean him away from his antiquated notions. I know the Tsar is anxious it should be so—he holds Count Borodinov in great esteem and regrets only his preference for our more archaic traditions.'

Kirsty sighed. 'I wish I knew how it might be done,' she said.

'I am quite sure that between us something may be

devised,' he told her, and led her back to the main body
of guests. 'Darya, my dear, my apologies for having
deserted you for this delightful young boyarina, but, see,
I have brought her back.'

Darya Menshikova did not seem the least put out that
her husband had been monopolising the attention of a
young and very beautiful woman. She smiled up at him
with a look of sheer affection which was, Kirsty realised
with a jolt, reflected in his own eyes. She felt a pang
of jealousy—not of the affections of Alexander
Danilovich, whom she did not even like, but of the fact
that the Princess so clearly had her husband's heart.
What would Kirsty not give to see such a look in Sergei's
eyes!

The exchange of glances was brief, and Darya
hastened to include Kirsty in the conversation. 'I cannot
blame any man for wishing to further an acquaintance
with Christina Alexandrovna—not even my own
husband! I fancy there were broken hearts in plenty in
Archangel when your betrothal was announced!'

Kirsty blushed. 'I think not, Princess. None that had
ever indicated an attachment, at all events.'

'No? And what about that handsome young man from
the German Suburb who was at the ball? Was he not
from Archangel?'

'You must mean John Harrow. No, Princess. I know
the family well; John was like a brother to me, and we
were always friends, but I do not think his heart was ever
touched.'

'Not in Archangel, perhaps,' Menshikov's silken
voice broke in. 'I fancy the situation may have changed
since your marriage.'

Kirsty was spared the necessity of answering by the
appearance of the Tsaritsa at her shoulder with a request
to be told the subject of so absorbing a conversation.

Menshikov bowed. 'We were discussing the felicity of

your recent nuptials, and regretting that Peter Alexeyevich feels it necessary to keep the matter secret still.'

Catherine laughed. 'I do not think you were, Alexashka, but it is like you to say so. Darya, Kirsty, one more glass of tea before you go.'

Kirsty had a great deal to turn over in her mind when she was once more in her palanquin and free, behind the drawn curtains, to think without fear of interruption. Even so, the journey, slow as it was, was too quick for her to have reached any conclusion before they arrived back at the Borodinov Palace and it was a very thoughtful Countess who made her way to her *terem*.

She remained thoughtful until her husband's return late next day. She looked at her servants with a new eye. One of them was in Menshikov's pay. One of them was reporting their conversations, their disagreements, and goodness only knew what else. Which of the many serfs it might be, she had no idea. She assumed they were all from families long dependent on the Borodinovs, which made it very unlikely that they would be disloyal.

The knowledge that what she and Sergei did was all being reported elsewhere was not comforting, and it certainly could not be allowed to continue. Thank goodness she had told Sergei of her intention to accept Catherine's invitation. There would at least be no embarrassment in telling him what had transpired, though perhaps it might be wiser not to mention John Harrow, as the references to him were in any case, hardly germane to the main issue.

The relief she felt at Sergei's return, because the problem could be transferred to his shoulders, gave her greeting a warmth he had hardly expected.

He smiled, pleased but puzzled. 'I am gratified that my presence was missed,' he said drily. 'I have only been gone two days. What sort of welcome shall I receive when I return from months on campaign?'

'Oh, you are mistaken,' Kirsty assured him, without reflecting upon the infelicity of her choice of words. 'It is just that there is something I must discuss with you. It is important—and it should be in private,' she added.

She did not notice that the warmth left his eyes or the irony that entered his voice. 'No, I must be mistaken, I suppose. I must confess to considerable curiosity, however. Can the matter wait until I have changed out of these uncomfortable clothes?'

Looking at the mud-stained bottle-green of his uniform and his bespattered boots and breeches, Kirsty conceded that it could wait until he had bathed and changed.

'You had best come to my *terem*,' she told him. 'I shall send the women away; we can then lock the door and not be . . . disturbed.' She had been on the verge of saying 'overheard', but it seemed unwise to give any listening ears so broad a hint.

Sergei's face was expressionless. 'I am overwhelmed,' he said politely. 'I had not looked for such an invitation. To what do I owe the honour?'

'I am just being practical.'

'I see. Doubtless all will be explained eventually. I shall keep you waiting no longer than I must.'

When he knocked at the *terem* door and was ushered in by Anna, smiling broadly, Kirsty was waiting for him. He noticed a mixture of anxiety and impatience on her face, which cleared as soon as she saw him.

'At last!' she said, and then, turning to the maid, 'Anushka, you may leave us.'

The maid's heavily rouged cheeks beamed, and her knowing grin grew even broader as she bobbed a quick curtsy before leaving.

Kirsty looked after her a moment before closing the

door and turning the key. 'I cannot imagine what has got into the girl, grinning in that idiotic way.'

'One does indeed wonder,' Sergei said, his voice perfectly serious, yet with something undefinable about it that caused Kirsty to cast a quick glance at his face, which told her nothing.

'We had better go through to the bedroom, where we cannot be disturbed,' she said, leading the way through from the private sitting-room.

'Very wise, I'm sure,' Sergei murmured. Whatever might be on his wife's mind, it was perfectly clear that it was sufficiently important to have rendered her quite oblivious to the more usual interpretation that most people would have put upon her invitation to him to visit her in her *terem*—an interpretation that Anna had most certainly put upon it.

She invited him to sit down, and herself curled up, tailor-fashion, on the heavy brocade counterpane of the bed.

'Did you receive my message?'

'I did.'

'I hope you were not too angry.'

'On the contrary. You had little choice but to accept the invitation, and I was glad that you kept me informed.'

Kirsty looked at him suspiciously. 'Are you being sarcastic?' she asked.

He seemed surprised. 'Not at all. Why should I be? I meant precisely what I said. Did you enjoy yourself?'

'I did at first. It was pleasant to have some acquaintance, and the conversation was most interesting—and I was made to feel very welcome, which was something I appreciated.'

'As a guest, it could hardly be otherwise, surely?'

'Well, no: one would not expect the Tsaritsa to ignore a guest, I suppose! But I felt a special effort was made, particularly by the Tsaritsa and Princess Menshikova.'

'They are two women noted for their lack of the arrogance so often engendered by high position,' Sergei conceded. 'This is all very interesting, my dear, but does it merit the efforts you have made to tell me about it? Forgive me, but I have not so far learned anything of high importance.'

'I haven't reached that yet,' Kirsty told him impatiently. 'You asked me if I enjoyed myself, and I have told you.'

'My apologies. Clearly I spoke out of turn.'

There was no mistaking the sarcasm this time, but she chose to ignore it. 'Altogether, it was a very pleasant afternoon,' she said. 'But then Prince Menshikov and some of his friends came in—mostly husbands of those present.'

'And you felt—because you know my views on the subject—that you should leave?'

Kirsty looked at him, surprised. 'Not at all. How could I? To walk out at precisely the moment that the highest minister in the land walked in would look sufficiently pointed to occasion comment, do you not think?'

'Of course. How foolish of me. I feel sure there must be some significance attached to the arrival of Alexander Danilovich, and find myself on positive tenterhooks wondering what it might be.'

'You don't *appear* to be on tenterhooks!' Kirsty said suspiciously.

'That is because I have schooled myself to present an inscrutable expression to the world.'

'Prince Menshikov said as much, as a matter of fact!' At this, she had the unexpected satisfaction of seeing all inscrutability disappear, to be replaced with something close to displeasure.

'Indeed? I gather you discussed me.'

'Prince Menshikov introduced you as a topic. I tried to

turn the conversation, but failed. He is a clever man.'

'It would, I imagine, take more *savoir faire* than you as yet possess to deflect him from a topic upon which he was determined—and I mean that remark in no way as a critical one.'

'It is perfectly true,' Kirsty said ruefully. 'At all events, I failed, and he persisted. Sergei, he knows we disagree about the position of women in a household.'

Sergei looked surprised. 'I imagine he might. I have never made any secret of my views on the matter.'

'You do not understand. Something he said made it perfectly clear that he knew you had forbidden me to pay visits after the ball—and I cannot imagine you had told people that—and that my invitation by Catherine had been at his instigation.'

Sergei was very still. 'You are correct. It is not the sort of domestic detail one imparts to others.'

'Then, if he knew it, he must have been told by a member of our household. There must be among our serfs one who is in his pay, who has overheard our conversations—and our disagreements,' she added diffidently.

'Obviously. Fortunately we do not have to look very far to find him.'

'What do you mean?'

'Prince Menshikov's wedding present was a man-servant, Pyotr. I could not return him for fear of offending the Prince, but I did suspect there was more than generosity in Alexander Danilovich's mind. I set the man to work in the stables. He was less than delighted, having been trained as an indoor servant, but I did not want Menshikov's creature free to roam at will through my house. I cannot ban him from communication with the rest of the serfs, and he has obviously picked up the gossip.'

Kirsty shivered. 'I do not like the thought that what we

say and do is being reported to anyone. But only think, Sergei: you have on occasion made remarks which could, given the right degree of ill-will, be interpreted as treason.'

There was a long pause, during which Sergei paced up and down. Then he looked at her curiously. 'You are right, of course, and more astute than I had given you credit for. Have you paused to reflect that, were I convicted of treason, you would be free of this uncongenial Russian husband?'

'I do not wish to be free of you,' Kirsty whispered, her face suddenly pale. 'Is that what you think? It is not so, I assure you.'

Sergei reached out his long fingers and gently stroked her cheek. 'I am pleased to have such an assurance. You must admit there has been little in your manner to suggest otherwise.'

'As there has been little in yours to provoke compliance with your whims,' Kirsty retorted, disconcerted by the unexpected gesture and unsure what had prompted it.

He smiled. 'At least I have the consolation that you warn me of the possible consequences of my sometimes ill-chosen words. I should not wish to die a traitor's death.'

'No, indeed, and I should not wish it for you,' Kirsty said warmly, and added reflectively, 'it would not be a very satisfactory way to dispose of a husband—I am sure poison would be more sure and less lingering.'

'If such thoughts are going through your head, you have need to be grateful to the Tsar's sister, the Regent Sophia, who ameliorated the punishment for women who killed their husbands which, until her rule, had been burial alive.'

Kirsty shuddered and then, intrigued, asked, 'What is it now?'

'Decapitation.'

'It is hard to think of that as an amelioration.'

'You find it so? It has the merit of speed.'

'Perhaps I shall discard notions of poison,' Kirsty said. 'They grow less attractive by the minute. Besides, we must be serious. It is more important to decide what to do about Yuri. Can you get rid of him?'

'No, that is the one thing I dare not do. I think I shall promote him to a house-serf again.'

Kirsty's mouth dropped open. 'To a . . . a *house*-serf again? Why? Is that not playing into Menshikov's hands? Sergei, I do not want an eavesdropper anywhere, but certainly not in the house!'

'Allow me to conclude, my dear. Pyotr will be thus promoted, and then will stay here while we go to Zubstovoy for the summer. When we return from the country, he will be sent there to take charge in our absence.'

'Sergei, I vow you are a genius!'

He bowed modestly. 'I have my moments, my dear. You would do well not to forget the fact.'

CHAPTER
EIGHT

THE WEEKS before they could depart for Zubstovoy were largely uneventful and entirely peaceful domestically: aware that everything that reached the kitchen would also reach Prince Menshikov, both Kirsty and Sergei behaved and spoke with the utmost circumspection, like strangers who frequently encountered one another at social functions but who remained none the less strangers. Kirsty was not again asked to the Palace, but Sergei made no objections to her resuming her visits to the German Suburb, nor to the ladies of the Harrow family visiting her at the Borodinov Palace.

On only one occasion had anything happened to discompose her, and that was at the Harrows' house shortly before the Borodinovs' planned removal for the summer. Both Master Harrow and his son entered the drawing-room while Kirsty was there, their arrival clearly unexpected and vexatious to Mistress Harrow, who protested to her husband.

'My dear James, you know it is not fair to Kirsty, married as she is to a boyar, that you and John should present yourselves when she is here without her husband. You place her in an intolerable position.'

'Since the Countess is never here *with* her husband, how else can I see her?' her husband replied, unperturbed by her reproof. 'Kirsty, I would not wish to discomfort you, but you will be gone for several months and I would like to wish you well. We are all very fond of you, you know, and I feel that I stand in some sort as your father, since Alexander's return to Archangel. Your husband would doubtless not see it in that light, but that cannot change how I—indeed, how my entire family—feel about you. I hope it will go well with you at Zubstovoy.'

'Your good wishes are appreciated, sir,' Kirsty told him. 'I am sure Count Borodinov will understand your feelings when I tell him of your presence.'

James Harrow smiled at her warmly and turned to say something to his wife, and in those brief moments when no one was engaging Kirsty's attention, John, who was at her elbow, leant forward.

'I know you have not been happy,' he said in an intense undertone. 'It grieves me to see you so ill content in the lot that has befallen you, particularly when I recall the lively girl you were before your marriage.'

Kirsty could not but be touched by his evident sincerity, but she kept her manner formal. 'You are mistaken. I am not ill content: I am fully conscious of the fact that if one weds outside one's own society, the adjustments that must be made will take time. It would be wrong to construe that as unhappiness.'

'Would it? I think not. Kirsty, this man seeks to remove you further from western influences by taking you to his country estates. You will be totally isolated.'

'You know as well as I do that it is customary for Russians to spend the summer months on their estates,' Kirsty reminded him. 'There is nothing sinister in our doing the same.'

John shook his head. 'It is to your credit that you should say so; it indicates a loyalty that is to be admired, but I cannot believe you wish to be so totally cut off from your friends.'

'Doubtless I shall make other friends at Zubstovoy,' Kirsty said with forced cheerfulness. She was touched by his concern, and it brought a quiver to her voice which she sought to depress and which told more, both of her unhappiness and her appreciation of John's sympathy, than she would have wished.

John patted her hand briefly and felt it move as if she would clasp his own for strength and reassurance. He glanced anxiously round the room, but his family had observed nothing. 'You are a brave woman, Kirsty, but if life becomes intolerable, you have only to get word to me and I shall contrive to get you away.' There was no opportunity for Kirsty to reply, for Margaret came over to beg her to write to them.

'The truth is, we are all dying of curiosity,' she said. 'Zubstovoy is said to be the largest estate in Russia, and very grand. We want to know all about it, and are depending upon long and interesting letters to tell us. You won't disappoint us, will you?'

'I will not, if letters are all it takes, but Zubstovoy might! I cannot easily imagine anywhere grander than our town palace,' Kirsty replied, laughing.

Zubstovoy was so different from Moscow that Kirsty felt she had moved to another continent. It was certainly a huge estate, though not, Sergei told her, the largest in Russia. Situated several days' journey west and slightly north of the capital, much of it consisted of forests. The house itself was huge, but, despite its size, its character was more of a *dacha* than a palace. Built of wood and on two floors, it was relatively sparsely furnished and entirely in the traditional style. The only interior decoration was that given by ikons and brightly-coloured rugs. These were sufficient to overcome any hint of asceticism, and Kirsty found that the relative simplicity of her surroundings was, in itself, a welcome change.

The village of Zubstovoy was some distance from the house, and there was little about it to tempt the new Countess to visit more often than obligatory attendance at the little church necessitated. The houses of the serfs were single-roomed hovels called *izby*, built of wood with roughly thatched roofs. One or two of the slightly more prosperous ones had wooden roofs or carved fretwork ornamentation over the doors, but the general impression was one of poverty. Only the little wooden church with its gilded dome appeared to have any degree of prosperity, but Kirsty was soon to learn that the impression of abject poverty was somewhat misleading. Zubstovoy was a well-managed estate on which famine was unknown and hunger very rare, and, even allowing for the legendary stoicism of the Russian peasant, those she came across seemed content enough with their lot.

There was one feature of the estate that particularly delighted her: all the roads leading from the house itself and those going to the village were lined with fruit trees, most of them cherries, and when she and Sergei arrived, these were in full bloom so that they drove through arcades of sweet-smelling blossom. Sergei told her that the fruit was for the peasants to take, so that they could thus devote the whole of their half-acre plots to the cultivation of vegetables, knowing that fruit, like the mushrooms and berries of the fields and the forests, were there for the picking.

In keeping with the traditional atmosphere. but purely for reasons of comfort, Kirsty discarded her heavily boned and corseted western clothes in favour of the unrestricted comfort of the *sarafan*, an embroidered *kokochnik* replacing the inconveniently high *fontange*. She would have preferred nothing more cumbersome than a lace cap, but Anna threw up her hands in horror.

'You are a boyarina, *barinya*,' she said. 'You must dress to match your station. How dreadful it would be were a visitor to think you a serf!'

Since serfs did not customarily wear lace caps, Kirsty thought this was a mistake unlikely to be made, but it was not a sufficiently important issue to risk upsetting the servants over, so she confined herself to the traditional *kokochnik*, knowing that, for once, she had succeeded in pleasing everyone, not least her husband.

She had welcomed the move to Zubstovoy because she had hoped the complete change it represented might provide the opportunity for a fresh start, a hope that had been fuelled by the more civilised nature of their relationship enforced upon them by the discovery of Menshikov's spy. When she arrived there and found that the *terem* was a concept only nominally observed, she became even more optimistic, and repressed with some difficulty the giggle that sought expression when Sergei, opening a door on their tour of inspection, said apologetically, 'This is your *terem*. I regret it is hardly as extensive as that to which you are accustomed, but here in the country we are rather less precise in our observance of some traditions.'

The room before her was handsome enough and comfortable, though rendered a trifle gloomy by an exceptionally large apple tree outside one of the two windows, but it was just that: one room. In a European household it would simply have been regarded as the mistress of the house's bedchamber. To dignify it with the word '*terem*' was to venture into the realms of hyperbole. Kirsty was delighted.

'It could not be better,' she assured her husband. 'I shall not feel isolated, and shall be so much more free to wander round the house. Must I always have a servant with me?'

'Not so long as you remain on the demesne of the *dacha* itself. I would prefer you to take someone with you if you venture further afield.'

Kirsty assured him that she would, and continued her inspection of the *dacha*, her heart lighter than it had been for many weeks.

But gradually her cheerfulness receded. It was almost as though Sergei had found the pattern of their lives in those few weeks after the discovery of Pyotr's perfidy to be very much to his taste, for he made no attempt to bring their relationship any closer. True, he produced some pleasant surprises. The first had been his willingness to allow her two borzois to accompany them. On arrival at Zubstovoy, the dogs were handed over to a serf, and when Kirsty later went to see how they did, she realised why Sergei had considered them to be superfluous: his kennels already held fifteen couple, as well as the black-and-white bear-hounds from Karelia and the small fox-red ones from that same province that treed capercailzie better than any dog yet bred; then there were the wolf-grey dogs captured from the Swedish army at Narva—'The only good thing to come from that defeat,' the kennel-serf told her bitterly—and used for hunting elk. Kirsty could see much to admire in all these dogs, but confided to the head kennel-man that the elegant wolfhounds were her favourites.

'You show good taste, *barinya*,' he told her. 'These are truly Russian hounds. You must persuade Sergei Ivanovich to let you see them at work. They are aptly named borzois, for they are very fleet of foot. To watch them streak over the ground after a wolf is something worth seeing.'

The second surprise came after breakfast a few days after their arrival.

'I would like you to come down to the stables with me when you have finished,' Sergei said.

'Of course.' Kirsty was surprised: the stables were not considered part of a woman's domain.

She followed him down, and as soon as they entered the yard it was clear they had been expected, and that there was something out of the ordinary in this visit. At a nod from Sergei, a door was opened and a handsome bright bay horse was led out, bridled, and wearing the broad, flat, single-horned saddle that was customary for English ladies to use.

'This is Babak,' Sergei said. 'I recalled your father telling me in Archangel that you had been used to ride in England and that you missed the chance to do so in Russia. You have yourself mentioned the fact. It is not usual for Russian women to ride, of course, but Babak has been trained to this saddle.'

'He is superb!' Kirsty exclaimed. 'I fear I shall not do him justice, though; I have not ridden since I came to Russia, and he does not look like a slug!'

Sergei shuddered. 'You will find no slugs in my stables! I would advise you to ride only in an enclosed *manège* to start with. Volodya here taught me to ride, and there is no one better suited to bring you to a level where you can handle Babak confidently. You will find him comfortable, but treasure him: he is from Turkmenia, the kind of horse they call Akhal-Teke, and was obtained with difficulty. He is not the sort of mount one immediately thinks of as suitable for a lady, but I fancy you prefer something with spirit.'

'You know me better than I thought!' Kirsty exclaimed. 'Babak will be a challenge—and I do not often back down from a challenge.'

'So I have observed,' Sergei remarked drily.

So, under the careful supervision of the old groom, Kirsty refreshed her riding skills and learned to handle Babak. Sergei appeared to take no interest in her progress—he certainly expressed none—and she was consequently surprised one suppertime when he referred to it.

'Volodya says you are perfectly capable of handling Babak in the open country. Would you do me the honour of riding with me tomorrow? I shall have the opportunity of showing you more of the estate than you would otherwise see.'

'It will be a pleasure. Does Volodya really think I shall be all right?'

'He would hardly have recommended it otherwise. He will accompany us as he used to accompany me when I first rode abroad.'

After that first day, Kirsty rode out regularly, sometimes with Volodya, sometimes with Sergei, but never alone. This was not because her husband placed any restriction on the activity, but for the purely practical reason that she knew she was still very much a novice where Babak was concerned, and realised that it would be unwise to risk riding him unsupervised until she was a great deal more proficient.

She hoped these rides would bring about a greater familiarity between them, but they did not. Sergei was unfailingly pleasant and courteous, but she might as well have been a favoured guest. In some strange way, she felt they were further apart than they had been in the days when they seemed always to be in conflict. Insidiously, her spirits began to sink until she was asking herself once more whether this was really all life held for her.

And then they had a visitor.

Dressed for riding, Kirsty had been about to set off with Volodya when a servant came rushing out of the *dacha*.

'*Barinya, barinya!*' he gasped. 'There is someone to see you and Count Borodinov.

'But Count Borodinov is inspecting the mill and will not be back for some time,' Kirsty replied, and then, reluctantly, dismounted and passed the reins over to the groom. 'It looks as if I shall be unable to ride today. What a pity we had not already left! I suppose I must exert myself to be welcoming and polite, whoever it is.'

When Kirsty entered the drawing-room, she was extremely surprised, and by no means entirely delighted, to see before her the thin-lipped, calculating face of Alexander Danilovich Menshikov, Prince of Russia.

'Good gracious!' she exclaimed involuntarily. 'I mean, what a pleasant surprise, Prince! I did not realise we were expecting you.'

'Why should you? I gave no warning. I was, I must confess, sufficiently conceited to think that you would not be entirely averse to my making a brief visit, but if I have arrived at an inconvenient time . . .'

'No. No, not at all,' Kirsty assured him. 'I shall send someone to fetch Sergei Ivanovich; he will not otherwise be back for some time.'

'There is no need. I would not wish to interrupt his work.' Menshikov's smile stopped at his mouth, and she felt it advisable to move a few paces further away from him.

'You are very kind, but my husband would never forgive me if I did not advise him immediately of the arrival of so important a visitor.'

It took only a few minutes to send someone to the stables with a message that Count Borodinov was to be fetched, and very few more to light the flame under the samovar.

'You will take tea, Prince?' Kirsty asked.

There was a hint of self-deprecation in his voice. 'Do we not know each other well enough, Christina Alexandrovna, to cease using our respective titles? It puts a distance between us that I would wish to see reduced.'

Privately forming the opinion that she would rather see it increased, Kirsty had little choice but to incline her head graciously and accede to his wish.

'May I enquire what brings you to Zubstovoy, Alexander Danilovich?' she asked.

'Apart from my desire to renew my acquaintance with the beautiful English Countess, you mean? I am on my way to St Petersburg for the summer—at least, if Charles of Sweden holds back, it will be for the summer! It seemed churlish to pass so close and not to visit.'

'But you cannot, surely, be travelling alone? Yet I saw no servants, no baggage train,' Kirsty said.

'I have two body-servants with me, but the rest of my entourage has gone ahead. I felt I could hardly impose so many unexpected visitors upon you.'

'You are very considerate,' Kirsty said politely, though she suspected that consideration for the convenience of others was not normally at the forefront of the Prince's mind.

She sent for a servant to bring *pirozhki* and a plate of the ratafia biscuits she had succeeded in teaching her Russian cook how to make.

'I hope you will taste these,' she told her visitor. 'It has not been easy to teach the cook some English receipts, but her ratafias have been particularly successful.'

While the Prince politely sampled the small, crisp macaroons, Kirsty indicated to the maid that she was to remain in the room and dispense the tea, but when, this having been done, Prince Menshikov airily dismissed the girl as if he were in his own house, there was nothing Kirsty could do to prevent it without being obviously ill mannered. She was sure now that he had some ulterior motive in visiting Zubstovoy, and could only wonder how long it would be before it was revealed.

Kirsty asked after the Princess Menshikova and the Tsaritsa, and received the effusively unspecific answers that such questions normally elicit. Both were well, it seemed.

In her turn, she confessed to finding country life entirely agreeable and expressed regret that the summer could not last for ever.

Menshikov shook his head. 'That would be a great loss for those close to the Tsar,' he said.

Kirsty was puzzled. 'What do you mean? I do not quite follow you.'

'If summer were to last for ever so that you could remain in the country, the Court would be deprived of the pleasure of looking upon so beautiful a creature as the Countess Borodinova.'

Kirsty laughed a little self-consciously and sought to turn the subject. 'You are too kind, Prince.' She rose from her chair. 'Some more tea?'

Menshikov rose too, putting his glass down beside the samovar before relieving Kirsty of her own.

'Thank you, but I thirst for other refreshment,' he said, catching hold of her wrist and pulling her towards him.

'You forget yourself, Prince,' she said, trying to twist her arm from his hold.

'On the contrary, that is something I never do—and I thought we had agreed on the more familiar mode of address, Christina Alexandrovna.'

'I beg you, let go of me!' Kirsty pleaded. 'You much mistake matters if you think such advances are welcome.'

'Indeed? I seem to recall that the last time we met, we agreed that between us we would devise a way to wean your estimable husband away from his old-fashioned ideas.'

'Behaviour such as this is more likely to confirm him in them.' The voice from the door was cold, hard and menacing. Neither Kirsty nor the Prince had heard it open, and Kirsty, at least, was aghast to see her husband standing there. The Prince seemed unconcerned, but he let go of her wrist and bowed to Sergei.

'How very like you, Sergei Ivanovich, to return at precisely the wrong moment,' he remarked.

'Yes, I suppose you would regard it in that light. You will not be surprised that I do not, however.'

Menshikov bowed, managing to inject a degree of insolence into the action that rendered it offensive, and Kirsty saw her husband stiffen.

When he spoke, it was obvious that Sergei was restraining his fury with difficulty. 'You may seek to conspire with my wife to wean me from my old-fashioned ideas. You will not, however, seek to wean her from me: a much more probable explanation of the behaviour I have just witnessed.'

'You mistake,' Menshikov said, still smiling. 'I do not seek your wife's affections. Merely a little dalliance to pass the tedious summer months.'

The Prince had barely finished speaking before he was sprawled on the floor, one had tenderly cupping his jaw, while the tall figure of his reluctant host stood over him.

'Get up!' Sergei commanded. 'Get up and get out! Or must I kick you to your feet like the serf you once were?'

Menshikov struggled to his feet, no longer able to sustain the patronising dignity that was such a characteristic of his general mien.

'This is a matter you will have cause to regret,' he hissed. 'No one treats a Prince of Russia in such a way. I shall bide my time, but of one thing you may be sure: when opportunity occurs—as occur it will—I shall take advantage of it.'

He flung out of the room, closely followed by Sergei, determined both to see him on his way and to give the departure at least the outward appearance of normality.

Kirsty sank into a chair, trembling. She looked up apprehensively when her husband re-entered the room.

'I am so sorry,' she whispered.

'For what?' he answered, surprised. 'I was standing in the doorway long enough to see that his attentions were hardly being encouraged. The man is a peasant.'

'A very dangerous peasant.'

'As you say. It is, however, too late to alter anything. Come, have some cognac.'

He had already poured her a small measure and offered it to her, smiling. Kirsty was surprised to observe that there was no hint of reproof in his tone. 'I know you do not much care for it, but it will calm you. Come, to please me, just this small measure.'

Kirsty did as he bade her and felt the liquid warmth filter through her veins until the trembling stopped.

'Sergei,' she said at last. 'I did try to keep a servant in the room, but he dismissed her. What could I do? I swear I did not seek to be alone with him.'

'I believe you: Menshikov's propensities are well known. At least you now have a good reason, should a similar situation seem likely to arise, to insist on the presence of a third person.'

Kirsty shuddered. 'I cannot bear the thought of a repetition of this day.'

'Then do not think of it. It is unlikely in the extreme that he will again overstep the bounds of propriety where you are concerned.'

'But I do not think he will let the matter drop.'

'On that you may depend. He is a vindictive man and he has been humiliated. He will seek vengeance. But that is my problem: you need not concern yourself with it.'

Kirsty put a hand on his arm and looked up at him, anxiety in her eyes. 'What can he do, Sergei?'

'My estates could be confiscated and we could be banished to Siberia,' he told her lightly. 'I rather fancy that is unlikely, however, for he could not persuade the Tsar to such a drastic step without the events of this morning becoming general knowledge, and I imagine our Prince will wish to avoid becoming the laughing-stock that such a revelation would create. No, his revenge, when he exacts it, will be both subtle and devious.'

Kirsty found little comfort in this undoubtedly accurate forecast, but she sought refuge in the consolation that at least Sergei did not seem to hold her in any way responsible for the Prince's behaviour.

Any hope she might have had, that the barrier of politeness between them could be lowered by Sergei's acceptance of her having in no way invited Menshikov's advances, was soon squashed.

Life at Zubstovoy was easy and pleasant, but more than ever Kirsty sensed there was something missing. It was true she was glad to be free of the confrontations that had characterised their life in Moscow, yet she had felt that perhaps—just perhaps—they had betokened some deeper feeling that knew no other way of manifesting itself. Now that was gone, and she sometimes felt she was no more than a guest. Admittedly, a guest who managed the household, but a guest for all that. There was not even any sense of partnership, of coping with the estate's minor crises or making decisions together. She did not feel Sergei was interested in how she dealt with household matters and was sure he would resent her expressing any opinions as to the management of the land.

Sergei watched her ride out one day in the company of Volodya. It seemed she preferred the company of the old groom to his own, and he was loath to press his presence where it was not sought. He did not regret buying Babak: Kirsty was turning into a first-rate horsewoman and had enormous pleasure from her daily rides. Life in the country suited her.

Not for the first time, Sergei wondered why she had married him. When Alexander Benmore had brought her answer, he had assumed that she had remembered him from the Archangel contretemps with feelings similar to his own. She had made it clear that she had had no idea he was the same man. Her motives could therefore only have been practical: status, wealth, and the degree of security such an alliance would afford a foreign resident.

She ran his household to perfection, but exhibited no interest in his affairs or in the running of the estate generally. There had been occasions—few enough, to be sure, but some—when he had sensed a passion, a sensuality, that it must surely be possible to arouse. Yet such hints as he had detected had vanished completely after the discovery of Menshikov's spy. He had hoped that, in the more relaxed air of Zubstovoy, they might somehow succeed in drawing closer, but that had not happened: Kirsty seemed entirely content in this superficial existence that their marriage had become.

His greatest fear was that, sooner or later, some man would inevitably succeed in gaining Kirsty's love. He had hoped, by bringing her to Zubstovoy, that it might be he, but they were further apart than ever. He knew that the polite, courteous life they currently led distanced them far more than raging fury could. He had no fear that Menshikov was the man to dread: he had seen how Kirsty shrank from his touch. He feared the arrival of some other—perhaps as yet unknown, perhaps not —and dreaded the time when custom and impending winter should determine their return to the social life of Moscow and the inevitable renewal of acquaintance with the Harrow family.

CHAPTER
NINE

SERGEI WAS less than pleased when John Harrow arrived with a small baggage train and an official escort. It seemed that the acquaintance was to be renewed earlier than he had expected.

John dismounted and took papers from the satchel at his side. 'Count Borodinov? We have met—at the Tsar's ball in Moscow.'

Sergei inclined his head. It was not a gesture which indicated any pleasure in the recollection.

John bowed and handed him the papers. 'I am John Harrow, sir: I do not know if you remember me. I have been ordered to St Petersburg, as my papers show, to survey and oversee the paving of the streets. It is a considerable challenge, since the city is being built on a marsh and I gather difficulties are being encountered. As you will see, I am advised to break my journey here.'

Sergei glanced through the documents in deepening dismay. He did not doubt that they said exactly what young Harrow claimed, but he could think of no visitor whom he wished less to accommodate. His interest in the papers lay in the signature of whoever had decided to send the Englishman here. As he expected: Menshikov. He handed the documents back.

'Forgive me if I speak bluntly. This is not the most convenient time to accommodate visitors, but the Prince's wishes naturally have precedence. We shall endeavour to make your stay—which I imagine will be brief—as comfortable as we can. I believe you are well acquainted with my wife?'

'Indeed I am,' John replied with unnecessary warmth.

'I have letters for her from my mother and sisters, which I hope I may be able to present.'

'I am sure the Countess will take pleasure in receiving them,' Sergei said stiffly, and stood aside for their visitor to enter.

Kirsty's pleasure in seeing this reminder of happier days was unmistakeable, and Sergei felt a tightening of his heart that she was so unreserved in her welcome.

'John Harrow! I cannot believe it! Is it truly you?' She rushed to him, hands outstretched, in a way she had never greeted her husband, and John, in return, kissed her hands with a warmth that surely was more than that condoned by long acquaintance.

'I could not believe my good fortune when my orders included an instruction to stop here briefly. I have letters from Mama and the girls. I hope my arrival is not too inconveniently timed?' he added.

'Not at all. How can the arrival of old friends be thought inconvenient?' she said, unaware of her husband's earlier remark. She tucked her hand in his arm and led him to sit down. In the pleasure of seeing someone from the days when she still led an English life, she forgot that so friendly a gesture, which would occasion little comment in an English household, would be open to misinterpretation in a Russian one. 'What genius thought to have you break your journey here?' she went on.

'It was Prince Menshikov's suggestion,' John told her. 'It seems he recalled that our families had been close in Archangel, and thought we might both enjoy a short reunion.'

'Yes, indeed,' Kirsty assured him warmly. 'I must say that I do not like the Prince, but he earns my gratitude on this occasion. I had not credited him with such thoughtfulness.' So delighted was she that she did not even notice the glowering expression on her husband's face.

John saw it, though. He recalled his parents' misgivings about Kirsty's marriage. Count Borodinov's welcome had been grudging in the extreme, and now he seemed positively angry, though there was nothing in his voice to indicate anything other than politeness. If the marriage was unhappy, as he and his parents suspected, it was no wonder Kirsty was so pleased to see him. Besides, had he not indicated in the past his willingness to help her? What clearer indication could she give him, in the presence of her husband, at least, that she needed his help than to welcome him thus warmly?

Sergei observed the interchange between them with increasing despair. The warmth and very obvious pleasure Kirsty showed at John's arrival seemed to confirm his worst fears. This must surely constitute a warmer welcome than would normally be accorded to one who stood in place of a brother?

He had feared that sooner or later a man other than he would reach Kirsty's heart, and he had already suspected that John Harrow might be he. Now it looked as if he might be right. It did surprise him that Kirsty should be so lacking in circumspection in her welcome, but probably that could only be an indication of the depth of her feelings.

Sergei cursed Prince Menshikov. He suffered from none of Kirsty's illusions that the Tsar's dear friend had acted from motives of pure thoughtfulness. There was one way in which he could thwart the Prince's interference, and on that he was determined: John Harrow would have little opportunity to pursue his interest while he stayed at Zubstovoy.

How John was to be able to render to Kirsty the help he was sure she was seeking, he could not immediately perceive, for it soon became clear that the Count had no intention of leaving them alone, even in the company of servants whose presence would surely have been enough to ensure propriety. John had established very early in his visit that the Count spoke no English, but since one could hardly conduct a conversation with one's host's wife in the presence of one's host, in a language he could not understand, this was not something he could turn to much advantage. Nor was it a visit that could be extended indefinitely, since, quite apart from any other considerations, he must get to St Petersburg. He was full of an excitement about the new city that Kirsty would have found infectious were it not for her memories of the mud and confusion of her brief visit last autumn.

'It was chaos,' she insisted. 'I cannot see that anything habitable can be built there in the foreseeable future.'

'I understand that it progresses very fast—that is why the paving of the streets has already begun,' John told her. 'The Tsar throws in thousands of serfs to do the work and when they die, he sends in more.'

Sergei concurred with John. 'You would not recognise the place, my dear, even after so short a time. The city is to be built regardless of expense in terms of both money and lives: neither is begrudged.'

Kirsty grimaced. 'I imagine the serfs concerned might begrudge their lives in such a cause.'

Sergei looked surprised. 'Why should they? Their lives are their masters', after all.'

'Will there be a Borodinov Palace there, Count?' John asked.

'Oh, yes,' Kirsty broke in. 'That is, if they get any higher than the foundations.'

'I told you you would not recognise the place,' Sergei reminded her. 'Your assumptions are behind the times. The exterior is finished. Only the interior ornamentation and the furnishing have yet to be finished. Like my Tsar, I begrudge neither money nor lives,' he added provocatively, but Kirsty refused to be drawn.

'I hope I may have the opportunity of choosing some,

at least, of the furnishings,' she said.

'Of course, if you wish. Most women, however, would be happy to find it all completed before they saw it.'

'I am not "most women",' she retorted.

Sergei bowed. 'How very true, my dear.'

John looked from one to the other, puzzled. Although the exchanges between husband and wife seemed civilised enough, there were undercurrents here that he did not comprehend though he sensed that they ran deep. He was sure Kirsty was unhappy, yet she seemed unperturbed; the Count smiled urbanely but without humour, and the topic was changed.

On the second, and final, morning of John Harrow's visit, the Count's plans never to leave his wife alone with their guest went awry with an urgent request from his bailiff for an interview. Sergei was tempted to tell the man to wait until the morrow, but since the bailiff felt it was urgent and was not a man given to exaggeration, he agreed to see him.

'I regret that I must leave you,' he told his guest. 'I hope you will be able to occupy yourself. I fear I shall be an hour or two with Grigor Pavlovich.'

'We can hardly leave Master Harrow to his own devices!' Kirsty exclaimed.

Sergei frowned. 'It grieves me to do so: one does not wish to be considered inhospitable, but the circumstances make it necessary. I am sure our visitor appreciates the situation and will forgive me the discourtesy, just as I am sure he would welcome some time to write to his family. I have a courier returning to Moscow in a few days who will be happy to convey letters to the German Suburb.'

John was about to express his willingness to amuse himself, thinking that here, at last, might be the opportunity for which he had been searching, when Kirsty butted in.

'Nonsense, Sergei. We cannot be so rude. Why do I not take Master Harrow round the estate? He has seen little enough of it so far.'

Sergei bridled. 'Certainly not. It would be most unseemly. I am sure Master Harrow fully appreciates the impropriety of wandering about the countryside accompanied only by another man's wife.'

Regretfully, Master Harrow did, but before he could say so, Kirsty again took up the cudgels.

'Oh, Sergei, such a fuss about nothing! I sometimes think you seek wilfully to misunderstand me! I had no intention that I should be his only companion: naturally, I intended that Volodya should accompany us. You can have no possible objection to that!'

The irony was, Sergei thought, that had his visitor been anyone else, he would have been entirely satisfied with that arrangement. Indeed, it was most probable that, had their visitor been anyone else, he would have suggested the expedition himself. Then it occurred to him that a ride securely chaperoned by Volodya might be far safer than leaving his wife and her childhood friend with time on their hands. So, reluctantly, he agreed.

Volodya kept very close to his mistress, but saw nothing untoward in the two foreigners speaking to each other in their own tongue, especially since it was frequently apparent from their gestures that they were discussing what they saw around them.

John was only marginally interested in Zubstovoy. This was the first chance he had had to have anything approaching a private interview with Kirsty, and since it was likely to be the last, he was certainly not going to waste the opportunity. After complimenting her on Babak, he broached the more important matter.

'Are you really happy, Kirsty? My mother, I think, doubts it.'

'Of course I am,' Kirsty said, rather too brightly. 'Why should I not be? I have everything I want.'

'Including a jealous husband.'

'Jealous? What do you mean, John?'

'I fancy Count Borodinov does not like my presence here.'

'I do not think that has anything to do with jealousy,' Kirsty said a trifle wistfully. 'Your orders to visit were from Menshikov, and there is no love lost between those two.'

'Perhaps. But, Kirsty, can you truthfully say that the life Count Borodinov offers you is the one you want?'

Kirsty's silence gave him the answer he hoped to hear.

'Your position is not irretrievable, you know,' he went on. 'It is possible to escape from it.'

'To be sure, I have two choices, do I not?' Kirsty's voice was heavy with mingled sarcasm and despair. 'I can, like the Tsaritsa Eudoxia, enter a nunnery—or I can kill myself. Neither seems preferable to my present life.'

'You mistake, Kirsty. It need not come to either. If you can but return to England, the matter is solved.'

Kirsty stared at him. 'Have you turned simple-minded, John Harrow?' she demanded. 'How on earth could such a thing be achieved? I could not even get out of Russia! And your family and my father would certainly be penalised.'

'It could be arranged,' John said, his voice hinting at mystery.

'Indeed? And what happens when I get to England, without money, family or protection? Do not take me for a stupid woman, John. It is true that my marriage is not what I had hoped for, but I assure you, it is infinitely preferable to any option you have so far suggested.'

'You speak as if I were an impulsive schoolboy,' John protested. 'I am not. I have thought about this most thoroughly. In the first place, if you could only persuade the Count to take you to St Petersburg, it would be relatively simple to find a boat going to England, Holland or Sweden. The new city is, after all, on the coast. As for your being without protection . . . I would be there too.'

Kirsty looked at him, her face expressionless. 'How so?' she asked.

John cast a warning glance at Volodya. 'I wish we were alone: I could then express the depth of my feelings for you.'

Kirsty coloured. 'I was not aware your feelings for me were of any depth greater than those of brother for sister. You certainly gave no indication of them when we were in Archangel.'

'A matter I have long since regretted,' he told her. 'In Archangel I thought as a boy. It took the move to Moscow to make me a man, and by that time you were married.'

'You should not allow yourself deep feelings for a married woman,' Kirsty protested.

'Do you think I am not aware of that? Since our first meeting after your marriage, the knowledge of how I should behave has been in constant conflict with the way in which I wish to behave, but most important of all is my desire to see you happy—which you patently are not.'

Kirsty looked at him. 'Do you think I should be happy as a fugitive from Russia, living under your protection?'

'It would be a temporary measure only,' he assured her.

'How so? I should be even less happy were you then to abandon me.'

If John noticed the astringency in her tone, he chose to disregard it. 'Foolish Kirsty,' he said fondly. 'As if that was what I meant! If you flee Russia as I suggest, can you doubt but that Count Borodinov would obtain an annulment of your marriage? You would then be free to marry me.'

Kirsty made no answer. She did not doubt that he meant every word and the scheme sounded perfectly feasible, although fraught with danger. She realised, too, that to flee with a man and live under his protection it was first necessary to love him, and no sooner had that realisation struck her than it was followed by another: had Sergei—the tender, gentle Sergei that she had almost forgotten—made a similar suggestion, she would have counted the world well lost. The truth was that she did not love John Harrow, and at the thought of an annulment of her marriage, her heart grew chill and her mind withdrew. This was not what she wanted.

'I think we have gone far enough—both on our ride and in our converse,' she said at last, turning Babak. 'I will show you the new mill on the way back.'

Kirsty might have curtailed their conversation, but her thoughts were not so easily cut short. She did not know to what extent John Harrow really loved her, or whether, as she more than half suspected, his love, though sincere enough, sprang largely from her unattainability. If that were the case, it would die soon after she had proved attainable. At the same time she did know that, no matter how flattering his attention or how comforting his concern, she did not love him.. She would have to be desperate indeed to flee with him.

They were in sight of the house before John referred again to their discussion. 'I shall be in St Petersburg, Kirsty. If you need me, you have only to get word to me.'

'Thank you. I shall not forget.'

Sergei, his business with his bailiff completed, saw them return. Something in Kirsty's expression made him wonder what had transpired. He could hear old Volodya grumbling under his breath as he led the horses away, and laid a hand on his arm.

'What has upset you now, old man?' Sergei asked.

'Foreigners!' Volodya said, and spat. 'Begging your pardon, Sergei Ivanovich, seeing as how the Countess is one, not that you'd notice . . . most of the time. But foreign they talked, the whole of the ride. I know well enough that what's said is none of my business but I tell you this, Sergei Ivanovich, a long ride is a deal less tedious if there's talk to listen to—talk a man can understand, that is. Not that I'd ever pass on what I'd heard,' he added hastily.

Sergei laughed grimly. 'I trust you, Volodya,' he said. 'But it is natural for the Countess to want to use her native tongue sometimes.'

'To be sure,' the groom agreed. 'I don't know as how she was all that happy with whatever they were saying, though. Not to go by her face, that is.'

Since that confirmed his own impression, Sergei said no more and hoped that nothing would occur to delay his guest's departure. It gave him considerable satisfaction to provide young Master Harrow's small entourage with an escort that stayed with them until he reached the northern limits of Zubstovoy land.

As Sergei turned from saying farewell to his unwelcome guest, he caught sight of Kirsty's face as she stood close behind him, and was shocked and more than a little hurt by the wistful expression he saw there as she watched John Harrow ride off.

She had assured him once that there had been nothing between them, and he had believed her. Had this visit changed that? He did not think John Harrow was entirely indifferent to Kirsty, and had not thought so since seeing them at that ball. Could it be that this visit had resulted in a change in Kirsty's feelings? He put a guiding hand under her elbow as they went indoors, a gesture of intimacy that surprised her by its unexpectedness.

'You are sorry to see our visitor go?' he asked, his voice expressionless.

'In some ways, of course,' Kirsty said. 'He is a link with my childhood and it meant I had the opportunity to converse once more in my own tongue. A small thing, perhaps, but it suddenly seemed important. You, I think, were less than happy that he should be here.'

'I hope I treated him with every courtesy.' Sergei's voice was stiff, as if he had inferred some criticism.

'You were politeness itself: Master Harrow can have no cause to complain of his reception. Let us just say that your courtesy lacked the warmth that would have been evident had he been really welcome.'

'I am sure that any warmth lacking in my welcome was more than compensated for in yours.' There was a bitterness in his voice that made Kirsty glance quickly at his face, but it told her nothing.

'I hope you do not wish to suggest that I betrayed a degree of warmth that passed the bounds of propriety,' she said.

'Not at all. Merely that he cannot have doubted your pleasure in seeing him.'

Kirsty looked at him doubtfully. She knew that she had behaved precisely as any hostess—any English hostess, that is—would have behaved; only the conversation during her ride on that last day had been improper. She should not have allowed herself to be drawn into a discussion of either her husband or her marriage; to do so had been reprehensible, and had it not been for her constant, nagging unhappiness, she would have stifled the topic at birth. Could Sergei be referring to this, perhaps? She turned the possibility over in her mind and rejected it: he probably knew they had talked entirely in English, but he could not be aware of its content since Volodya, she knew, had no knowledge of any language other than his own.

John had described Sergei as a jealous husband, and that was a thought that was by no means unpleasant, since jealousy implied that there must first be love. Sometimes it had almost seemed as if love might be there, but always subsequent events had disproved it. No, for whatever reason Sergei had married her, it was not for love.

Over the following days, Sergei watched his wife with some unease. There was an abstraction, a withdrawn quality, about her which disturbed him. He could not doubt that she was unhappy, and, since it followed so soon upon John Harrow's visit, he could only conclude that that was the cause.

He had thought that, before John's recent visit, they had established a pattern for living which was acceptable to them both, though it lacked the ingredient he had sought. Even Menshikov's visit had not suceeded in upsetting it. Now it seemed that the Englishman had somehow managed to throw it out of kilter.

Sergei had expected things to return to at least such normality as had existed before John's arrival, but as the days went by and Kirsty continued withdrawn and melancholic, the bitterness increased until the concern at her unhappiness which he had originally felt gradually changed into an anger against the man who had initiated the change in his wife. Since he had no way of venting the anger he felt in the direction of its true cause, it was not long before he found himself blaming Kirsty.

Kirsty watched her husband with increasing despair. John had indicated that there was an escape from her predicament and for that she was grateful. None the less, she wished he had never come.

Sergei had been displeased to see him, and his departure had by no means eased that displeasure. Their easy, if not entirely satisfying, relationship had been destroyed in two short days. It had not been the relationship she longed for, but it had been infinitely preferable to the strained atmosphere that now lay between them. If only there were some way of reaching out to him, some way of saying: 'We have managed things awry; can we not start again?' but she dreaded the cold, impassive expression that would enter his eyes; the harsh, unfeeling voice with which he would indicate his failure to admit a fault.

So she said nothing, and was surprised when Sergei himself referred to the matter at breakfast one morning, after he had dismissed the servants.

'You are unhappy, Kirsty.' It was a statement, not a question.

'I have nothing to be unhappy about,' she said cautiously, fearing to say anything that might provoke either his anger or his cold, biting sarcasm. Had there been warmth in his eyes or in his voice, she might have tendered a less equivocal answer.

'Nevertheless, you are so.'

Kirsty returned no answer. If she agreed with him, how could she explain why she should be so? She hardly knew herself. She was sure only that Sergei would be unable to accept any explanation that implied a criticism of himself. His next words seemed to reinforce that opinion.

'I have observed it, and it concerns me that it should be so. It is a matter to which I have given much thought. I fancy you do not have enough occupation to fill your time. You are not by nature indolent, and even with Babak to exercise, time must hang heavy on your hands. You need occupation.'

Kirsty stared at him, torn between curiosity as to his solution and amazement that he so little understood her.

'I presume you have thought of just what I need to keep me occupied,' she said, unable to keep all hint of irony out of her voice.

'I think I have,' he replied, and Kirsty wondered if it was her imagination that there was a touch of savagery in his voice. There was certainly no warmth, and as his cold voice continued, Kirsty felt its chill grip on her heart tighten. 'I have been too indulgent a husband,' he went on. 'The time has come to remind you of your responsibilities. I have hardly made excessive demands upon you, my dear, but I do feel the time has come to consider supplying the House of Borodinov with an heir. You have had time in plenty to accustom yourself to the management of a Russian household, and I have not begrudged that time. I need an heir—and a child will most assuredly give you occupation.'

Miserably, Kirsty could only agree. She had wondered that, after those two disastrous nights, he should have made no more demands upon her in all these months, and she knew it was her duty to provide him with an heir. There were no arguments to offer against his case. She nodded.

'Very well. I shall visit you tonight.'

Any pleasure Kirsty might have had from the day was destroyed in apprehension of the night to come. There were circumstances in which to give Sergei the heir he needed would have been the pinacle of her desire, the visible evidence of her love. But this cold acceptance of a duty to be performed was the negation of love.

Any faint hope Kirsty might have had that he would come to her that night in a mood of courtship was destroyed when she retired. Anna had been notified of Count Borodinov's intent to visit his wife, and had duly made the appropriate preparations. Kirsty was bathed and sprinkled with perfumed oils; barley- and flax-seeds, symbols of fertility, were strewn by the bed, and when Kirsty reached for the chemise that she customarily wore in bed, Anna removed it from her, shaking her head.

'Not tonight, *barinya*. It would not be fitting.'

She had no choice, therefore, but to allow the girl to assist her into bed and cover her naked body with its sweet-smelling sheets before she tiptoed out.

She must have advised her master that all was ready, for he came shortly after her departure. He tapped on the door, but awaited no answer before he came in and stood before her.

'I trust the Countess Borodinova is ready.' His harsh voice struck a blow at her heart. She nodded and turned her head as he removed his *kaftan*. With one swift movement he stripped back the bed covers and stood staring down at the unconsciously sensuous curves of her slight body. It was a night warm with the heat of summer, yet Kirsty shivered at this cold inspection. If this was what he wanted, thus be it.

Sergei felt his heart beating. This woman he had chosen was so beautiful that it was hard to believe. If only she could bring herself to respond! Once, no twice, he had thought she might and had been proved wrong. He longed to stroke, to caress, to see whether she might not still be brought to joyous acceptance, but there was no sign in the fragile, trembling body of any such willingness. He remembered her screams on her wedding night and the moans that followed. He knew well how a woman could scream with delight and moan with pleasure, and thus enhance his own pleasure. But Kirsty's cries had been cries of pain, discomfort and terror that it would never end, and he would never forget those silent tears trickling down her cheeks.

No, he would not again try to arouse her desire. He would do what he had come to do and then go. Could he but ensure an heir, he would bind her to him through the child. The child would make them one.

He threw himself down beside her and briefly, tentatively, caressed her breast. He felt her tremble, but could not delude himself it was with pleasure. He turned her face so that it looked at his own and was startled at the blank expression he saw there. Did she hate him so much that she must wipe all trace of feeling from her face? Could she not at least make some pretence of welcoming him? Sergei pushed to the back of his mind the thought that pretended pleasure was only a more subtle form of rejection, and it never occurred to him at all that the manner of his arranging this visit was scarcely likely to encourage Kirsty's willing participation. He saw only the blank expression and the unresisting body. Hurt and angry, the impulse he felt when he saw her lying there, the impulse to kiss and caress, to coax and excite, was expunged.

'I will give you a son this night,' he said savagely, 'if I must take you until cock-crow.'

'It is your right,' Kirsty murmured, and Sergei felt a sudden surge of anger. Could she not see that it was not his rights that he wanted?

Kirsty offered neither resistance nor response. He had required her to do her duty, and she had obeyed. That her husband had achieved no satisfaction from this enforced union she neither knew nor cared, and when, his anger finally appeased, he looked again at her unresponsive face, he knew that whatever action had been needed to bring her closer, it had not been this. In his heart of hearts he suddenly knew that any child conceived in this manner, while it might bind his wife to him, would never make them one.

Sergei took his *kaftan*, and pausing only to draw the bedclothes over his wife's still trembling body, left the room. Not until she heard the door close behind him did

Kirsty's tears begin to flow. Only she knew how much of that night was spent in weeping.

Only he knew how much of that night was spent in impotent anger at his own ineptitude.

CHAPTER
TEN

SERGEI HAD begun to regret his arbitrary action almost as soon as he realised that all his wife was prepared to offer was mute obedience. He pursued it from a mixture of pique and pride, a mixture which made it difficult for him to acknowledge that he would have done better to let matters be. It was also a mixture which led him, when he encountered his wife next day, to treat her with a politeness so distant and so icy as to render any communication between them difficult and anything beyond the briefest of basic civilities, impossible.

Determined not to let him see how deeply hurt she was by his ruthless assumption of his dues, Kirsty responded in kind.

The breach was complete.

Sergei immersed himself in the management of his estates; Kirsty sought the companionship of Babak and her hounds. She rode with only Volodya in attendance, and the only people with whom she conversed at any time were the servants.

It was not very long before she knew beyond doubt that the purpose of Sergei's visit to her room had failed. She did not know whether to be glad or sorry. She did not want a child conceived thus, in antipathy, yet she could not overlook the possibility that, once she had given Sergei his heir, he might look on her with approval, if nothing more. Now she faced the dilemma of whether she would tell him: he would find out soon enough, in any case, but Kirsty knew she should let him know as soon as she was herself certain.

Several times she steeled herself to broach the subject, but did not. She made excuses as to why she had held her tongue: the time was inauspicious; it would be better to wait until the harvest was in. The truth was that she dreaded a repetition of that last night, and if she told Sergei that no heir was to be expected, would it not be tantamount to an invitation to him to visit her again?

So she said nothing, and, as the weeks passed, did not know how to interpret Sergei's own silence on the subject. It seemed to Kirsty that, since he must realise by now that she was not with child, he had lost such interest as he had ever had. His cold indifference, his total lack of interest in her, could only mean that he was planning to put her away. Annulment was possible, of course, but it was more likely she would be required to retire to a nunnery, as had the Tsaritsa Eudoxia. The marriage would be deemed to be over and Sergei would be free to marry some plump, be-rouged Russian girl who would be perfectly content with the life he had to offer.

It would be preferable by far to return to England. John Harrow had intimated how it could be done. Once there, she would be an outcast, of course, but surely that would be easier to live with than was her present existence? However, John Harrow's plan could not be executed unless she could first reach St Petersburg, and that could not be done without Sergei's co-operation.

When little beyond 'good morning' has passed between a husband and wife for several weeks, it is not an easy matter for one of them to suggest, quite suddenly, that they might remove several hundred miles at short notice. Kirsty turned over in her mind several schemes by which she hoped to start a conversation out of which a reference to St Petersburg might arise with seeming naturalness. She rejected them all. She could imagine all too clearly the look of icy surprise that would for an unguarded moment flash across Sergei's face before his habitual inscrutability re-asserted itself once more. Besides, he would be suspicious of an indirect approach, and was extremely unlikely to be deceived by it. She must raise the subject without preamble—and with no more delay.

Breakfast was nearly over the next day before she had nerved herself to speak.

'Sergei Ivanovich,' she began hesitantly, and took some comfort in the fact that, while he looked surprised at what was obviously the beginning of something more than a polite enquiry about the fields, he did not seem to be instantly on his guard. Encouraged, she continued. 'You said that our house in St Petersburg was nearly finished. If you do not mind, I should like to visit it before the summer is over. I should like to see the progress that has been made and perhaps make suggestions as to its furnishing.'

'There is no need to put yourself to the trouble,' Sergei replied. 'The house is virtually finished, and I have already made arrangements for the internal ornamentation and furnishing: it is in the western style.'

Slightly daunted, Kirsty nevertheless pressed on. 'It sounds quite habitable, which is most encouraging! I own I did not precisely enjoy living in a log cabin, even for only a few days. Perhaps we might leave fairly soon?'

She realised that the mask of polite inscrutability had descended once more. 'I prefer you should not see it until next year. We shall visit St Petersburg then.'

'A whole year!' Kirsty exclaimed. 'Oh, Sergei, do not say so! *Please* may we go this summer?'

'I am touched by this sudden interest in the place,' Sergei said sardonically. 'Nevertheless, you will wait till next year. I would present you with a *fait accompli*.'

Kirsty sprang up from the table, knocking her seat over as she did so and throwing her crumpled napkin down on the polished surface. 'You treat me as if I were but five years old and stupid!' she exclaimed. 'Should I then have pestered you remorselessly about the house? Is that what you wanted?'

'Not at all. I have been happy to have it left to me. I am merely at a loss to understand this sudden desire to visit what is, after all, still an unsalubrious swamp. It crosses my mind that it may not be entirely unconnected with the residence there of your English friend from the German suburb.'

'John Harrow?'

'The same.'

'That is ridiculous!' Kirsty retorted, but her voice sounded unconvincing even to herself, so, rather than pursue an argument which she could not win, she stormed out of the room and up to her chamber where she obtained very little relief to her feelings by hurling a Bohemian crystal scent-bottle across the room.

She sent a servant to order Babak to be saddled and pulled her habit out of its coffer, cursing, not for the first time, the green dimness which the tree outside cast across an otherwise pleasant room.

Kirsty was no sooner thrown up into the saddle than she put Babak into a sudden plunging canter before Volodya had even had time to gather up the reins of his own mount. The stable-lads fell back before her, startled: never had they seen the Countess leave the stable yard at anything faster than a walk. By the time Volodya was mounted and out of the yard, she was so far ahead, pushing Babak at a flat gallop, that he knew his sturdier horse could not hope to catch up until the Countess drew rein to let Babak breathe. Nevertheless, it would not do to lose sight of her, and he rode as hard as he reasonably could with that end in mind.

Babak was dark with sweat and flecked with foam before Kirsty drew rein and eased his pace. She knew she had pushed him far too hard and that she had no real justification for doing so; her only excuse was that it had in some small degree served to relieve her feelings, and that was not an excuse any horsemaster would consider justified. Now she must ease him down gradually, lest he take chill. She had given no thought at all to the possibility that someone might have followed her and so was genuinely surprised when Volodya drew alongside, his own horse hard-pressed but less distressed than Babak.

The groom wasted no time on courtesies. 'Whatever has come over you, *barinya*?' he demanded. 'Have you no thought for your horse? Do you want to kill him? If so, it would be kinder to use a musket—or slit his throat. What are you doing, for the love of God?'

The criticism was justified, Kirsty knew. Nor could she deny that such a disrespectful address from a serf to his mistress was also justified in the circumstances. But she would not admit it. She stiffened. 'You will not speak to me in that manner, Vladimir Stefanovich, and I should not have to remind you that I am not answerable to you.'

'Oh, it's "Vladimir Stefanovich", is it?' Volodya did not seem in the least discomposed by the unwonted formality of her address. 'Very well, *barinya*: as you say, you are not answerable to me, but we are both answerable to Sergei Ivanovich. I hope you have some good reason for half-killing one of the best horses in the stable, because you will need one when he finds out, and *I* certainly have no explanation.'

Kirsty flushed. The old groom had analysed the situation to perfection. There was contrition in her voice when she spoke.

'It was unpardonable, Volodya. I know that and I am truly sorry. Does Count Borodinov have to know?' she added wistfully.

'If Babak drops dead, he can hardly fail to. After all, he is bound to ask why, don't you think?'

'Then we must see to it that Babak does not!'

Volodya looked the horse over with the eye of experience. 'Then we must hope he can take a further hour's riding—he'll need at least that if he is not to take a chill. Your temper, *barinya*, will just have to accommodate an hour's steady walking.'

Kirsty said nothing but shot him a quick glance: the old groom was no fool, it seemed.

By the time Volodya considered Babak might be safely returned to his stable to be thoroughly rubbed down, Kirsty's temper was well in hand, or so she thought. Certainly she was able to ignore the speculatively curious looks of the stable-lads who saw her come in. She noticed that Sergei's own horse was not in his stall. Was the man never at home? she thought irritably, not pausing to consider that he had as little incentive to be at home as she, and considerably less need.

Back in her room, she exchanged her habit for the comfort of a *sarafan*. The maid had opened one window, but it was a hot day and the room seemed stuffy. Kirsty went over to the other one, intending to open that as well. Some air at least must filter through the tree outside. The catch was rusted: clearly this window had not been opened for some time, and when she finally succeeded in releasing it, the casement moved only a couple of inches before its path was blocked by a huge, gnarled branch.

The thin thread that held Kirsty's temper in check snapped. This really was the last straw! She had tolerated having her room made permanently gloomier than it need be by this ugly and unproductive old apple tree and now it even prevented her letting in such breeze as there might be. Well, there were many things she could do nothing about—going to St Petersburg, for example —but this was one she could remedy. She went downstairs and out into the garden.

It took her a little while to find Dmitri, the gardener,

who was tending his own tobacco-patch. Had Kirsty been less cross, she would have found his expression, when he heard what she wanted, ludicrous. As it was, it simply aggravated her already impatient mood.

'Cut down the old apple tree, *barinya*? But it can't be done!' he protested.

'Nonsense,' Kirsty said bracingly. 'All it needs is a saw and an axe, and I know you have both. Get one of the woodsmen to help you if necessary. I want it down before dusk.'

'It isn't as simple as that: we'd have to take the branches off first, or we can't control where it falls.'

'Then do so. The sooner you start, the sooner you finish.'

'But, *barinya*, it is nearly time to eat!'

'Then eat—but do not expect to spend the afternoon asleep. Today you will ignore the customary afternoon doze and work until the task is completed. Do you understand?'

'I understand well enough, *barinya*.' Dmitri sounded decidedly churlish. 'May I ask if the Countess has Sergei Ivanovich's permission to cut down the tree?'

'The tree does not incommode Count Borodinov,' she snapped. 'It does incommode me, and as mistress of this house I tell you to chop it down. Or would you prefer me to report your disobedience to the Count when he returns?'

Dmitri turned away, grumbling under his breath. He was reasonably certain that Count Borodinov knew nothing of his wife's intent and would be angry when he found out. On the other hand, he would be still angrier if he learned that Dmitri had disobeyed. Sergei Ivanovich was a good master, as masters went, but disobedience meant a beating. Better to let the Countess risk the beating when her husband found out what she had done. Better still to have the task completed and be well away from the scene before Sergei Ivanovich returned.

Kirsty was therefore very agreeably surprised that work started on the tree with no more delay than that caused by fetching and honing an axe. Her room grew steadily brighter as the branches were lopped, and when the old tree finally fell with a thud that shook the house, her room became as light and cheerful as she had always felt it should be, and her spirits lightened accordingly. So, by the time she went downstairs before dinner, her temper was almost restored to what it had been when she had first come to Zubstovoy.

Such improved spirits were to be short-lived.

She had not been long at her tambour-frame, waiting for Sergei's return so that the evening meal—one of the few western customs which he had been prepared to adopt—might be served, when she heard his boots on the wooden steps and the front door first opened and then slammed shut with unnecessary force.

'Where is the Countess?' she heard him demand. She heard no answer, but whoever he had been addressing must have given some sort of reply, for a few seconds later the door of the room in which she was sitting burst open and Sergei's tall figure, white with anger, stood there.

'So here you are, Countess—and so innocently engaged with your embroidery. Such a charming tableau. I congratulate you, but it will not serve.' The words were softly spoken, almost hissed, Kirsty thought, though why they should be, she could not think. Nor could she imagine why his tone should be so laced with venom, unless—the thought struck her with unwelcome force —unless Babak had died. Surely Volodya would have got word to her if that were so? It was certainly enough to account for Sergei's present fury, but why had she heard nothing about it?

Pushing her frame aside, Kirsty rose. 'You have me at

a disadvantage, Sergei. Has something happened to Babak? I know I rode him harder than I should, but Volodya did not think he would take chill.'

He stared at her. 'I know of nothing amiss with the horse, though it would not surprise me if you set about destroying all you could. Or do you think to divert me from my purpose? If so, you will be disappointed. I refer—as I am sure you are perfectly well aware—to the apple tree outside your room.'

Kirsty's brow cleared momentarily. 'Is that all?' she said and then the frown returned. 'Was it so very bad to cut it down without your permission? I am sure I have mentioned often enough how gloomy it makes my chamber.'

'It was unforgivable,' he hissed between his teeth.

'Oh, come, Sergei, you overstate the case! It was an old tree that rarely blossomed, and last year it produced only three apples, I am told. There were none on it this year, and if you look at the remaining stump you will see it is quite hollow.'

'Yes, it was dying.' His voice was grudging. 'Nevertheless, it would have continued for several years yet, had you not interfered.'

Kirsty stared at him. 'Do you keep everything until it dies, then?' she asked. 'The old dairy cow past bearing a calf? The horse whose working days are over? Do you not slaughter them and put the meat to good use? Why, then, should a dying tree not be cut down and its wood help to keep us warm in the winter?'

'Not that tree,' he said, his voice harsh and adamant as if there were no arguments that could change his opinion. 'When my mother came here fifty years ago as a young bride, she planted that tree and always came back to Zubstovoy in time to see it bloom. It was fifteen years before she had a child, and when I was born, it was in that room with the tree in bloom. She loved that tree as she loved her husband and her long-awaited son. I vowed it would remain until it fell, in memory of her. Do you think I did not know it was rotten through and through? I have long dreaded the sudden storm that would take it from me. But it needed no storm, did it? All it took was a thoughtless wife.'

Kirsty was aghast at the realisation of what she had done. 'I did not know,' she whispered, and reached out to touch his arm in a gesture of sympathy and contrition. 'I had no idea.'

He turned curtly away from the proffered gesture. 'And cared too little to seek my approval first,' he said bitterly. 'Did Dmitri not warn you?'

'He was unwilling to cut it down, and asked if I had your permission,' Kirsty admitted reluctantly. 'But his unwillingness seemed to stem largely from laziness. I did not dream that there might be more to it than that.'

'And made no attempt to find out. You were willing enough to marry the rich Count Borodinov, but, having done so, you have made little effort to become a wife in any but a purely social sense.' The bitterness in his voice was almost tangible.

'That is not true,' Kirsty whispered, though she sensed that, in his present mood, nothing she could say would make any impression on him.

'Perhaps you believe that,' he said flatly. 'For my part, I can only regret the foolishness of my action in marrying a foreigner. I was advised against it, and I ignored the advice. I can only blame myself. Fortunately, as it turns out, we have no children. I will enquire whether the marriage can be set aside. It may be possible and will be best for us both, I think, but it will take many months.'

'No, Sergei, no!' Kirsty's whispered plea was barely audible.

He looked at her with contempt in his eyes. 'Do not worry, Countess, I shall see that you will not starve

—and I am sure matters may be arranged so that you may keep your title.' He stared down at her for a few moments. 'I had not thought to envy my father the love of his wife,' he said. Then he turned and left her staring after him, tears blinding her eyes.

When the door had closed behind him, Kirsty sank down, her face in her hands. So her premonition had been right. This was how it was all to end.

The despair in her heart was not lightened by the knowledge that, when she had agreed to this marriage, it had been for no more reason than that no better alternative offered or was likely to do so. Only when she had realised that her new husband was the very man who had been the source of her dreams since he acted on her behalf in Archangel did she realise that her marriage could become more than a matter of convenience, of duty. Those hopes had come to nought; indeed, it now seemed she had lost even that which she had originally settled for: a marriage of convenience.

Sergei had refused to take her to St Petersburg, thus cutting her off from her only escape. It was true there was little to choose between the social ostracism she would encounter in England if she returned there under the protection of a man to whom she could not be married and that which she would encounter in either country as a woman who had been set aside. Nevertheless, ostracism in one's own country must surely be preferable to the same situation elsewhere, a feeling reinforced by the fact that she was not at all sure what the setting aside of a Russian marriage entailed for the wife. It was certainly customary for unsatisfactory wives to be expected to enter a nunnery, preferably for them also to take the veil, though Sergei had said she would retain her title and an income. Surely neither of these would be required in a convent?

She forced herself to ponder these practical considerations, but it was with great difficulty she concentrated
her mind on them at all because, over-riding all other
considerations, would be the inescapable and unwelcome fact that she would have lost for ever the only man
she thought she had loved. It did not matter that he did
not seem to have loved her. That, she suddenly realised,
was something with which she could come to terms. How
bitter it was that that realisation should have come too
late.

Briefly Kirsty toyed with the thought that she might,
even at this late stage, seek Sergei out and beg him to let
them start again, but the idea had no sooner taken shape
in her mind than she rejected it. Sergei was not the most
flexible of men, and there was his pride. Nor did he
particularly admire humility in others: she could imagine
all too clearly the contempt in his face were she to plead
for the marriage to continue, since he had made it very
clear he believed that material considerations alone lay
behind her actions. Then, too, she doubted a positive
response to such a plea: having failed once, the proud
Count Borodinov was hardly likely to risk failure a
second time.

Such thoughts as these went round and round in her
head. When the maid came to make her mistress ready
for bed, she found the Countess strangely abstracted and
reported, on her return to the kitchen, that they might
mark her words that an upset was in the offing.

Sleep did not come easily that night. With her
thoughts in a turmoil, Kirsty tossed and turned in a
fruitless search for a solution and when exhaustion
finally closed her eyes, the sleep that ensued was far
from being either deep or dreamless so that, when she
awoke in the unaccustomed light of dawn, no longer
filtered through the leaves of a tree, she felt neither
rested nor refreshed.

She lay there, heavy eyed, thinking at first that the time was further advanced than it was, and then remembered that more light was coming into the room because she had cut down the tree outside. It was not a felicitous realisation. Her agony of mind returned anew and she sought once more for a solution.

Suddenly, through the convolutions of her questing, just such a solution appeared with the clarity of Bohemian crystal. Why should she not go to Sergei, now, and convince him of her true feelings in the hope, the expectation, that the force of her sincerity would induce him to think again? The burden suddenly lifted, it was with as light a heart as she had had these many weeks that she swung her feet out of bed and into the slippers that lay ready. She reached for a wrap and, throwing it round her shoulders, put her hand to the door.

As the chill of the latch touched her fingers, the brief moment of unfamiliar lightheartedness dropped away and cold reality replaced it. Of what use would it be to see Sergei? She had considered that solution yesterday and discarded it. Nothing had changed. No matter how strong, how sincere, her feelings, he would suspect them, and consider they masked her true reasons for wishing to remain his wife—reasons he had already convinced himself were the real ones. There was no solution in that direction.

All the same, her fingers closed over the latch. She lifted it and went out. She paused momentarily outside Sergei's room as if, for a tiny chip of a second, she would plead with him after all. The pause was barely a hesitation in her step before she passed on, down the stairs and out of the front door.

As she went down the short flight of steps to the drive, she did not notice the startled look on the face of an old woman crouched beside her hobbled cow, milking-pail between her feet. It was early for the Countess to be out, the old woman thought, and why should she be dressed like that? Then she reminded herself that the Countess was a foreigner, and shrugged. There was no more to be thought.

Oblivious to everything, uncertain even, as to just what was driving her on, and with no clear idea of her destination, Kirsty kept walking down the avenue of cherry trees and on in the direction of the little village.

Just before the dusty road forked, she met the village priest, bearded and rotund in his black *kaftan* and tall hat. He was as startled as the old woman, and a great deal less ready to attribute the Countess's abstracted air and strange apparel to her foreignness.

'Countess?' he said, and laid a hand gently upon her arm.

Kirsty smiled vagely. 'Good morning, Father Mikhail,' she said, and walked on, heedless of his mildly restraining arm.

Father Mikhail looked after her, troubled, and seeing her take the left-hand fork which led to the mill and not the right-hand one to the village, his troubled look deepened and he pondered whether to follow her or whether to make all speed to the Count.

He could think of only one reason why an incompletely attired woman whose manner was uncharacteristically vague should be heading for the mill—and the river. Father Mikhail knew that if he was right and if he could not dissuade Countess Borodinova from her intended sin, he could not save her, for he could not swim.

On the other hand he could, if he hurried, get to the Count before the Countess reached the river, the fork in the road being nearer the house than the mill. So, removing his hat and lifting his *kaftan* as a woman lifts her skirts, he ran.

The household was well astir when he got there. Panting heavily, for such exertion was not his custom,

Father Mikhail had the forethought to go first to the stables and order horses, including one for the Count, to be saddled.

Then he rushed into the house. 'Is Count Borodinov not up yet?' he demanded.

'At this time? When there are no manoeuvres? Have you lost your wits, Father?' the old house-serf, Fedor, answered.

'Then wake him! Tell him I am here, that it is urgent. No, better still—take me to his room,' the priest commanded.

Fedor stared at him. 'And be beaten for it? You *have* lost your wits!'

'I promise you, Fedor Ilyich, that that would be nothing to the beating you will get when Count Borodinov finds you kept me waiting.'

There was a grimness in the priest's voice and on his normally cheerful features that had a stronger effect than any threats. Fedor said no more, but grudgingly led the way upstairs and tapped gently on his master's door.

Impatiently, the priest pushed past him, hammered on the wooden panels and then, almost before the reverberations had ceased, he opened the heavily carved door and went in.

Count Borodinov was half-lying, half-sitting in bed, very much a man who had been sound asleep half a second ago.

'What, in the name of all that's holy . . . ?' he began, and then stared at the unexpected sight of the priest at the foot of the bed. 'Father Mikhail? What are you doing here, looking for all the world as if you are about to administer the last rites? If you have been told I was dying, you were misinformed: I merely sleep—or would be doing so, were it not for this intrusion.'

His sardonic reception flustered the priest more than mere anger would have done. He flushed and bowed.

'Your pardon, Sergei Ivanovich,' he began. 'This is an intrusion indeed, and the last rites may yet be administered, though not to Your Excellence. You must hasten. Sergei Ivanovich: I have but a short time since passed the Countess and I feared she makes for the mill.'

Sergei was wide awake now. He stared at the priest. 'What makes you think Christina Alexandrovna does not simply ride early?'

'She does not ride; she has no escort; and she wears, if I mistake not, her night-clothes and a brocade wrap. I have ordered horses to be saddled,' the priest added.

Sergei was already on his feet. 'Did you not seek to stop her?' he asked.

'I spoke to her and she answered, but her mind was elsewhere. She was oblivious to my restraining hand and I was not willing to wrestle with her: to do so might only provoke what one would hope to prevent.'

Sergei pulled on his boots and stood up. 'Do you ride, Father?' he asked.

'I ride—but I do not swim,' the priest replied.

'It is fortunate then that the Tsar insists his officers do so,' Sergei replied grimly, leading the way to the stables where Volodya waited with horses, not only for the Count and the priest, but for himself and another groom as well.

Father Mikhail's instincts had been wise. Since he had made no overt attempt to delay or divert Kirsty, she experienced no wish to hasten, and once on the narrow, dusty cart-track to the mill, her pace slowed so that she gave more the appearance of one drifting aimlessly than of one with a definite destination in mind. As a consequence, she did not reach the mill-race so very much in advance of the pursuing party.

She stood by the river that fed the mill's launder, deceptively placid as it moved inexorably towards the wooden building itself. She remembered all that she had heard about the river at this point: that it was not particularly deep, but that under the calm, smooth surface was a heavy undertow which had been known to drag even the occasional cow off its feet as it waded in to drink just too far.

Kirsty stood staring down at her reflection. A passer-by would have judged her to be deep in thought, but this was not so: she stared down unseeing, and her mind was completely empty with that numbed emptiness that is a waking unconsciousness. After a few minutes of this apparently rapt contemplation, she drifted round to the other side of the mill, where the water tumbled and foamed from the wooden wheel into the race below. The sudden turbulence of the stream disturbed the surface calm of Kirsty's mind much as it disturbed the surface calm of the river. She shook her head as if unwilling to acknowledge this boisterous interruption and returned to her former vantage-point. She paced slowly up and down on the bank within the small compass of two or three yards. Still no conscious thought, no formalised intent, had taken shape; she merely felt herself drawn to the cool calm depths of the river.

Thus, when Sergei, the priest and the grooms rounded a slight bend in the track, they saw the cerulean blue of Kirsty's brocade wrap straight ahead of them, and all four riders immediately drew rein.

'Thank God we are not too late,' Sergei whispered.

'Thank God, indeed,' the priest echoed.

The two men dismounted, and handing their reins over to the grooms, made their way as quickly as they dared towards the figure in front of them, anxious above all not to precipitate an action that was still only contemplated.

But Kirsty neither saw nor heard them, and when she felt Sergei's hand on her arm, she looked up at him, genuinely startled.

'Sergei? And Father Mikhail?' A frown settled briefly on her brow. 'Did I not see you earlier, Father?'

'You did, indeed, my child, and Count Borodinov shares my view that the morning air is too chill for a visit to such a spot.'

Sergei's arm was round her shoulder now, and he turned her from the river, grateful that he encountered no resistance.

'I could not sleep,' Kirsty told them, 'so I came for a walk.'

'And now you must return home,' her husband said gently, beckoning the grooms forward with the horses. 'We did not think to bring Babak,' he went on. 'Will you ride before me, Kirsty?'

Kirsty nodded, and was lifted on to Sergei's saddle. When he had mounted behind her, the little party moved off towards Zubstovoy in silence. Kirsty leaned back against the warm strength of Sergei's body, suddenly, unaccountably, quietly happy. Never had they been as close as this before. Never had she felt before that he was concerned for her well-being.

The feeling uppermost in Sergei's mind was one of relief that they had reached Kirsty before the lure of the river had proved too strong. Allied to that relief was a deep sadness that she must be so unhappy in this marriage that she could not await its formal ending. He did not reflect that it was he who had suggested that formal ending. Nor, strangely, did it cross his mind that, had Kirsty drowned, all the problems that had arisen as a result of this marriage—and all the problems attendant upon ending it—would have been solved with that single plunge.

CHAPTER
ELEVEN

KIRSTY SPENT several days confined to her room, her maid detailed to sleep in a truckle bed made up at the foot of her mistress's own bed. On Sergei's orders, Kirsty was not left alone, day or night.

At first, Kirsty scarcely noticed this close attendance: once put to bed, the housekeeper had brought her a tisane which sent her into a deep and dreamless sleep from which she awoke physically, if not mentally, refreshed. After the second night she told Anna she need no longer sleep in her room but might order the truckle bed removed and return to her usual quarters.

Anna bobbed a curtsy. 'Begging your pardon, *barinya*, but Count Borodinov's orders are that I stay.'

Kirsty opened her mouth to protest, but then closed it. There was nothing to be gained by arguing with the girl, who was undoubtedly, telling the truth. It was a matter to be discussed with Sergei, who seemed to be avoiding her.

In fact, Sergei had sat by her bedside for several hours while she slept, watching that fragile beauty, so peaceful in repose. How sad it was that that expression should manifest itself only in a drugged sleep, and what an indictment of this misconceived marriage that such a sleep should have become necessary!

It was the need to catch up on his own sleep and to attend to the management of his estates that led to Sergei's absence from her side when Kirsty awoke, so that, when he did present himself once more, it was after her conversation with Anna, and she was much dispirited.

He sat down on the edge of the bed and looked down at her, observing the tentative, puzzled smile she gave him.

'You do not object to my company, I hope?'

Kirsty shook her head, her dark curls tumbling on the pillow, framing her pale, fine-boned features.

'I trust you are rested and fully recovered,' Sergei went on. 'Father Mikhail, also, sends his wishes for your recovery.'

'My recovery? Have I been ill, then?'

'What else would make you leave your bed at dawn and wander by the mill-race? We took it to be some fever.'

'Is that what the servants have been told?'

'What else would you have me tell them? That your hatred of me is such that you would sooner drown than wait for the slow processes of law to end this marriage?' He tried to keep his voice light, but the bitterness crept through.

Kirsty shook her head again. 'That is not true, Sergei. I do not know what drove me to the river, but it was not hatred of you.'

'Revulsion—dislike—the word does not matter. It matters to me that I, who have never been a hard master, should not acquire the mantle of a brutal husband, and so it has been given out that you have been ill.'

'And Father Mikhail?'

'Is a good man who believes that the sin of suicide can be contemplated only by one who is ill and therefore unable to make rational decisions.'

'I had not, I think, gone out with the intention of killing myself,' Kirsty said thoughtfully.

'That is a view shared by Father Mikhail. He feels you would have been walking with a greater sense of purpose and would have been beyond help by the time we arrived, had your mind already been made up.'

'He is wiser than I had thought.'

'He has that wisdom that is not infrequently shown by those who combine simplicity with a wide knowledge of people.'

Kirsty said nothing, but turned her head so that her gaze went through the window; that same window whose view was no longer obscured by a leafy mass of gnarled branches. Almost at once she turned back to Sergei.

'I am truly sorry about the tree,' she whispered. 'I had no idea of the significance it held for you.'

A cloud drifted across his face, but his voice was not unkind.

'It is over and done with now. Perhaps the blame is mine. Had I been more forthcoming when we came, the misunderstanding would not have arisen.'

'Nevertheless, I should have waited until you came back before insisting on its removal,' Kirsty said.

Sergei smiled, a wry smile. 'I had not looked for such contrition.'

Kirsty flushed. 'What a picture you must have of me!' she exclaimed. 'Obstinate, impulsive and a stranger to regret!'

'That is not the picture I have of you.' In the long pause that ensued, Sergei took the pale hand that lay on the coverlet and raised its tapering fingers to his lips and found them unresisting. 'We should have dealt together better than this,' he said softly and saw the tears spring unbidden to Kirsty's eyes. 'Forgive me—such unhappiness as I have brought you is not what I intended. You cannot know how much it haunts me that you were driven to the step you almost took.'

Kirsty longed to say, 'Then let us try once more, let us see whether we cannot make something better of it,' but the words would not come, choked as they were by tears so they remained unsaid and the moment passed.

Sergei took a paper from the deep pocket of his coat. The seal was already broken and he spread it out on the counterpane.

'Our unhappy situation may be more quickly resolved than I had thought,' he said.

'What do you mean?' His remark had been so far removed from Kirsty's thoughts that she could not immediately follow his drift.

'It is a slow and tortuous business to have a marriage annulled and I did not think I could begin the process until winter, when the Court returns to Moscow. But I have orders here to proceed to St Petersburg and report to the Tsar. I shall seek an audience with him and plead our case. He will not be pleased. We must pray God he will be understanding.'

'So you go to St Petersburg,' Kirsty whispered, feeling events were accelerating beyond her control and in a direction she did not want. 'When do you leave?'

'No. *We* go to St Petersburg,' he told her. 'Was it not to our future capital you begged me to take you so short a time ago? Well, you have your wish—at the Tsar's command. A few more days should see you sufficiently recovered to undertake the journey. We may be thankful that our palace there is so far advanced. Do you know, we even have glass in the windows? Even the Tsar cannot boast that yet!'

Kirsty smiled dutifully. In truth she cared little whether they had glass or mica or only wooden shutters, and even less what the Tsar had, but Sergei's remark was clearly intended to raise her spirits, and she had no desire to disappoint him.

Mistaking her quietude for fatigue, Sergei took his leave, promising to return when she should once more have rested.

Kirsty lay still enough, knowing that Anna sat by the window mending linen and would bustle around her like a broody hen if the turmoil of her thoughts transferred itself to her body.

Clearly Sergei was set on the annulment of this marriage, and his chief concern was to expedite it with all possible haste. Very well, she must bow to the inevitable, but she had the power to hasten matters still further. They were going to St Petersburg. There was no reason that Kirsty could think of for not executing John Harrow's plan. She would flee, with his help, on the first foreign boat that would take her. Once she had left Russia in the company of a fellow-countryman, the annulment of their marriage would be a mere formality, and Sergei would be free to marry the sort of wife he really wanted.

Curiously, Kirsty found little comfort in this eminently practical conclusion.

The journey to Peter's new city on the Baltic was a great deal more pleasant than had been that earlier one. For one thing, it was high summer, and although that meant the days were very hot, it also meant the roads, fields and forests were dry and they could make good speed. For another, Kirsty had prevailed upon her husband to let her ride. He was undoubtedly influenced by the fact that, if she did so, they could make much better speed than would be possible if they had to keep pace with a lumbering carriage or a palanquin, and when Kirsty offered to wear a veil over the broad-brimmed hat that would be her protection from the sun, his last objections were swept away and there remained only his concern that she might find it was too fatiguing after her recent 'illness', as he persisted in calling it.

'I shall not find it nearly so fatiguing as rattling along in that uncomfortable carriage,' Kirsty assured him.

Sergei looked doubtful. 'I must say that a long journey in that estimable vehicle would try my own temper sorely, but I am accustomed to long journeys on horse-back. Will you undertake to tell me if you should find it too much?'

Kirsty assured him that she would, mentally resolving that, since nothing could be worse than to be obliged to travel any distance beyond a few versts in her father's wedding present, she would make sure she betrayed no hint of any fatigue she might feel.

As it turned out, she felt none. To be sure, at the end of each day she tumbled into bed at the various post-houses with considerable alacrity and fell asleep instantly, but she awoke each morning completely refreshed and ready to be on her way again. Any tired-ness she felt was entirely physical, and a sound sleep soon remedied it.

Both she and Sergei were agreeably surprised to find considerable pleasure in each other's company. It was as though, having agreed on a solution to their problems and awaiting only that, there could be no more friction.

Kirsty rode well and had no difficulty keeping up with Sergei, and since she was the only member of their entourage who was neither serf nor servant, Sergei found it possible to converse on a level of equality and familiarity that would otherwise have been denied him. It was an experience he had previously enjoyed only when travelling with his fellow-officers. Even then, this was subtly different since it included the disconcerting unexpectedness of a woman's view of things.

Kirsty commented on the fact that, through whatever villages they passed and wherever they stopped, the women were quite conspicuously not in seclusion. True, they often wore a shawl, the end of which could be drawn across their face when a strange man approached, but few women bothered and many, with their rouged cheeks and bold stare, seemed, to any woman brought up in a western society, to be positively forward.

'Has the Tsar's instruction concerning the abolition of the *terem* reached these remote villages?' she asked as they left one such.

Sergei seemed surprised. 'What place has the *terem* in such a community?'

It was Kirsty's turn to look surprised. 'But we are strangers! Yet they make no effort to withdraw from the gaze of the men in this party.'

'Nor would the women at Zubstovoy.'

'I observed that they did not withdraw in your presence, but took that to refer to the fact that, as their master, your position was one of father,' Kirsty said doubtfully.

'I imagine it may have started so,' Sergei conceded, thinking about it for the first time. 'However, seclusion is hardly practicable in the country.'

Kirsty stared at him. 'I should have thought it a great deal *more* practicable in the country, where there are fewer people, than in a city,' she said.

'Nonsense! How would they help with the harvest or milk the cows if they were obliged to stay hidden from men?'

'Then why is a boyar's wife expected to scuttle for cover like a frightened mouse whenever a man appears?'

'Is that what it seems like?' Sergei laughed. 'How else may their virtue be protected?'

'A chaperon would do just as well,' Kirsty commented. 'It is, after all, a concern for western men as well as Russian. Though I am interested to observe that the virtue of village women does not seem to concern you. Do you consider them to have none, or is it of little importance?'

'It is simply not practicable,' Sergei reiterated.

'No, it is not,' Kirsty agreed. 'Nor is it practicable for a boyar's wife, I assure you. Your arguments lack logic, you know.'

'What does a woman know of logic?' Sergei began, and then stopped, laughing. 'All right, I concede that if a woman's virtue needs protection, it makes no difference whether she be boyarina or serf. But a chaperon can be bribed, a *terem* cannot, and I think a boyar holds his honour dearer than a serf does.'

'That is a completely different argument, and to pursue it would provoke more questions than it would answer,' Kirsty told him. 'Since you have been sufficiently honest to admit the illogicality of the system, I will concede that not all chaperons exhibit the trustworthiness expected of them. Thus may we each feel the argument won and continue our journey charitably disposed towards one another.'

'I have not felt otherwise towards you since this journey started,' Sergei said, his voice suddenly serious.

Kirsty looked at him, and their eyes met in a momentary gaze that caused Kirsty's hand to tremble on the reins as her heart beat inexplicably faster.

An outrider intruded with an important message. 'Sergei Ivanovich . . .' he began, and once again Kirsty had the feeling that a moment when much might have been said would now be lost for ever.

Sometimes they conversed; sometimes they simply rode in a companionable silence. For both of them, an otherwise tedious journey became a pleasant interlude, and neither was entirely glad to see the distant tower of the Admiralty rising above the forested skyline.

Were she not seeing it for herself, Kirsty would not have believed so much progress could have been made so quickly since her previous visit to the Tsar's favourite project. There were three reasons for so much progress having been made: her earlier visit had been at the very end of the last season, when the weather and the darkness were slowing down almost every facet of advance and now she arrived at a time when there had been several warm, dry months in almost permanent daylight; the long, laborious work of sinking foundations strong enough to bear the stone buildings was largely completed, and now those actual buildings were rising from the swamp, their very visibility making progress more noticeable; lastly, and of supreme importance, Peter did not care how many lives were lost in the completion of his enterprise—if ten serfs died, twenty more would be forthcoming to replace them. The dream would be realised, cost what it might.

The Borodinov Palace was outwardly complete. Only that of Prince Menshikov on Vasilevsky Island was further advanced, although it was to be so magnificent that it would take another three years to be finished. Many of the rooms in the Borodinovs' new home had furniture in them, and teams of Latvian craftsmen were laying the intricately convoluted parquet floors that were so striking a feature of great Russian houses—and which rendered unnecessary the new-fangled English fashion for patterning floors by covering them with carpet. Nor, of course, were wooden floors as cold as the stone flags of English houses, another reason behind the current English fashion.

One English fashion that had been adopted was that of open fireplaces in the larger rooms, though Kirsty was amused to notice that each also contained its far more efficient Russian stove, decorated with glazed and patterned tiles, many of them from Holland.

The Borodinov Palace was certainly habitable. It was not yet sufficiently finished to warrant entertaining on any but the most intimate scale. Significantly, in Peter's own city, its *terem* was but a private suite of rooms, permitting seclusion to whatever degree its occupants wished. It was an arrangement that would not have been at all out of the way in an English home of comparable size.

This palace was much larger than their Moscow one, but laid out in accordance with a more logical western prearranged plan rather than developing over the years with wings and additions as their home in Moscow had done. Nevertheless, Kirsty wondered how long it would be before she was familiar with its endless corridors and antechambers, and tried not to reflect that she might not live in it long enough to become so. She found it quite refreshing to learn that Sergei, too, more than once lost his way—and that was without his attempting to penetrate the servants' quarters and the kitchens, the pantries, laundries and dairy, as she did.

To Kirsty's surprise, it seemed that the Tsar himself had made no effort at all to build himself a palace in keeping with his rank. Indeed, he still lived in the small two-roomed wooden cottage on the embankment that had been the first residence built in the new city. From here it was but a short walk to the small island on which the city's central stronghold, the Peter and Paul Fortress, was being built. The Tsar could therefore easily supervise the work, the most urgent of which was currently the replacing of the fortress's protective earthworks with ramparts of bricks, an urgency underlined by the proximity, in the Gulf outside, of the Swedish navy. It was said that no fewer than twenty thousand workmen laboured on the fortress at any one time, and Kirsty, watching them scuttling like ants, believed it.

Sergei acceded to her wish to see the city in detail, and conceding that this could hardly be done either from a closed carriage or from a curtained palanquin, agreed to her exploring on foot, provided only that she was veiled, and that he accompanied her. Since Count Borodinov knew far more about what was planned for the city than any attendant manservant would have done, and since he seemed perfectly happy to walk with his wife, this suited Kirsty very well. She had thought Sergei might prove impatient to cover as much of the city as he could as quickly as possible or be reluctant to answer questions, the answers to which might seem self-evident to anyone familiar with St Petersburg, but this was not so: Kirsty did not feel he was in any haste to complete her exploration nor impatient with her many questions.

Several times she found herself contemplating the companionable relationship that they seemed to be establishing, and found it hard to believe that Sergei planned what amounted to an annulment, or that she had planned to make her escape before he had had the opportunity to do more than broach the matter to the Tsar. The dispiriting fact was, however, that he gave her no hint by word, gesture, or even look that he, too, might be having second thoughts. Then occurred a small incident which made it clear that he was as determined upon his plan as ever, thus reinforcing Kirsty's own determination.

They were strolling along one of the embankments that flanked the Neva. Kirsty was masked, in the English fashion, for she found it easier to see clearly through the eye-holes of the complexion-protecting mask than through the misty folds of a veil, and the effect of the mask was to make her much more noticeable as a westerner than the western clothes which were now *de rigueur* among the nobility of this emerging city which was so shortly to be declared the new capital of all the Russias. A man and a woman in western clothes aroused no interest, but the mask attracted the curious stares of those passing by.

The embankment along which they strolled was paved with cobbles for most of its length, and they eventually came to a place where the cobbles ended and a broad swath had been cut through the forest at right-angles to the embankment. This broad cutting was to become the Nevsky Prospekt, a big perspective road that was soon to become one of the greatest thoroughfares, not only in Russia, but in Europe. As yet nothing was to be seen but the surveyors' marks, the beginning of the tree-clearing, and the pile-driven foundations of the very first buildings.

As they paused to look down the line of marker posts and Kirsty tried to visualise what would be the final appearance of this incredibly broad street—and failed —she caught sight of a familiar figure deep in conversation with one of the surveyors. It was John Harrow. Since his purpose in St Petersburg was to supervise the paving of the streets, it clearly facilitated his work if he was involved in the early stages of any roadworks, and, difficult though it might be to imagine what this particular road would finally look like, it was not difficult to realise that it would be of a length, breadth and straightness unequalled in any other city.

The two men glanced up from their consultations as they noticed the approach of two well-dressed strangers, their attention caught by the unusual fact of the woman's being masked. John Harrow gave a start of recognition when he caught sight of the tall form of Count Borodinov, followed by a flush of consciousness as he realised who the masked woman at his side must be. He removed his hat and bowed.

'Count Borodinov,' he said. 'Countess.'

Kirsty felt Sergei stiffen. 'Master Harrow, I believe. We have met, of course.' His voice was not calculated to inspire anything less than the utmost formality of manner.

Kirsty intervened gently. 'You will recall, Sergei Ivanovich that, quite apart from Master Harrow's recent visit to Zubstovoy, it was with his family that I stayed before our marriage and, besides having a great respect for them, I hold the family in great affection.'

'I had not forgotten. I naturally share my wife's

gratitude for the support your family has given her in the past.' Sergei's voice was still icily formal.

John bowed again. 'It was no onerous burden—Countess Borodinova had long been a friend.' He turned to Kirsty. 'Now that you are settled in St Petersburg, I trust that I may call to pay my respects.'

Kirsty opened her mouth to assure him that he might, but before any words could be uttered, Sergei pre-empted her courtesies. 'Alas, Master Harrow, our palace is far from complete and we do not entertain as yet, not even on the most simple scale. I trust you will understand.'

'Indeed, I understand perfectly,' John said, glancing from one to the other and taking note not only of Sergei's implacable manner but of the embarrassed flush on his wife's cheeks. Matters did not seem at all improved between the couple, he thought, and wondered whether Kirsty's presence in the city indicated a readiness to fall in with his suggested plan. He could not immediately see any way of communicating with her on the subject, her husband having just disposed of the only feasible excuse for converse that he could think of. Still, it could do no harm to lay some more detailed plans.

As they retraced their steps along the embankment, Kirsty turned to her husband. 'That was discourteous, Sergei,' she said, her voice tight with embarrassment. 'His request to call was a customary English politeness, and there is no reason why we should not receive him: besides, he must know that our home is sufficiently advanced to make it perfectly suitable to receive the occasional visitor.'

'I am sure he does,' Sergei replied, unmoved. 'That is precisely why I said it. It can leave him in no doubt that his acquaintance is one I wish my wife to discontinue.'

Kirsty stopped and stared at him. 'How . . . how *dare* you!' she said. 'The son of people who have treated me as if I were their own daughter! How *dare* you allow him to infer that you wish the acquaintance discontinued! You are *intolerable*!'

Sergei smiled grimly. 'I am aware that that has ever been your opinion, though you have never stated it quite so unequivocally before. Take comfort in the fact that you will not long be obliged to tolerate me.'

'Oh, I do, I do!' Kirsty retaliated. 'You can have no idea what consolation that thought provides!'

'You underestimate my imagination,' Sergei told her in a tone that caused Kirsty to glance swiftly up at him. Did she detect a note of irony? It was hard to tell: those slavic features so easily adopted that expression of inscrutable impassivity with which she had become so familiar. How much easier it would be to deal with a man who, like John Harrow, let his emotions range across his face!

Sergei's hand under her elbow guided her on. 'Let us not stand here providing entertainment for every serf in Russia,' Sergei said softly. 'If you wish to continue this . . . discussion, perhaps it could wait until we are within our own walls.'

'There is nothing to discuss,' Kirsty stated flatly. 'I am only happy to find I have not misjudged you in any way.'

'So gratifying to find oneself in the right, is it not?' Sergei murmured, making no attempt to disguise the sarcasm of the comment.

Kirsty searched rapidly for an even more biting retort but could think of none, and, wisely, appeared not to have heard the remark.

Their exchange was not referred to again by either of them, but what has been said cannot be unsaid, and the memory of it lay between them, tacit and corroding, so that the comfortably companionable quality that had attached to their little expeditions was gone and they walked together like polite strangers.

The visit that Kirsty liked most was to the Summer
Gardens, a formal garden of geometrically arranged
walks that would one day soon house the Tsar's Summer
Palace. Laid out as it was in the style reminiscent of an
English knot-garden, though on a somewhat larger
scale, it reminded her of gardens seen but hardly noticed
during her childhood, and she felt oddly at home there.
It would be some time before the gardens were complete, but there was always the added interest of seeing
what new statues had been added since their last visit.
The Tsar was very fond of statues.

The tall figure they met there two days after the
dispute about John Harrow was no statue, however, but
the Tsar himself, talking in his energetic fashion to the
friends who accompanied him. He stopped when he saw
Count Borodinov and his wife, and smiled with obvious
pleasure.

'Sergei Ivanovich!' he exclaimed, 'and his delightful
Countess. I am flattered that you choose to walk in my
new gardens, Christina Alexandrovna.'

'It is one of my favourite excursions, sir,' Kirsty told
him.

'I fancy you find the place more to your liking than on
your last visit,' the Tsar went on.

'I did not see it in the best of weather conditions,'
Kirsty told him tactfully. 'So much progress has been
made! You must be very pleased with your new city.'

'I shall be when it is completed, but there is much still
to be done, and I intend to oversee it all.' He looked
from one to the other and then uttered a short, sharp
laugh. 'Indeed, it seems that is all I do this summer.
Alexander Danilovich, it is time we diverted ourselves.'

Prince Menshikov bowed, an ingratiating smile on his
face.

'As you wish, Peter Alexeyevich. Invitations will be
sent out.'

The Tsar turned to the couple before him. 'We shall give . . . a ball, I think. I look forward to seeing you there.'

Kirsty stared at him. 'Forgive me sir, but a ball? How may that be?'

'It shall be because I decree that it shall be.' The Tsar seemed irritated by her question, but then noticed that she seemed genuinely puzzled. 'What gives your wife such difficulty in believing I can hold a ball, Sergei Ivanovich?' he demanded.

Sergei smiled. 'I think Christina Alexandrovna refers to your cottage, sir. You will admit that it would be hard to hold more than a very small tea party there.'

Once again, the Tsar's sudden laugh rang out. 'When we wish to entertain, my dear Countess, we appropriate Prince Menshikov's palace. It is by no means finished, but it has a roof, and Alexashka has a genius for making it look festive—and I do not question too closely the source of the roubles that pay for it! Sergei Ivanovich, we would have your company tonight!'

With this adjuration the Tsar swept on, resuming his conversation with his friends as if there had been no interruption. Sergei seemed displeased.

'I have no desire to form part of his Merry Company, as he calls them. It is not a circle into which I wish to be drawn, but I can hardly ignore an Imperial command,' he said.

'Would it not be to your advantage to be drawn into the circle of favourites?' Kirsty asked.

'In some ways, yes, it would. I prefer not to have to choose between this faction and that, nor do I wish to be thought to ingratiate myself with the Tsar: I like the man despite his sudden rages and his westernising ideas. There are good men in his Company, too: who could not but admire Golovkin? Pinch-purse though he be, he is at least incorruptible. But Menshikov? The less I have to do with that noble Prince of Russia, the happier I am. Besides, I get little pleasure from drinking myself into a stupor, and that is how their riotous evenings end.'

This was very true, Kirsty reflected. Sergei was quite extraordinarily temperate by the standards of his fellow-country men. She rather thought it sprang, not from any dislike of spirituous liquors, but from a determination never to be seen in a situation in which he was not in control.

CHAPTER
TWELVE

THE FIRST invitation to be delivered was not, however, to the Tsar's ball, though it came from Prince and Princess Menshikov. It was to what was described as 'an intimate dinner' for the noble couple's friends, among whom, Sergei drily observed, he would not have regarded himself and his wife.

'"An intimate dinner",' Kirsty said thoughtfully, fingering the beautifully hand-written card of invitation. 'How small a party will it be? It would not do to over-dress.'

Sergei laughed. 'I doubt that will be possible!' he said. 'It would not surprise me at all if Alexander Danilovich's idea of an intimate dinner included the entire population of St Petersburg.'

Kirsty thought crossly that such comments were of little help in deciding her costume for the event, and selected a fashionable but discreet gown of lemon satin with very little train but some fine lace at neck and cuffs, and a rope of even finer pearls.

She was well satisfied with her appearance and fully expected at least a smile of commendation from Sergei when she appeared. Instead, he looked her up and down, unsmiling, and then said, 'Very pleasant, my dear, but we are not taking tea with your friends the Harrows. A little more magnificence is called for.'

'But Sergei, this is but a dinner party for a few of Menshikov's friends!'

'Among whom we do not figure. I think you misread the man, Kirsty. Prince Menshikov is not one for the understated gesture. I told you as much before but you seem to have disbelieved me. Your rose brocade and the rubies will be more in keeping—with an infinitely higher *fontange*, tell Anna. Go and change.'

'Are you sure, Sergei? I do not wish to be over-dressed in such company; it would be an impertinence.'

'Your discretion does you credit, my dear, but it is misplaced, I assure you. You will not be over-dressed.'

When she had changed, Kirsty surveyed herself in the mirror with considerable misgivings. The deep, soft rose—almost the colour of crushed strawberries—of the Italian brocade over its gleaming silver underskirt was nothing short of magnificent, the demi-train was sufficiently long to make walking—or at least, turning—a feat requiring skill and dexterity, and the three wired and starched tiers of her *fontange* obliged her to hold her head absolutely erect if she were not to feel as if one small push might overbalance her. When to this was added a rope of rubies cut like beads and so long that it wound three times round her neck, yet still hung to her bosom, she felt herself attired more appropriately for a coronation than 'an intimate dinner'.

When they entered the Menshikov Palace, her misgivings deserted her. Sergei had been wrong in only one respect: the entire population of St Petersburg included tens of thousands of labouring serfs. They had not been invited, but it would not have surprised Kirsty to have learned that they were the only exceptions.

Kirsty could not but feel that some embarrassment must be attendant upon an encounter with Prince Menshikov, their last one, if one discounted the brief meeting in the Summer Gardens, scarcely having been uneventful. If the Prince felt any embarrassment, however, he hid it well. His manner was as urbane and smoothly polished as always, and if his welcoming smile seemed not to reach his eyes, that was, after all, a characteristic she had noticed before. Despite the

Prince's seeming to have forgotten their previous unfortunate meeting, Kirsty felt some awkwardness at encountering him again. She was pleased to greet the Princess at his side, for no unwelcome recollections lay between the two women, and each genuinely liked the other.

Because the palace was unfinished, guests circulated and chatted within the huge entrance hall, and it was not long before Kirsty caught sight of John Harrow and his father among a little band of foreigners. James Harrow greeted her with unalloyed pleasure, and if his son's greeting was a shade formal and restrained, that was hardly surprising when one recalled Sergei's recent rudeness.

Once the Tsar and his wife had arrived and had begun to circulate, the Prince and Princess were able to do the same, since it was unthinkable that any should arrive after the Imperial couple. Sergei and Kirsty were deep in conversation with Gavril Golovkin, a man of culture and intelligence, with a handsome, sensitive face who was, Kirsty knew, one of the very few of Peter's intimates for whom Sergei felt any respect at all. While Kirsty listened, having little to contribute on the subject, the men discussed the design for the cathedral which Peter planned to build in the fortress.

'The spire will be visible to all who approach the city from whichever direction they come,' Golovkin was enthusing. 'A truly fitting focal point for all perspectives.'

'And a reminder to all that even in his innermost fortress, the Tsar does not forget his Maker,' added Menshikov's smooth voice from a point just behind Sergei's elbow.

'It would never do to allow the people to imagine the Tsar was careless in his observances,' Golovkin agreed. Kirsty looked at him speculatively. There was nothing untoward in the words or tone, and yet she had the feeling that there was an irony implicit in what he said. She also had the feeling that Golovkin's opinion of the Prince did not differ enormously from Sergei's, and this feeling was confirmed when he made his excuses, leaving the Prince with his guests.

'We are pleased to see you here, my wife and I,' he said, and then paused, looking from one to the other as if to read whatever expressions he saw on their faces. 'It crossed my mind that you might not come,' he continued blandly.

'I cannot imagine why,' Sergei remarked. 'I fancy people do not lightly decline an invitation from so influential a courtier.'

Menshikov smiled. 'Not when they recall that I am a courtier. You, however, Sergei Ivanovich, do not always recall that fact.'

'I forget it only when the courtier's behaviour suggests that he has forgotten it himself,' Sergei answered, and the barb brought a flush of recollection to the Prince's cheeks.

'Yet you risk laying your Countess open to insult by bringing her to a mixed gathering such as this; a gathering such as everyone knows does not meet with Count Borodinov's approval. I wonder you did not oblige her to remain in her *terem*.'

'Countess Borodinova will encounter few insults while I am with her,' Sergei said. 'Should any be foolish enough to overstep the mark, he will answer to me.'

Menshikov threw up his hands in mock horror. 'No bloodshed in my new palace, I implore you, Count: my wife would not wish to see the floors so inappropriately stained!'

Sergei laughed reluctantly. 'Rest assured, Alexander Danilovich, in the unlikely event of so distasteful a situation arising, the matter will be settled elsewhere at a mutually convenient time and in the western manner.'

'Swords rather than *knouts*?' Menshikov commented.

'Precisely.'

'Then let us hope it is not a European who oversteps the mark; he is likely to be the more adept with the sword.'

Sergei bowed, and Menshikov, observing that no riposte was forthcoming, inclined his head and moved on to another group of guests.

Kirsty stared after him.

'Was that wise, Sergei?' she asked. 'You reminded him of Zubstovoy and then laid yourself open to an insulting remark about your swordsmanship.'

'A lure to which I refused to swoop. Do you fondly imagine he had forgotten Zubstovoy? On the contrary, it rankles, as I knew it would. I have no intention of letting him think I have forgotten. If he seeks revenge, as I do not doubt he will, at least he will know he has not lulled me into thinking the matter over and done with.'

'Might it not be better if he did?' Kirsty asked doubtfully.

Sergei looked at her sharply. 'What do you mean?'

'Only that he need not be so devious if he thinks you have discounted the possibility of his taking revenge. His ploy would then be the more easily spotted and countered.'

Sergei stared at her. 'Do you play chess?'

'What an extraordinary question! No, I do not, though what that has to say to anything, I cannot imagine.'

'Then it is perhaps as well for my own self-esteem that our marriage will not now endure long enough to enable me to teach you. I fancy I should not long remain the master.'

With this enigmatic remark, he guided Kirsty into the line of guests now filing slowly into the room being used as a dining salon. Two immensely long tables ran the length of the room, and the guests sat where they would. Since, on this occasion, the Borodinovs had received no hint that they should place themselves anywhere in particular, they were able to take seats at some distance from the royal pair and their intimates.

The food put before the guests was sumptuous and superbly presented. Unfortunately it was also stone cold, since no one had realised that the choice as a temporary dining-salon of one of the few completed rooms—and one which happened to be at the opposite end of the vast building to the kitchens—was not an arrangement whereby the food would arrive at the table in the condition in which it left the kitchen.

Because of the numbers of people involved and the incomplete nature of most of the palace, it was not feasible for the ladies to withdraw and so both sexes, at a signal from the principal guest, rose from the tables and withdrew to the hall where servants and samovars awaited. Chairs had been placed for the Tsar and his wife, but other guests had to circulate with their handleless glasses of tea—no easy feat, as Kirsty soon discovered, when one had a train to control as well.

The wine that had flowed freely during dinner had compensated for the disappointment of the cold food, and had very successfully relaxed the formality that had attended the pre-dinner assembly. As a consequence there was a great deal more movement between groups of guests, and lively conversation was very much in evidence. It therefore became inevitable that the Borodinovs should sooner or later be parted by the attentions of this acquaintance or that, and it was on one such occasion, when Sergei was some distance off, and Kirsty could only see his dark unpowdered head towering over his companions, that John Harrow approached her.

'Has your husband deserted you?' he asked in Russian.

'Not at all,' Kirsty replied, smiling. 'He is over there talking to the Trubetskoys. It is so easy to be temporarily parted in such a crush as this.'

'A fact which raises my spirits,' John told her, and then continued in English. 'I had hoped to be allowed to pay my respects, for it is important that we talk, and I had almost despaired of the opportunity to snatch a word with you.'

'You would not have had such an opportunity had you visited us—we certainly would have had no private talk, I assure you,' Kirsty told him.

He smiled ruefully. 'I suppose you are right. All the more fortunate that we have these moments. I must ask you: are you still of a mind to flee Russia?'

Kirsty's heart leapt to her throat. The question should not have been unexpected when one considered their conversation during the ride at Zubstovoy, and yet somehow it had taken her by surprise to have it so bluntly put. For some extraordinary reason her instinct was to say 'No', to indicate a change of mind, of heart. Then she recalled that only this evening Sergei had referred to the impending end of their marriage, thereby indicating that his mind was still set on it. She recalled, too, that whenever it seemed that she and Sergei had found common ground and she began to hope that matters might change for the better, something—some small incident—occurred to set them back where they were. It was foolish, in the light of the evidence, to go on hoping. Better by far to accept the reality—and any offer John Harrow might be going to make.

'My mind is still so set,' she told him. 'I have never been more glad of anything than I was when Sergei told me that we were invited this evening. He had previously refused my request to come here, and I would not otherwise have been in a position to do more than think, on occasion, about what we have discussed.'

'Very well. Now listen carefully. In the hope that that you might be still of the same mind, I have made enquiries, and it seems by no means impossible. The master of a Dutch boat that left here some days ago returns in three weeks, and is prepared to take us both. He naturally has no idea who you are, only that you are English, and otherwise unable to leave Russia.'

'Will he not have second thoughts in the weeks before he has to take the risk?' Kirsty asked.

John shook his head. 'I think not. I know him well, and he deplores the lack of freedom to return to their own countries that so many foreigners here experience. He will not fail us.'

'Then what are the arrangements?'

'That I cannot tell you until he returns and can let me know when he plans to set sail again from St Petersburg. It is crucial that we do not board until the last possible moment. It would never do for Count Borodinov to have time to hunt for you.'

Kirsty shuddered. It was always possible, of course, that Sergei would not bother to search for a wife he was proposing to discard, but that was not a possibility on which she would be prepared to lay odds. It was one thing for Sergei to annul the marriage, but it was quite another for his pride to tolerate her running off with someone else.

'But we will have no opportunity to talk again! How will you let me know?' Kirsty's face betrayed her anxiety for any bystander to see.

'I do not know but I promise you, I will contrive.'

With this assurance Kirsty had to be satisfied, and it was perhaps fortunate that her attention was claimed by another guest. John, well satisfied that he had been able to explain to her how matters stood, took a discreet leave and became engaged in a discussion with a German stonemason about the relative merits of granite and limestone as facing materials.

Neither of them observed the thin and devious figure of Alexander Danilovich Menshikov, Prince of Russia, standing quietly and observantly by an alcove whose mirror had not yet arrived from the glazier. Nor would it have occurred to either of them that the noble Prince, who had accompanied Peter during his stay in London, might possibly have understood part, at least, of anything he might have overheard.

When Sergei rejoined her later, his manner suggested that he had not observed her somewhat protracted conversation with the foreigner by whom he seemed so much to feel threatened. Kirsty was glad of it: for some reason she could hardly explain, the conversation with John Harrow had overturned her composure, and she was happy to escape the half-expected icy chill of Sergei's displeasure.

Sergei did, however, observe that she was not in her usual spirits. He watched her polite but perfunctory replies to various of their acquaintance, and drew her slightly to one side.

'You seem tired, my dear. Do you wish to return home?'

It seemed to Kirsty that his voice was unexpectedly concerned—even tender—but perhaps it only seemed so because already she felt guilty at the wrong she planned to do him. She smiled faintly.

'I am, a little. Would it be wise to take our leave already?' she asked.

'We shall not be the first, and I certainly have no intention that we shall be the last!'

Princess Menshikova expressed concern that her 'dear friend', as she called Kirsty, should seek to go so soon, but observed that she did look a trifle haggard, an observation which Kirsty felt might have been more tactfully phrased, and was disconcertingly aware, from the half-smile on his lips, that Sergei, too, had noted the infelicity.

The Tsar was more jocular.

'Already, Christina Alexandrovna? You must acquire some Russian stamina! Model yourself on the sturdy cranberry that covers our woodland floor; the delicate English harebell would not long survive our climate, you know!'

In spite of herself, Kirsty felt her lips twitch. She curtsied.

'As you say, sir, though I confess I had never quite thought of myself as a cranberry!'

Peter looked at her. Then his short, barking laugh rang out. 'No, indeed, Christina Alexandrovna. Perhaps the model to put before you is our graceful silver birch, a tree which captures the heart of all Russians, for, like the people, it has a tenacity of purpose which its beauty often belies.'

He turned, feeling his wife's touch on his brocaded sleeve. Catherine had been observing the couple before them and had realised that with Kirsty, at least, all was not well.

'I hear the Countess Borodinova had exhibited great stamina in her excursions to explore this new city of ours,' she said. 'I am sure it is hardly surprising if she now feels a little tired.'

'To be sure, not many women have your strength, my dear,' the Tsar conceded, patting Catherine's hand affectionately. 'Very well, then, Sergei Ivanovich. Take your wife home.'

Nobody observed the glint in Prince Menshikov's eyes as he listened to these exchanges. Nor would they have attached any significance to it if they had, beyond recalling the liberality of cognac that had been flowing.

Sergei handed Kirsty gently into their barge which was waiting for them by the palace steps, and they were rowed in silence up the Greater Neva to their own home.

It was a slow journey that might have been tedious had Kirsty not had so much to occupy her mind. Three weeks! If John Harrow had said, 'We leave tomorrow', she would have been startled, but the impetus of the surprise would have been sufficient to carry her through the twenty-four hours. But she had three weeks to wait; twenty-one stretches of twenty-four hours—and quite possibly longer, since the Dutchman would be at the mercy of tides and winds. Three weeks in which to behave with complete normality. Three weeks in which an unguarded slip of the tongue might provoke a comment in the servants' quarters which might find its way upstairs again to the master of the house. Three weeks! Kirsty shivered as she began to have some comprehension of the scale of the dissimulation she must embark upon.

She felt Sergei's strong hand over her own. 'You shiver,' he said. 'Have you taken chill?'

She shook her head. 'I think not. It is just the night air.'

Sergei unfastened his cloak and put it round her shoulders, over her own.

'What troubles you, Kirsty?' he said gently.

'Why, nothing! What should trouble me?' she answered, a shade too quickly to carry conviction.

'If I knew that, I should not need to ask,' he said reasonably. 'But something troubles you, of that I am sure. Just as I am sure it arose this evening,' he added. 'Tell me, can it be laid at Menshikov's door?'

In the turmoil caused by John Harrow's pronouncement, she had all but forgotten the earlier exchange with their host, and now fastened upon it with relief as the cause of her woes.

'He frightens me a little,' she said truthfully. 'Would it not be wiser to adopt a more placatory manner to the man?'

'Wiser, perhaps, in some ways, but I'll not play the fawning spaniel to some upstart peasant who would wean my wife away from me if he could.'

'Surely not?' Kirsty exclaimed. 'He might very well try to seduce your wife—in fact, we have good reason to be sure of it—but I am sure none would be more surprised —or displeased!—than he if your wife left you for him!'

Sergei laughed. 'True enough, but you make it sound as though your seduction would be less serious to me than your desertion.'

'I cannot imagine why either should bother you unduly.'

'Can you not? Do you imagine I relish the thought of becoming a laughing-stock?'

'There is that, of course. I had forgotten how much that consideration would rankle with you.'

'Had you, indeed? May I enquire whether you were planning to be seduced or to desert me?'

Kirsty blessed the darkness that prevented him from seeing the colour that she felt rising in her cheeks. 'I don't think one *plans* to be seduced,' she said, avoiding the wider implication of the question.

'I am not at all sure that some women do not do precisely that,' he told her. 'I take it you are not one of them?'

'Of course not. Who would I make my target? Of course,' she added, unable to resist the imp of mischief that jumped unbidden into her thoughts despite her low spirits and mistrust of the turn the conversation had taken, 'there is Gavril Golovkin—a most attractive man.'

'But not for you, I think.' Sergei seemed genuinely amused, and the concern there had been in his voice was now quite absent. 'You would find he kept far too tight a hold on his purse-strings to suit your ideas.' He fingered the ropes of ruby beads round her neck. 'I cannot see Golovkin arraying you in these, much though he might admire the effect.'

'I would remind you, Sergei, that these were entirely your idea when you saw the colour of this overdress —which was also a suggestion of your own. I proposed neither.'

'True enough, and I had no desire to portray you as extravagant. I sought merely to point out that, because of the expense involved, Golovkin would not notice if you were in rags!'

'Now that *must* be an exaggeration!' Kirsty protested.

Sergei laughed. 'It is, of course, for the Tsar would most assuredly draw his attention to the shortcomings of your wardrobe.'

'Is *that* why you insist upon my dressing so opulently? I had often wondered. I must confess it is a little lowering to realise that it is only done to preclude an Imperial rebuke!'

Sergei chuckled and put a hand under Kirsty's chin, lifting it so that he was looking down into her eyes. Swiftly and unexpectedly, his lips sought hers in a brief and gentle kiss.

'At least I have succeeded in raising your spirits,' he said. 'Nevertheless, I would give a great deal to know what was troubling you. I fancy it was more than our noble Prince of Russia.'

Kirsty was not sorry to be spared the necessity of replying as they then arrived at their own landing-stage.

CHAPTER
THIRTEEN

LIKE HIS father, John Harrow had been agreeably surprised at the invitation to the Menshikovs' dinner. True, most westerners in St Petersburg had been invited, but it was none the less gratifying for that. His surprise on that occasion was nothing, however, compared to that with which three days later he received a request to present himself at the Menshikov Palace the following morning.

Carefully worded as a request, there was nevertheless more than a hint of a command in the message, as James Harrow was quick to spot.

'No, I have no idea what it may be about,' he told his son. 'All I know is that you go: if it is for ill he wishes to see you, your absence will only make matters worse; if for good, your absence will hardly be to your advantage.'

John tried very hard, but could think of no way in which he could have angered the man who stood second only to the Tsar in power. There were sins of neither omission nor commission that might be expected to bring down Menshikov's displeasure. It must therefore be only to commend him upon some aspect of his work that the Prince wished to see him, a conclusion which could only serve to demonstrate how unfamiliar John Harrow was with the workings of the Prince's mind.

The study into which he was ushered was small and of a surprisingly human scale when compared with the rooms in which the dinner party had been conducted. It appeared to be decoratively complete, too, though since much of the decoration consisted of shelves of ledgers and the parquet was of simple wooden blocks, it revealed a businesslike side of the Prince that few would have recognised in the more usually presented flamboyant peacock-figure.

'Sit down, Master Harrow,' the Prince said, graciously indicating a stool. 'You will join me in a cup of chocolate, I trust. A western indulgence I grew to enjoy in London.'

John took the seat offered and indicated that the trust was not misplaced. He began to feel considerably less apprehensive. Any lingering fears that he might inadvertently have done something that merited flaying alive were rapidly vanishing in the affability of his welcome.

The chocolate was delicious, as were the macaroons that accompanied it, and the Prince was affability itself, clearly intent upon putting his visitor at his ease.

'You have been here some months now, Master Harrow. What are your impressions?' he asked, sipping delicately from a fine china cup.

'I am amazed at the imagination that can conceive such a project,' John told him truthfully. 'I cannot yet imagine what the completed city will look like, but that it will be superb is already evident.'

'And what of the Nevsky Perspective, the paving of which you are to supervise?'

'A task to which I hope I shall be equal: a road more than twenty yards wide, well over a mile long and as straight as an arrow: it must compare only with the roads of the Roman Empire.'

'So the Tsar believes. And what of our climate? Do you enjoy living here?'

'The summer has been very pleasant. Winter, I imagine, will be less so, though having lived so long in Archangel I shall not find it unduly harsh, I think.'

'Ah, yes, of course—Archangel. That, I believe, is where you met the Countess Borodinova, is it not?' Menshikov's tone was as bland as ever.

'Kirsty Benmore as she then was. Yes, her mother being dead, my own mother took her under her wing, so to speak, and Kirsty became like a sister to me. She was married from our house in Moscow, you know.'

'A sister? So that is how you regard her.'

John flushed involuntarily. 'That was how we all regarded her—in Archangel.'

'And in Moscow?'

Suddenly realising that what he had taken to be firm ground had become as spongy as the Neva swamps, John began to step more warily. 'In Moscow she became the Countess Borodinova, which obviously entailed a change in the relationship.'

'Indeed? And would the marriage of your sister Mary change the relationship between you in any way?'

'No, of course not, but that is different!'

'Precisely so.' Menshikov's smile invited confidence.

'However, had Borodinov not made his offer, I fancy we should have been married in time,' John told him, thinking that perhaps frankness was called for.

'You had discussed it?'

'No, no, nothing like that: Kirsty had seemed so young, you see. But I had always assumed it had been so.'

'I see. And Christina Alexandrovna? Had she, too, always so assumed?'

'I don't know. I mean, I haven't asked her. But what alternative was there for her—until Sergei Borodinov made his offer, of course?'

'Very true.' Menshikov mentally discarded any idea he might have formed that an attachment of long standing might lie between the two young foreigners. John's ingenuous comments made it clear enough that any attachment was one-sided and probably the result of a fantasy entertained in the knowledge that its target was safely married.

'You must find it very painful to be obliged to watch the object of your affections living as the wife of another man,' he said sympathetically.

'I should not find it painful, were they happy together,' John said with a nobility that impressed himself more than his host. 'But that is not the case. Kirsty is miserably unhappy in this marriage,' he added in a burst of injudicious candour.

'How very strange that you should say so! She has always seemed to be remarkably content with her lot —which you will admit is a most comfortable one! Sergei Ivanovich, too, always seems most attentive. To an excessive degree, I have sometimes thought.'

'He is most assuredly very dog-in-the-mangerish,' John said bitterly. 'He would be happiest if she were locked away and spoke to no one. Kirsty puts a good face on things, but she is far from content, I promise you.'

'And you, being a noble soul and much in love, are proposing to rescue her, I gather?'

John stared at him. 'What makes you think that?'

Menshikov spread his hands in a gesture of apology. 'Forgive me—something I overheard. It involved a Dutch sea-captain, I believe.'

If the ground on which he stood had been spongy before, John now had the unpleasant feeling that it had given way completely and he was floundering in deep water with undercurrents he sensed but did not understand. He struggled desperately to keep his head above the tide.

'You misunderstand, Prince; you must have done. My only recent converse with the Countess was in English.'

'You have overlooked the fact that I accompanied Peter Alexeyevich to London some years ago. It is true that I would not wish to conduct a conversation in English, but I am quite capable of understanding most of what I hear.'

John's high colour faded, to be replaced with a deathly pallor as he realised the possible consequences of this revelation. To plot to abduct the wife of a boyar, a captain in the Preobrazhensky Guards, one of the richest men in Russia, at whose wedding the Tsar himself officiated? For the first time he realised the enormity of his scheme. If Menshikov had offered him a passport out of Russia and told him to leave within the hour, he would have accepted with alacrity.

Menshikov had other plans.

'I think the time has come for frankness,' said the man in whom frankness was a rare commodity. 'Make no mistake: I am fully aware of your situation. I have, however, no cause to love Count Borodinov; rather the reverse, though I am disinclined to elaborate upon the matter. Let me say only that I shall be perfectly happy to help someone to do him a bad turn. Tell me, why have you selected this Dutch sea-captain to aid your enterprise?'

'I know him well and can trust him,' John said, contenting himself with the thought that this was at least partly true. 'My acquaintance with such as he is limited.'

'And how exactly do you propose to get Christina Alexandrovna on board without her husband's knowledge?' Menshikov went on.

John frowned. 'That is the most difficult part of all. I have given it much thought and have been able to formulate no plan so far, but doubtless something will occur to me before it becomes necessary.'

'A touching faith in chance!' Menshikov commented. 'I, on the other hand, leave nothing to chance. This is what I suggest.'

Outside the study door, Yuri Denisovich Popov was obliged to subject his ears to considerable strain in order to catch what ensued, but it proved well worth the effort. Alexander Danilovich was a wily one, and no mistake! It was an honour to be one of these new-fangled footmen in his house, that was a fact, worth the hours of boredom for these odd little snippets of intrigue. It would make good listening in the tavern, too: a snippet here and a snippet there—worth a vodka or three, for sure.

Several good nights' sleep seemed to do little to restore Kirsty's spirits, Sergei observed. Indeed, she did not look as if she had had much sleep at all. Her naturally pale skin had become wan and had an unhealthy transparent look about it, and although she made an effort to join him in any conversation he initiated, she seemed unable to sustain it for long and soon lapsed into what appeared to be apathy, had he not had a strong suspicion her mind was elsewhere.

She seemed in a remarkably few days to have changed completely from the spirited and perverse creature he had married to a subdued and biddable one, offering no opposition to anything he proposed and venturing no suggestions or ideas of her own.

He was honest enough to admit to himself that she had, in fact, become the sort of wife he had thought he wanted. Now that he had such a wife, he was far from happy about it. Kirsty's perversity and wilfulness had irritated him to the point of exasperation, but now he realised that those very characteristics had given life with her an interest that it now lacked, and had provoked him into thinking, into questioning assumptions that he had thought unassailable. He had resented the compulsion so to question, but it had had its effect: his attitudes had subtly changed; the sort of wife he had thought he needed was no longer the sort of wife he wanted.

It occurred to him briefly—very briefly—that perhaps this new complaisance was simply a device on Kirsty's part to be the sort of wife he had indicated often enough that he wanted, in order to persuade him to change his mind about ending the marriage, but its onset had been too sudden. Whatever had caused the change had happened at the Menshikovs' dinner. He cast his mind back. Could it have been that dreadful cold meal? It might well have made anyone ill, but he had heard no rumour of anyone else being affected. St Petersburg was not the most healthy city, of course. Fever seemed more rife here than elsewhere, though this summer had been better than most in that respect. Nevertheless, Kirsty had been very active. Perhaps she had done too much. Looking back, it occurred to Sergei that the rigours of the journey to St Petersburg, followed by Kirsty's daily excursions of exploration, were in sharp contrast to the weeks of relative indolence at Zubstovoy—weeks which had culminated in her contemplating suicide. That brief, unhappy phase had also been characterised by a sort of inertia.

Whichever way he turned things in his mind, Sergei could come to no conclusion that would account for his wife's present mood. When the inevitable invitation to the Tsar's ball arrived, he found himself in a dilemma. He paced up and down the breakfast-salon, the card in one hand, tapping it against the fingers of the other. Then, his mind apparently made up, he ran quickly upstairs, pausing at the door of Kirsty's bedchamber and knocking lightly before going in.

Kirsty was breakfasting in bed, propped up by pillows across which her dark curls tumbled in artless disarray. Her face expressed her surprise at this unwonted visit, but she smiled, and Sergei did not feel unwelcome. He perched beside her on the edge of the bed, much as he had done on that last visit to her bedchamber at Zubstovoy.

'How are you feeling?' he asked.

'As well as ever,' she answered. It was her invariable

reply to that question and therefore meant nothing, he observed a shade bitterly.

He handed her the Tsar's invitation and waited while she read it. Her expression told him nothing.

'Do you wish to go?' he asked.

Kirsty smiled. Thinly, he thought. 'Do we have a choice?'

'I suppose not, unless you choose to plead illness. Do you wish to do so?'

'If you wish me to, then I shall be happy to.'

'I wish nothing that you do not wish for yourself,' he snapped. 'There are problems attached to going to a ball on that date, but they are not insuperable if you wish to attend. My only concern is your health. I fear you are not well—or, if your health is good, as you insist it is, then something is troubling you. Whatever may be the problem, if the ball will make matters worse, we shall decline.'

'I must say that I am curious to see how they manage to hold a ball in a house with so few completed rooms,' Kirsty said, a spark of her old spirit showing through.

'I have heard that a ballroom will be complete by then,' Sergei told her. 'That is to say, it will have walls and a roof. What ornamentation there will be, I cannot imagine, but Menshikov will contrive something, you may be sure.'

'Then we go,' Kirsty told him. Then an afterthought struck her. 'You mentioned problems attached to that date. What did you mean?'

His face clouded. 'Only that I am suddenly on guard duty that night. All this time in St Petersburg, and suddenly I must report for duty.'

'Can you not exchange your duty?'

He shook his head. 'With whom? All officers will be invited. No, you must go alone, and I will join you there when I have been relieved.'

Kirsty stared at him. 'Alone?' she echoed. 'Go to the ball alone? Sergei, you cannot mean it! Even in England it would not be at all the thing!'

'Let us say, without me, then. You will be safe enough in the barge and when I accept the invitation I will, if you have no objection, inform the Tsar of the circumstances and request his protection for you. That will be sufficient to avert all gossip, I assure you.'

Kirsty nodded her acquiescence in this scheme. 'I presume you will wish me to have a new toilette for the occasion?' she asked.

Sergei smiled grimly and an unaccustomed glitter in his eyes took Kirsty by surprise. 'Most assuredly. You will outshine Darya Menshikova on this occasion. Diamonds, I think. Your taste is always unassailable, my dear. I leave the toilette to you, but you will wear diamonds with it and you will surpass yourself.'

Kirsty smiled. 'A challenge, I perceive.'

'One to which I have no doubt you will rise,' Sergei told her, more than a hint of a smile in his eyes. When he saw the answering but tentative smile in her own eyes, his voice softened and he took her hand gently in one of his, covering it with the other and feeling it flutter like a captive moth. 'Tell me, Kirsty, what troubles you? I have no wish to see you unhappy.'

The agitation between his cupped hands before she withdrew from his hold was sufficient to tell him that he had touched a nerve.

'I am not unhappy. Nothing troubles me. I have told you so before.'

'Yes, you have—and you lie. Something does trouble you, and you are, I think, very unhappy. Can you not confide in me?'

Kirsty stared at him. What could she confide in him? That she was so unhappy at the thought of the impending annulment that she was planning to leave him before it could be put into effect? And what if he asked her why the dissolution of their marriage should make her unhappy? He had convinced himself that she had married him for his money and position and she was hardly likely to be able to persuade him of anything else at this late stage. So she just smiled, albeit a shade apprehensively.

'There is nothing to confide,' she said simply and untruthfully.

The words were no sooner uttered than she regretted them. Although he remained in the room, the coldness of his manner was a withdrawing from her as effective and conclusive as if a door had shut behind him.

'I see,' he said. 'There would not appear to be much more to say, would there?'

He rose from her bed and was gone, physically this time as well as emotionally.

Kirsty pushed the tray from her and turned restlessly on her pillows. She was making a success of nothing! Every so often she had the fleeting feeling that Sergei did not want to end their marriage, whatever his protestations to the contrary. She had had that feeling during this present interchange. He had not spoken as if there was any temporary facet to their marriage. Did a man planning to put aside his wife, tell her to outshine his enemy? Regretfully, Kirsty was obliged to conclude that, if that man was Sergei with his not inconsiderable Russian pride, he did. Very well, then. He was not to know that the Tsar's ball was likely to be the last function she would attend in Russia, for only five days remained after the ball before the probable date of her flight. Sergei would have his wish. She would outshine Princess Menshikova —and the Tsar's unacknowledged wife, if it came to that, though that was less difficult to achieve. Sergei would have a few days' satisfaction before she was gone for ever.

It flashed across her mind that the injury to his pride

when he discovered she had gone would be infinitely the greater, the more successfully she achieved his desired effect at the ball—but she pushed the thought aside. What difference did it make, after all? In a few months she would no longer be his wife. The result was the same. The only difference was that her planned ending would happen first. Thus fired with self-justification, she sent for Anna.

'They say that Madame de Fontainebleau comes to St Petersburg for the summer. Send a message to her to expect me this morning. We must plan my toilette for the Tsar's ball. Tell her she is expected to excel herself. When you have attended to that, lay out the blue morning toilette and order the palanquin. We enter the lists of fashion.'

Anna was not at all sure what the Countess's last remark meant, but she was delighted to see her mistress's return to her former vigour. She bobbed a curtsy.

'With pleasure, *barinya*,' she said, and hesitated. 'It gives me much satisfaction to see you return to your usual spirits. Sergei Ivanovich's visit has done you good. He will be pleased. He has been much worried about you, as we all have.'

Kirsty gave her maid a long, searching look. 'Is that so? Well, then, we must make up lost time, must we not? Be off with you and get that message to the dressmaker. I do not wish to be last in her queue.'

Not that there was any danger of that. Madame de Fontainebleau's reputation had been made in Moscow by the patronage of the beautiful young Countess Borodinova. No sooner had the Tsar's invitations been received than the talented French-woman was inundated with requests for her services from the prominent ladies of St Petersburg. The Countess's request was not, by several hours, the first to be received, but it was the first to receive Madame's attention. The Countess Borodinova had beauty, figure, taste and style. She also had a husband who begrudged no expense and who, unusually in any country, settled his accounts in full within a few days of their being rendered. It would display a remarkable lack of business acumen not to carry out Countess Borodinova's instructions before all others, and a lack of business acumen was not one of Madame de Fontainebleau's shortcomings.

She ushered the Countess and her maid into the large single-storey house she had taken for the summer, through the workroom where her Moscow seamstresses laboured, and opened the door of a long, narrow stockroom, for she not only made up her customers' own materials, but bought in bolts of fabric from Italian, French and Persian merchants, fabrics that her clients would not otherwise have seen. She knew her clients' tastes, and bought accordingly. They, if they considered the matter at all, regarded it as a happy chance that one of Madame's purchases had so precisely matched what they had in mind but could not quite put into words.

'Was there anything in particular you had in mind, Countess?' The introductory question was standard: if the lady had come with firm ideas, Madame need not make suggestions.

'Only that my husband desires me to outshine them all, and that I shall be wearing diamonds,' Kirsty told her.

Madame beamed. 'Then I have just the thing. The Countess will not object to setting, rather than following, a style, I take it?'

A smile and a glint in Kirsty's eyes told her all she wanted to know, and the dressmaker expanded.

'I have made enquiries, Countess. The ballroom, which is unfinished except for the walls, the roof and a

quite exceptional floor, is to be draped from ceiling to
floor in sapphire silk, gathered and festooned, so that,
from within, one appears to be inside a huge silken
pavilion. It will be lit by double rows of chandeliers of
the best Bohemian crystal. (One cannot but hope that
they do not set fire to the silk, but I dare say that has been
allowed for.) The Princess Menshikova, who has a
desire to stand out against her sapphire surroundings,
will be dressed in crimson.' A scarcely perceptible sniff
indicated Madame's opinion of this solution to the
Princess's dilemma. 'The Tsar's consort will be wearing
cloth-of-gold. This is what I suggest for you, my lady.'

One of her apprentices lifted down two bolts of fabric.
Madame unrolled the first: a heavy ivory satin completely embroidered with a delicate design in silver
and the merest hint of pale metallic blue consisting of
flowers, on some of which had settled tiny moths. The
outline of their wings was edged with a thin gold thread.
The effect was both ethereal and sumptuous.

'The underskirt,' Madame explained.

The second bolt was a material such as Kirsty had
never seen before . It was too light in texture to be
cloth-of-silver, yet that was the closest she could come
to defining it. Interspersed with flashes of the same
metallic blue, it shimmered even in daylight.

'The overdress, Countess,' Madame said, holding it
against the satin so that Kirsty could see how well the
two fabrics looked together.

'I propose a style that is just beginning to appear at the
French Court,' Madame went on. 'There will be no train
and less bustle, and we shall use only lace of silver
thread. I shall puff the underskirt out with starched
petticoats, and the overskirt will be looped up. Every
gadroon will be fixed either with a bow, or . . . Olga,
fetch Mynheer Andela.' She turned to Kirsty. 'Forgive
the interruption, Countess, but in anticipation, I must

admit, of this discussion, I have taken the liberty of speaking to Mynheer Andela, a Dutch jeweller. You know his work?'

Kirsty was obliged to say that she did not, and wondered what part he would play in this, since Sergei had indicated that he would be obtaining the diamonds. The Dutchman was small and rotund, quite lacking the obsequiousness Kirsty knew was generally accorded to wealthy potential clients. She soon realised that this was because his pride in his craftsmanship far outweighed any other consideration: it was an honour to own one of Mynheer Andela's pieces, and any deference was due the jeweller.

He produced a well-padded, soft suede pouch and from it took, with great care, a small package of the softest tissue. This he laid on the table beside the fabrics and gently opened. The contents he placed on the back of his hand and held towards Kirsty. There glimmered a small moth, no more than an inch from wing-tip to wing-tip. The edges of the wings and the veins within were of the thinnest gold and the main fabric of the wings was of thin slices of aquamarine. The effect of setting each slice separately between the gold veins was not dissimilar to that of faceting a stone, and so they caught the light. At a nod from Madame, the apprentice lit candles and closed the shutters. Mynheer Andela put the moth on to a ball of the silver cloth and moved them across the light. The effect was magical. Kirsty was delighted.

'You wish to put one of these at every intersection?' she asked.

Madame shook her head. 'No. That would be too obvious. Most of them will have small bows, but just here and there we will have one of Mynheer's moths —just three or four of them in all. Their shape is not dissimilar to the bow: seen in the flickering light of a thousand candles, people will not be sure whether they are seeing bows or moths. Intriguing, do you not think?'

'Fascinating,' Kirsty agreed and turned to the jeweller. 'Will you be able to complete the work in time?'

He nodded. 'For the gown and for the Countess's hair,' he said.

'My hair?' Kirsty turned to the dressmaker. 'How so? It will surely conflict with the *fontange*?'

'There will be no *fontange*, my lady, if you will accept the suggestion. Instead your hair will be curled and worn slightly *poudré*. It would be too drastic to give no height: the eyes of the beholders are too accustomed to the *fontange* to accept its total absence. I suggest an aigrette —two or three white egret feathers springing from a diamond clasp; a clasp that will itself be a diamond moth.'

Kirsty smiled. 'Madame, I bow to you. You have the vision of a genius.' She turned to Mynheer Andela. 'And you, sir, the craftsmanship of an angel. I shall mention your work to my husband.'

It was the jeweller's turn to smile. 'He knows it, Countess. Your diamonds will be cut and set by me. It was I who fashioned your ruby beads—a task of technical complexity belied by the resulting simplicity.'

'You have good cause to be proud of your work,' Kirsty told him. 'I look forward to wearing it.'

She returned home in high good humour. 'I think Count Borodinov's expectations will be realised, Anna,' she remarked, as her maid helped her to change.

'Oh, yes, *barinya*. There can be no doubt of that!' the maid replied.

CHAPTER
FOURTEEN

PETER ALEXEYVICH, Tsar of All the Russias, ducked under the low lintel into the small bedchamber that also served as study in his tiny cottage. Catherine, his beloved, sensible Catherine, was still in bed, having eaten an extremely hearty breakfast, if the tray beside her was anything to go by. She did not normally indulge herself in this way, but she was increasing again and if she felt the need for more rest, he was not the man to deny it her.

He paced back and forth across the room as well as any giant can pace across a room no more than five yards wide and fully furnished. Then he stood looking out of the leaded window across the Neva. He was frowning and Catherine noticed the tic which indicated a disturbed state of mind.

'What do you know of the Borodinovs' marriage?' he asked at last.

'No more than you, I imagine. Why?'

'Are they happy, do you think?'

Catherine considered carefully. 'As to that, I know neither of them well enough to be sure, but I think perhaps the Countess is not entirely so. Sergei Ivanovich maintains such an inscrutable mien that I could not even hazard a guess. Why do you ask?'

Peter turned away from the window and sat on the edge of the huge carved and painted wooden bed which, made to accommodate his immense height, occupied so much of the small room. His frown deepened.

'When he sought my permission to marry this foreigner, I formed the distinct impression that it was a love-match. It would not be putting it too strongly to say that he was infatuated. He was certainly adamant that it would be Miss Benmore or nobody. Some incident in Archangel, I gathered. I have heard hints—nothing definite, you understand—that he now means to put her away. There has been nothing in his manner towards her to support the idea, not in public, at least, but if that is the case, I suppose it would do no harm if someone meddled.'

Catherine looked at him steadily. 'I do not understand. Explain, I beg you. My opinion is of little use if I am in ignorance of the facts.'

'I had a visitor at breakfast. An informer. A very minor informer who would not normally expect to contact his Tsar, but in this instance he had little choice, since it would otherwise reach Menshikov's ears.'

'From which I infer that he felt that would be unwise.'

'Very, I imagine, since what he had to impart involved our friend.'

'Alexashka has been a dear friend to us both, but I cannot deny that he has exceeded his powers in the past and will certainly do so again—it is his nature.'

'This is not precisely a matter of exceeding his powers,' Peter said. 'It seems that this informer frequents the same tavern as some of the Prince's servants, in particular a footman who, finding his occupation somewhat dull, relieves the tedium by listening at keyholes.'

'And is then sufficiently indiscreet to repeat in the tavern what he has heard in the palace?'

'Precisely. Menshikov must be warned, of course, but that is not my immediate concern. It seems that our friend is plotting with a young Englishman who has known the Countess since she first came to Russia. They propose to abduct her.'

Catherine stared at him. 'Does the young fool know the punishment if he is caught?'

Peter shrugged. 'With Menshikov planning it, it was unlikely he would be. It would certainly have been very difficult for anyone to learn of the plan, had it not been for our friend's footman.'

'You will have the young man arrested, of course.'

'I think not. He would implicate Alexashka, and I would be obliged to banish him for a time—a loss which is more severe than the offence. He is, after all, only meddling in the affairs of a man he hates. No, John Harrow must be allowed to continue in Petersburg as if nothing had happened. Should he later ask to return to England, his wish will be granted and we shall not be welcoming him back. I am, in fact, quite uncertain whether to let matters take their course. If Borodinov is mindful to put her away, it might be best to do nothing.'

'But you do not know for certain that that is his intention!'

'Which is why I need to know if you think their relationship is such as to make it probable.'

'The only way to find out is to ask him,' Catherine pointed out.

'I am loath to do so, however: if it is untrue, he will be deeply offended, and if it is under consideration, he will feel I am pushing him into it.'

'Do you know any more about this plan than its general outline?'

'Oh, yes, Menshikov has it all worked out. On the night of the ball Borodinov will be on duty—our friend has arranged that, of course. The Countess will therefore come alone. Borodinov has already asked me to keep her under my protection until he himself arrives.'

'Hardly the act of a man planning to divest himself of his wife, surely?' Catherine commented.

'Perhaps not, but it is the act of an honourable man, and that Sergei Ivanovich most certainly is. It seems that the Countess's barge will not go to the Menshikovs' palace, but on down river to the port where an English captain who owes our friend several favours will take the lady on board and set sail immediately for England.'

'Does Christina Alexandrovna know of this arrangement?'

'Apparently not. She is not expecting to be abducted until several days later. Neither is she to be told of any change in the arrangements,' Peter added.

'Then the plan cannot succeed,' Catherine declared. 'No woman would go quietly aboard a strange ship!'

'John Harrow will be on board to greet her. She will no doubt accept his explanation of a change of plan.'

That seemed extremely probable but Catherine shook her head. 'No, my dear,' she said. 'There is something wrong here. I feel it in my bones. I said I did not think Christina Alexandrovna was happy. That is true. But it does not mean that I think she does not love her husband. When he comes across a room towards her, her face lights up. I think he is oblivious of the fact, but I promise you, others are not. In the same way I have observed a tenderness in his eyes when he looks upon her and thinks he is unobserved. I do not know what may lie behind these rumours of divorce you mention, but I would not wish to see them parted at the instigation of another.'

'You do not think she might be in love with this John Harrow?' Peter asked doubtfully.

'When she has met Sergei?' Catherine's astonishment was evident. 'My dear, I promise you that *no* woman who had once been the object of Sergei Borodinov's attentions could *possibly* be in love with John Harrow! No, that is certainly not the case.'

Catherine sat in silent deliberation after this emphatic pronouncement and when she finally spoke, it was in tones of strong resolution.

'Petya, are you willing to leave this matter in my hands for the time being?' she asked.

'What do you propose to do?'

'I am not entirely sure, but I do have an idea. I would prefer to have your permission to develop it for myself. May I do so?'

'Of course.'

'Good. You will not look askance if I indulge in a course of action which seems . . . unconventional?'

'Probably, but I promise not to interfere.'

She smiled and patted his hand affectionately. 'How well we deal together,' she said. 'It was a lucky day for us both that Alexashka enabled us to meet. Now go away; you have given me much to do.'

Thus summarily dismissing one of the most powerful men in the world, she climbed out of bed and called for her maid.

CHAPTER
FIFTEEN

KIRSTY SURVEYED herself in the looking-glass, turning this way and that and finally commanding Anna to fetch another full-length glass so that she might observe the back. She was not sure that she was entirely happy with the powdered hair, but the overall result was undeniably effective. Sergei had told her to outshine everyone. She rather thought she would. She could not help wishing he were at home. He had never seen her in this gown, the complexities of its manufacture being such that it had only been delivered that very morning, and she was rather sorry to be denied that quick flash of admiration that her first appearance on such occasions usually provoked. It was not often that she won unqualified approbation from her husband, and its rarity made it the more to be treasured. She knew, too, how close a guard he kept on his expression, and she must therefore be sure to keep her eyes on the door so that she would not miss his first involuntary reaction when he saw her.

She sighed. Thinking of Sergei called up before her eyes the image of the man: tall and strong with the high Slav cheekbones that gave the handsome face an almost barbaric aspect: the long fingers that could grip like a vice yet be infinitely tender when occasion warranted. It was, she thought, one of the great sadnesses of her marriage that he had considered tenderness to be so seldom warranted.

It was too late to alter that, of course. This would be the last function they would attend together, for within the week she would be on her way to Holland and thence to England. She was a little perturbed to have heard no more from John. She supposed there was little he could do before his Dutch sea-going friend returned to St Petersburg, but, even so, some indication that John had matters in hand would have been reassuring. In all probability he would be at tonight's ball, so he should be able to find an opportunity of contacting her.

This thought, which might have been expected to be reassuring to a woman planning to abscond with a man other than her husband, had the opposite effect: any conversation would have to take place before Sergei's arrival, for he certainly would not permit it afterwards, and since she would be under the Tsar's protection to start with, it was unlikely that John would feel inclined to intrude upon the royal party. In fact, she realised suddenly, she was none too eager to meet John at all. John was not the man with whom she wished to spend the rest of her life, though she was undoubtedly doomed to do exactly that.

But that was for the future. Tonight she was still the Countess Borodinova and there was one thing of which she could make sure: Sergei would get his money's worth. Taking one last look at herself, she signalled to Anna to fetch the pale blue satin cloak lined and edged with Arctic fox, and arranged it around her shoulders.

She went down the sweeping staircase and across the hall, through the silently opened doors and down the steps to the embankment. She could see the barge waiting at the foot of their private landing-stage. At the top of these steps she hesitated. She thought she knew the Borodinov boatmen. These, surely, were strangers? She looked beyond them to the barge. This was not theirs, either. It was not entirely unfamiliar, but Kirsty had never taken much interest in the niceties of boat design and could not therefore decide precisely where she had seen it before. All she could be certain of was that the Borodinov barge was a plainer affair, lacking

the gilded gingerbread that adorned the superstructure
of this more sumptuous vessel.

She paused, annoyed. 'What is the meaning of this?'
she demanded. 'This is a private landing-stage, and you
are occupying the space needed for my own barge which
will be here presently.' She looked upstream as she
spoke, expecting to see the Borodinov barge hove to in
the vicinity. There was no sign of it.

'If you are the Countess Borodinova, there is no
mistake,' the boatman said, and produced a sealed letter
from his pocket. 'If you will but read this, *barinya*, you
will understand.'

Kirsty took the letter from him, and moving closer to
the light of one of the flaring torches that lit the steps
from brackets at either side, broke the seal. The seal was
the Tsar's. The brief letter bore Catherine's signature.

It said simply that since the Countess Borodinova was
to attend the ball under the Tsar's protection, it seemed
appropriate that this should be demonstrated, and that
it therefore gave the Imperial couple much pleasure
to send their own conveyance for her. It added that
Count Borodinov had been informed of the change of
plan.

Kirsty's brow cleared. It was a sensible plan, though
perhaps a pity that it had so obviously been thought of at
so late a stage: she would have preferred advance notice.
Presumably the barge had seemed familiar because she
had seen it when they left the Menshikov Palace after the
dinner: it would have been standing by to take the Tsar
and his wife home the moment they decided to leave.
She allowed herself to be handed down into the little
cabin, and leant back against the cushioned swabs to
enjoy the smooth journey downstream.

Her thoughts must have wandered, she realised with a
start, aware that the barge had bumped imperceptibly
against a landing-stage. Surely the journey had taken a

remarkably short time? Or had she simply not noticed, being lost in her own thoughts?

She glanced out, expecting to see the lights of the Menshikov Palace lining the embankment, but the embankment was in almost total darkness, the only illumination coming from the glazed windows of a small cottage. The Tsar's cottage! she realised with a start.

The boatmen had secured the barge now, and one came forward to help her to disembark.

'Why are we here?' Kirsty asked him. 'It is to the Menshikov Palace I am meant to be taken. That is some way further downstream.'

'That's right, *barinya*, and we shall wait here for that purpose. But our instructions are to bring you first to the cottage.' He noticed her uncertainty. 'In truth, *barinya*, I know no more. Those are my instructions. I do know, however, that Peter Alexeyevich went to the Palace alone,' he added helpfully.

The man seemed to be telling the truth, Kirsty thought, but it was all very strange. She accepted his proferred hand and stepped ashore, not displeased that he and a fellow-crewman accompanied her across the dark embankment. She was suddenly conscious, in this relatively deserted spot, of her diamonds.

Their arrival had clearly been heard, for the cottage door opened before the boatman had had time to knock, and she found herself in a tiny hall, a small antechamber between the two rooms.

The door of one of them opened and Catherine stood there, short, plump, smiling, and resplendent in cloth-of-gold. She came forward and kissed Kirsty on both cheeks before her visitor had time to curtsy. Then she stood aside to let Kirsty pass.

'Come in, my dear. You will find it crowded, but only with furniture. The living-room is crowded with people. At least here we may be private.'

The small room certainly was crowded, though this was largely because of the presence of the huge bed, but the room also contained a large desk, a small table with a looking-glass, and two chairs of the sort designed for utility rather than comfort.

Catherine chuckled. 'Rather different from the Borodinov Palace, by all accounts,' she said. 'Peter Alexeyevich plans a Summer Palace across the Neva eventually, but it will be quite small. He has rather grander plans for a country palace, but I am not supposed to know about that, so I shall be obliged if you would not mention it.'

Privately thinking that the opportunity to do so was unlikely to arise, Kirsty expressed her willingness to forget all about it. She was puzzled by Catherine's presence.

'Forgive my curiosity,' she said eventually, 'but I understood that the Tsar was already at the ball. I conclude, since you are here, that that cannot be so. Is it your intention that I shall arrive with you?'

'Oh, no, that is not my intention at all,' Catherine told her. 'It is perfectly true that Peter has gone on ahead and is at this moment receiving guests alone. As you see, I am temporarily indisposed, but I intend to join him later.'

Kirsty thought it would be difficult to look less indisposed than the Tsar's wife, who was positively bursting with health, but she wisely refrained from comment.

'Sit down beside me,' Catherine commanded, patting the bed and pushing out of the way a delicately embroidered lawn chemise that a maid had failed to put away. 'We use the bed as a divan—the room is too small to do anything else. I have gone to considerable trouble to arrange this little chat, and I must join the Tsar before too long. I shall not, therefore, waste time in preamble. Are you in love with John Harrow?'

'Good gracious, no!' Surprise brought out the truth without hesitation.

'I knew it!' Catherine declared triumphantly. 'How gratifying to be right! Now tell me: if you are not in love with him, why are you planning to elope with him?'

The colour drained from Kirsty's cheeks. 'How do you . . . ? I don't know what you mean!'

'How do I know? That was your first thought. That is too long a story to explain now. Let me just ask if you knew that you were to go tonight.'

Kirsty shook her head adamantly. 'You are mistaken, madame. It is planned for about five days hence.'

'So you did not know. Good. The original plan was for five days hence, weather and tides permitting. The changed plan was for tonight. You would not have been taken to the ball, my dear, but a replacement crew would have rowed you downstream to an English merchant-man with Master Harrow on board.'

How Catherine knew all this, Kirsty could not imagine, but her pronouncement was so precise that Kirsty was convinced of the accuracy of her facts.

'So Sergei would have arrived to find me not there. Oh, no! How humiliating for him!'

'Why should that trouble you if you are planning to leave him?'

'But I was not planning to leave him in so public a way!' Kirsty protested.

'You still have not told me why you are planning to leave him at all,' Catherine reminded her.

Kirsty's shoulders slumped miserably. 'He plans to annul our marriage,' she whispered. 'I thought it better to get away before he could do so.'

'So that rumour is true,' Catherine said thoughtfully. 'And why does he plan this annulment?'

'He feels that the marriage was a mistake, that I

accepted only because he had wealth and position. The trouble is that he is right: I did.'

'You surprise me! Forgive me, my dear, but I have observed you. You do not behave like a woman who married for money and station. Such a woman does not follow her husband with her eyes, nor do her eyes light up when he appears.'

Kirsty smiled ruefully. 'When my father told me of the offer, I had no idea that I had ever met Count Borodinov. I accepted the offer because no better one was likely to arise, and I had no objections to the marriage on any grounds.'

'But you had met Sergei Ivanovich?'

'Oh, yes, a year or so previously, in Archangel. He . . . he performed a small service for me which earned my eternal gratitude.'

Catherine privately thought that the same small service performed by an elderly boyar might not have provoked those shining eyes and that wistful voice, but she kept the thought to herself.

'When did you realise that the man who came to your help and the man who had offered for you were the same?'

'After the ceremony.'

'But surely all was explained on the wedding night?' Catherine asked.

Kirsty shook her head. 'I suppose it seems foolish, but I was too . . . too apprehensive to want to talk. And then the wedding night was not . . . was not what I had imagined; it was not altogether a success,' she finished lamely, the tears welling in her eyes at the recollection.

By all that's holy! Catherine thought, I declare the fool forced her! Surely the man realised what he had married! 'You were a virgin?' she asked.

'Of course!' Kirsty blushed as she remembered that Catherine had very definitely not been when she had married the Tsar, since she had already borne him children.

Catherine seemed oblivious to any implication the remark might have. 'Put out of your mind everything that has caused friction between you,' she said. 'Just tell me this: do you love Sergei Ivanovich?'

'Yes,' Kirsty said simply. 'Oh, yes.'

'And why do you think he offered for you?'

Kirsty frowned. 'I do not know. I have never been able to decide, and he has never given me any indication.'

'Peter says he was infatuated. Now infatuation is not love, and Peter Alexeyevich, much as I love him, is not the most observant man in matters such as this. If you had the chance to find out, to meet Sergei on a footing not based on misconceptions, perhaps even to start again, would you take it?'

Kirsty stared at her, not entirely able to see the object of this questioning. 'There is nothing I would like more,' she said. 'But matters have gone too far. We cannot retrace our steps.'

'Perhaps not, but you could set out on a different path. Do me just one small favour.'

'Of course. What is it?' It seemed a change of subject, and Kirsty could not hide the surprise in her voice.

'Stay here tonight. I have had a night chemise laid out for you,' and Catherine indicated the garment Kirsty had supposed was there by accident. 'I promise you nothing except a long wait. Ring the bell if you want food or drink.' She paused and surveyed Kirsty's gown. 'It seems a pity to let such exquisite workmanship go to waste, but you will probably have another opportunity to put us all in the shade! Make free of the toiletries on the table. You will be disturbed only if you wish to be. And now I must go. I have lingered too long. It would never do for people to think the Tsar had been deserted!'

With a final warm chuckle, she kissed Kirsty again and went quietly out. When Kirsty strained her ears, she could just make out the gentle splash of oars. She crossed the little room and closed the shutters. Then she began to unlace her bodice.

CHAPTER
SIXTEEN

IF GUESTS were surprised at Catherine's absence from the Tsar's side to greet them at the Imperial Ball, they took good care not to discuss it openly and to accept Peter's explanation that she was indisposed. It was very strange, for they did everything together, yet the Tsar seemed quite unperturbed by her absence: there was no sign of that nervous tic that so often forewarned of his displeasure and, indeed, there were those who thought he looked more like a man relishing a private joke. It was true that Catherine was said to be increasing again, but that had never kept her from Peter's side before, yet if she was unwell on this occasion, surely he would not look quite so much like a dog who had just purloined a goose?

Their speculation deepened with Catherine's arrival, plump and cheerful in cloth-of-gold, a fabric eminently suited to her putative station, if not to her figure. Peter was clearly delighted to see her and equally clearly not at all surprised. He led her immediately into the line of dance.

'I hope the delay was profitable,' he said when the movement brought them together.

Catherine had to wait until the dance repeated itself before she could answer. 'So far, it has been worth while. Let us hope the second stage will be equally so.'

When they left the floor, she whispered, 'You have given Alexashka no hint, I hope.'

'And give him time to adjust his plans? You know me for a better general than that! You know, too, that fond as I am of our friend, there is a not inconsiderable satisfaction in outwitting him. I think perhaps we should not mention that we shall require the loan of a sofa or two after you next return here.'

Catherine beamed at him. 'My own thoughts exactly,' she said.

It was nearly midnight before the tall form of Count Borodinov came through the doors. Still in his regimentals, he hesitated in the doorway as his eyes raked the room in search of his wife. He frowned, puzzled. Surely she would not have been indiscreet enough to absent herself from the throng, no matter for how innocent a purpose? He caught sight of Prince Menshikov watching him from across the room, a smile on his thin lips, and Sergei's frown deepened. He made his way as quickly as he could through the crowd towards the royal couple, and bowed.

'You have made good time,' the Tsar commented. 'We did not look to see you until after midnight.'

'I had an incentive,' Sergei replied, and his eyes once more swept the room and once more caught Menshikov's amused surveillance. 'I do not see Christina Alexandrovna. Does she take refreshment?'

Peter chuckled. 'Quite probably. My dear?' He turned to Catherine, who was frantically fanning a somewhat heightened complexion.

'Petya, forgive me. I feel *most* unwell. You must remain here, of course, but perhaps Sergei Ivanovich would be so very kind as to escort me back to the cottage?'

Sergei looked from one to the other of them. Catherine did not look unwell—rather the reverse, in fact, but one could hardly accuse her of lying. Neither could one decline what amounted to a command. But where was Kirsty? He was loath to leave the ballroom without a word to her.

He bowed. 'If Peter Alexeyevich has no objection, it

will be my privilege. But is it not possible for me to have a few words with my wife? I would not like her to think I had been delayed.'

'She will not be expecting you just yet,' the Tsar assured him. 'Meanwhile, Catherine is looking positively feverish, do you not think? Your escort would be much appreciated, and delay would not, I fancy, be desirable.'

Sergei was left with no choice. The only consolation he could find was in Menshikov's face. The thin-lipped, knowing smile had been replaced by a puzzled frown. There was a buzz of surprise from the assembled guests as their hostess, having arrived long after their host, departed again so unexpectedly. All eyes went to the Tsar's face. What was Peter Alexeyevich making of it all? But Peter Alexeyevich seemed quite unworried though possibly mildly amused at the interest, so they shrugged and returned to the pleasures of the evening.

Sergei handed Catherine into the barge and seated himself opposite her. The boatmen cast off and, as Catherine felt the oars push the barge out into the current, she sighed.

'That was the most difficult part,' she said. 'I was afraid for a moment that you would refuse to accompany me.'

'I could hardly do that!' Sergei said, surprised.

'Nevertheless, I think you came close to it,' she said shrewdly. 'Kirsty is not there, you know.'

Sergei started. 'Not there? What do you mean? Forgive me, madam, but she was promised royal protection!'

'Which she is enjoying, I promise you. Tell me, Sergei Ivanovich, is it true you plan to put her away?'

There was a silence while he weighed up the implications of her question, then he nodded. 'I had been trying to force myself to the point of petitioning the Tsar to that effect,' he said.

'If you had to force yourself, surely it suggests that annulment is not the answer?'

'Perhaps. I do not know. I keep hoping, and am always disappointed. It was a mistake. Kirsty wants no more than money and station. I can offer those, but I ask more in return than mere duty.'

'Is money and position all you offer her?' Catherine asked gently.

He stared at her. 'It is all she wants,' he said. 'It is the least I have to offer.'

'I think you do not understand your wife. Are you aware that she was planning to leave Russia before you could implement any scheme for annulment?'

Sergei sat very still. 'Why should she do that? I should have seen she was generously provided for.'

'I am sure you would, but that would only weigh with a woman who was concerned merely with material considerations. It would not unfluence a woman who was desperately unhappy.'

'She is not happy, that is true, though I have given her all I could to make her so.'

'No, Sergei, you have not given her all you could. You have given her all you thought she wanted, which is not at all the same thing.' She paused to give him time to absorb the implications of what she had said before she continued. 'Would it surprise you to learn that she was planning to elope with John Harrow?'

His shoulders slumped as if at the confirmation of an unwelcome truth. 'No, I suppose not,' he said grudgingly. 'I think she would have married him eventually if I had not come along with a more advantageous offer. I have often suspected that she loved him.'

Catherine threw her hands in the air in despair. 'Oh, Sergei, what a fool you are! She no more loves John

Harrow than she loves Peter Alexeyevich! Less, in fact, since, as the wife of a Russian noble she is obliged to love the Tsar. Now listen to me; we are nearly at the cottage. At my instigation Kirsty has been there all evening. All the servants except my maid have leave of absence until noon tomorrow, and there are two guards. Apart from that, the cottage is empty. Peter and I shall not return tonight. The place is yours. I suggest that you use the time to become better acquainted with your wife. I shall return to the ball—and to break the news to Prince Menshikov that we shall require a sofa when the guests have gone.'

Sergei looked at her doubtfully. 'Will it not look very strange that you leave the ball indisposed, under my escort, and return without me, perfectly recovered?'

'Very strange,' she agreed. 'It will give rise to endless chatter, but I am certainly not one to deprive people of the simple pleasures of life!'

'I was thinking of the Tsar. Will he not require an explanation?'

Catherine laughed. 'Not at all. If anything, he will be wondering why I have not already returned. Do you think I would meedle thus without his connivance? Go, Sergei. Waste no more time!'

He rose from his seat and turned to step out of the barge, and was aware of Catherine's restraining hand on his sleeve. He paused and looked enquiringly at her.

'Have a care, Sergei,' she said. 'Do not overlook the value of tenderness.'

The maid who let Sergei into the cottage said nothing, but nodded silently in the direction of the bedchamber. Sergei tapped gently on the door, and went in.

Kirsty looked very small and fragile in the vast bed, her dark curls, from which all trace of powder had been removed, framing the delicate beauty of her face against the goosedown pillows. The softly flickering light of a branch of candles cast a warm glow across the little room.

Kirsty looked up at him shyly. 'You came,' she said simply.

'Were you not expecting me?'

'Not precisely: Catherine was very cryptic. I guessed what she meant, and guessed, too, that she did not know whether you would agree.'

'There was nothing for me to agree to: the lady gave me no choice.'

'I see.' Kirsty's voice was suddenly flat.

'You sound disappointed. Can it be that you hoped I would come?'

'Would you believe me if I said I did?'

'Why should I not? I have never found you untruthful, and it is certainly what I would want to hear.'

'I have never told you only what you wanted to hear,' Kirsty reminded him.

'Indeed not. Quite the reverse, I recall.' He looked around the cluttered room before removing his coat, his boots and his cravat and tossing them on a stool. He sat on the edge of the bed and took her slender hand in his. He raised it to his lips and kissed her fingers, one by one. 'Kirsty, Kirsty,' he whispered. 'Where have we gone wrong?'

She raised her free hand and stroked his thick, dark hair back from his brow. 'I do not know. I have gone over and over and cannot pinpoint the moment. I only feel it would have been different had I known the offer came from the man from Archangel!'

He kissed her then, crushing her willing body so closely against his own that he felt the beating of her heart beneath her breast. And when that kiss, so long and tender, was done, he held her still, gazing down into her eyes as if to read her heart there.

'I have loved you from that day,' he said softly. 'I have had many women, but none that aroused such feelings in me as you did. I vowed then and there that, with or without the Tsar's approval, I would make you my wife.'

'And for me you formed the magic of dreams. I did not know who you were, nor enquired, for what good would it have done me? I never thought to see you again, but the memory of you stayed with me. I imagined that it would sustain me through a marriage of convenience.'

His hand strayed down her neck, loosening the drawstring of the chemise and thrilling to the unconscious thrust of her breasts through the thin material. His kiss was harder, and she matched it with a pleading urgency that fired his veins, an urgency far different from the innocent compliance that had begun their wedding night.

There were questions he longed to ask, but instinct told him that this was not the time. His open kiss forced her head back against his supporting arm, and as their tongues met in sensual dalliance, the modest barrier of the chemise was broken and the full glory of her body was his to explore. It was an exploration with no barriers, their mutual pleasure only heightened by the hiatus of her fingers gently unfastening the buttons of his shirt, and when they lay together naked after the brief interval, Kirsty welcomed the gentle resumption of his caresses.

When she sensed that the time had come when mutual desire had reached beyond caress, she gave herself willingly, inviting the exquisite pain of his entry, her mouth still seeking his demandingly, imploringly, until the thrusting crescendo within her reached its climax and Sergei knew that her cry was one of ecstasy—and he rejoiced in that knowledge.

The morning was well advanced before they awoke, and Kirsty knew the joy of awakening within the tender strength of a man's arms. They lay together in quiet embrace, listening to the sounds of the city muffled by the shutters of their borrowed room.

Kirsty turned to look at Sergei's eyes, still vague with half-remembered sleep.

'I love you,' she whispered.

His answer was a kiss that silenced speech, the gentle, loving kiss of one who needs no reassurance.

'There is something else,' she said hesitatingly.

'You have told me the only thing that matters to me,' Sergei replied.

It was several moments before Kirsty was able to resume the conversation.

'The apple tree, Sergei,' she insisted at last. 'Do you think . . . I mean, would you mind if we planted another one in the same place?'

He looked down at her for a moment before kissing her gently once more. 'I thought it made the room inconveniently dark,' he reminded her teasingly.

'It did, but all the same . . .'

'We shall plant our own apple tree, and we shall make sure that no future Borodinov bride finds it inconveniently placed. I like the idea.'

Kirsty smiled contentedly and Sergei looked down at the delicate features now, for the first time, in the full bloom of that beauty which flowers only when it knows its love to be fully reciprocated. No hint of sleep was in his eyes, replaced as it was by something akin to the glitter Kirsty had seen there once or twice before.

'Tomorrow, my love, I shall teach you chess,' he said.

She looked at him. 'What is wrong with today?'

'Today I would remain master,' he replied. 'Let me enjoy it while I may.'

'I would not have it otherwise.'

He smiled down at her. 'A fine sentiment, but one unlikely to survive our first disagreement.'

'At least believe me when I say I shall try to bear it in mind when that situation arises,' she said.

'I believe you implicitly, my love. Fortunately for our future happiness, I am resigned to your inevitable failure.'

If Kirsty felt his comment to be unduly harsh, she had to acknowledge that its severity was considerably mitigated by the embrace which effectively stifled her protest, an embrace which she made no attempt to evade. There would be no disagreement between them yet awhile.

Masquerade Historical Romances

New romances from bygone days

Masquerade Historical Romances, published by Mills & Boon, vividly recreate the romance of our past. These are the two superb new stories to look out for next month.

THE COUNTRY COUSINS
Dinah Dean

HOSTAGE OF THE HEART
Linda Acaster

Buy them from your usual paperback stockist, or write to: Mills & Boon Reader Service, P.O. Box 236, Thornton Rd, Croydon, Surrey CR9 3RU, England. Readers in South Africa-write to: Mills & Boon Reader Service of Southern Africa, Private Bag X3010, Randburg, 2125.

Mills & Boon
the rose of romance

The burning secrets of a girl's first love.

WORLDWIDE

ANNE MATHER

Hidden in the Flame

Author of the bestsellers STORMSPELL and WILD CONCERTO

She was young and rebellious, fighting the restrictions imposed by her South American convent.

He was a doctor, dedicated to the people of his war-torn country.

Drawn together by a sensual attraction. Nothing should have stood in their way.

Yet a tragic secret was to keep them apart …

Following Hidden in the Flame's tremendous success last year here's another chance to read this passionate story.

WORLDWIDE

AVAILABLE FROM JUNE 1986. Price £2.50.

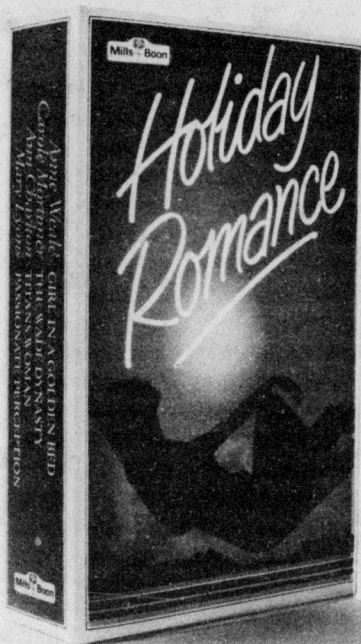

To be read with caution whilst sunbathing.

The Mills & Boon Holiday Pack contains four specially selected romances from some of our top authors and can be extremely difficult to put down.

But take care, because long hours under the summer sun, engrossed in hot passion can amount to a lot of sunburn.

So the next time you are filling your suitcase with the all-important Mills & Boon Holiday Pack, take an extra bottle of After Sun Lotion.

Just in case.

PRICE £4.40 AVAILABLE FROM JUNE 1986